"Why should I give you anything at all?"

She boldly stared back, a silent battle of wills.

"Because I'm from out of town?" Ross suggested, running a lock of hair between his thumb and forefinger. "Because I'm lonely and have no one to talk to?"

Dangerous, Paige decided. How could she have thought of this man in mild terms like *enjoyable* and *distracting* when what he really was was *dangerous?* She'd flirted with the flame longer than was wise. "Goodbye, Mr. Tanner."

One step. That was all he allowed her before his hand clamped around her wrist. She met his unwavering blue gaze. "You gave it a shot, but I'm not interested. Let's be civil and leave it at that."

"You're interested." Her pulse tripped beneath his fingertips. Ross smiled. "I'm rarely civil."

Dear Reader,

Welcome to Silhouette **Special Edition**…welcome to romance. Spring is here, and thoughts turn to love…so put a spring in your step for these wonderful stories this month.

We start off with our THAT SPECIAL WOMAN! title for April, *Where Dreams Have Been…* by Penny Richards. In this story, the whereabouts of a woman's lost son are somehow connected to an enigmatic man. Now she's about to find out how his dreams can help them find her missing son—and heal his own troubled past.

Also this month is *A Self-Made Man* by Carole Halston, a tale of past unrequited love that's about to change. Making the journey from the wrong side of the tracks to self-made man, this hero is determined to sweep the only woman he's ever truly loved off her feet.

To the West next for Pamela Toth's *Rocky Mountain Rancher*. He's a mysterious loner with a past…and he wants his ranch back from the plucky woman who's now running it. But complicating matters are his growing feelings of love for this tough but tender woman who has won his heart. And no visit to the West would be complete without a stop in Big Sky country, in Marianne Shock's *What Price Glory*. Paige Meredith has lived with ambition and without love for too long. Now rugged rancher Ross Tanner is about to change all that.

Don't miss Patt Bucheister's *Instant Family,* a moving story of finding love—and long-lost family—when one least expects it. Finally, debuting this month is new author Amy Frazier, with a story about a woman's return to the home she left, hoping to find the lost child she desperately seeks. And waiting there is the man who has loved her from afar all these years—and who knows the truth behind *The Secret Baby.* Don't miss it!

I hope you enjoy these books, and all the stories to come!

Sincerely,

Tara Gavin

Senior Editor

Please address questions and book requests to:
Silhouette Reader Service
U.S.: 3010 Walden Ave., P.O. Box 1325, Buffalo, NY 14269
Canadian: P.O. Box 609, Fort Erie, Ont. L2A 5X3

MARIANNE SHOCK

WHAT PRICE GLORY

SPECIAL EDITION®

Published by Silhouette Books
America's Publisher of Contemporary Romance

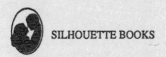 SILHOUETTE BOOKS

ISBN 0-373-09952-5

WHAT PRICE GLORY

Books by Marianne Shock

Silhouette Special Edition

Run Away Home #412
What Price Glory #952

MARIANNE SHOCK

has always been a romantic, and her happy marriage confirmed her belief in love at first sight. The encouragement to bring this romantic spirit to print came from her parents who, Marianne says, "had love enough for all ten of their children." Now the mother of four active children of her own, Marianne finds she is able to devote herself to family, some theater work, home decorating and, of course, her writing career. Finishing a book, she says, is a "very gratifying exhaustion."

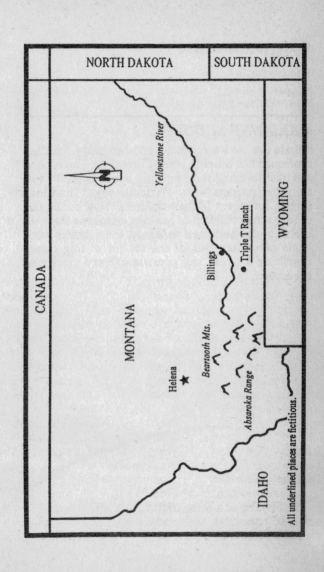

NORTH DAKOTA

SOUTH DAKOTA

Yellowstone River

WYOMING

Triple T Ranch

Billings

CANADA

MONTANA

Beartooth Mts.

Helena

Absaroka Range

All underlined places are fictitious.

IDAHO

Prologue

Paige slid a gold stickpin through folds of white silk, securing the snowy stock beneath her chin. The mirror she gazed into was narrow and hung crookedly. The hands she focused on were steady. Her eyes, wide and unwavering, conveyed an impression of deep concentration. Indeed, thoughts threatening to race ahead and scatter were determinedly confined to tucking, straightening, and smoothing out wrinkles. Head erect, she reached for the blond braid hanging down her back and began twisting it into a sleek knot at the nape of her neck.

Outside, the day and temperaments were heating. Warm dust and the faint sting of sweat scented the air. Tension was mounting, the sounds of it easily penetrating the door at her back: trainers barking orders at grooms; grooms snapping back before hustling to oblige; riders letting off steam in nose-to-nose shouting matches.

The first day of a horse trial was a strain on even the most seasoned equestrian. Paige told herself nerves were essential, that because of them she had an edge. Because of them she was never complacent or, worse, confident, though that was the image she strove to project. Confident, controlled, invulnerable. Her pulse might skip, but her emotions never showed, never got in the way of what she set out to do.

Braid anchored, she stepped back to give her reflection a critical study. White breeches fit snugly, molding hips she'd noticed recently were growing too narrow and legs she'd always thought had grown too long. Black leather boots glowed dully from a vigorous buffing. The gold at her throat was repeated at her ears, where unadorned studs discreetly glinted. Satisfied with what she saw, Paige nodded. Thirty minutes ago, she'd worn ragged jeans and a baggy sweatshirt. In ten or less, she'd be meticulously turned out in the top hat and tails of performance dressage.

It was a transformation she'd made hundreds of times over the years, at hundreds of combined-training sites. She'd entered her first competition, a prepreliminary, at the age of ten, dressing in the back of a horse trailer, with only a musty-smelling blanket to use as a curtain for privacy. Now she competed in international CCI events held at established horse parks boasting multimillion-dollar facilities. When she wasn't chasing world-class medals, she was moving midlevel backup mounts through the ranks, traveling from state to state, from hunt clubs to breeding farms to fairgrounds. This weekend it was a modest racetrack in Louisville, Kentucky.

Exceedingly modest, Paige mused, if one was to judge by the makeshift dressing rooms.

Her own cinder-block cubicle was hardly bigger than a closet. Nearly half the space was taken up by a battered wooden desk, suggesting that the room had once been an office. Now it stored discarded tack—dingy saddle pads heaped up in one corner, a tangle of frayed lead lines and broken bridles in another. Sunlight streamed through a window high on the wall, warming air that smelled of leather and liniment, a scent Paige rather liked.

Muted applause and the faint drone of the loudspeaker signaled the end of one rider's test, the beginning of another's. Soon it would be her name blasted through amplifiers, her performance scrutinized and scored. Refusing to hurry, she uncapped a bottle of ivory-toned foundation.

Except for the religious use of sunscreen, Paige rarely bothered with cosmetics. Appearances would hardly matter on tomorrow's cross-country course, where faces would wear sweat and dust, mud if it had recently rained. Speed, height and accuracy were all that counted in the third and final day's jumping arena. But for the classical disciplines of dressage, a scrupulously groomed rider was every bit as important as a scrupulously groomed horse. Precision and elegance were the goals, and everything, even appearance, was evaluated. Strong technical skills were crucial, a nerveless aloof attitude helped, and an attractive face—or a clever hand with makeup—didn't hurt. Paige had devoted her life to perfecting the skills and cultivating the attitude. Genetics had blessed her with the face.

From her father she'd inherited the Meredith bone structure, the high forehead, the patrician nose and the sweeping cheekbones. She had her mother's delicate complexion and thick silver-to-gold hair. Lashes uncommonly dark for a blonde framed eyes the color of smoky jade—a blend of the Meredith gray and the Anderson green.

Judges registered her to-the-manner-born looks the moment she entered the dressage ring. Paige had enough ambition to appreciate the advantage, but was otherwise unimpressed with herself. A face, after all, was primarily an accident of birth. She took far more pride in the titles and trophies earned through sheer determination and good old-fashioned sweat.

She was an athlete. An equestrian. Those two words both described and defined her. March through October she rode the circuit, zigzagging from her home in Maryland through a dozen states east of the Mississippi and half that many countries abroad. She wintered in Florida, taking specialized clinics and training—eight to eighteen hours a day. Exhibitors' banquets and the courting of corporate sponsors—the latter often done at the former—summed up her social life. Fortunately for Paige, her professional credits helped to ease the disagreeable ordeal of attracting financial backers.

Twenty-six years old, she'd been named horsewoman of the year the past three in a row. She was currently Leading Rider. She had a reputation for being driven, talented and fearless—no jump was too high, no chasm too wide. She'd finished last season by capping her individual silver medal at the American Invitational with a team gold at the world championship.

But there was one prize, one award for excellence, she had yet to claim. Number one in the country, Paige Meredith was going for best in the world.

Next week, and for the eleventh time in her seventeen-year career, she'd start in the Kentucky Three-Day Event. More prestigious than any horse trial, three-days were also more grueling, more nerve-racking. They challenged riders and asked the ultimate effort of horses—discipline, strength, stamina. Paige would be competing at two different levels, on two distinctly different horses.

Dual-eventing, she thought grimly. A daunting prospect. Nor could she forget that this year's Kentucky Three-Day was the final selection trial for the summer's Pan-American Games. Or that the Pan-Am Games kicked off the twelve-month countdown to the Olympics.

It was close now. And almost, almost hers.

Paige felt the jolt—half thrill, half panic. Her fingers, guiding a lip liner, faltered. Breathing a curse, she thumbed off the uneven line and started over. She would not, she vowed now, think about the months ahead. Seventy-two hours. She would think only of getting through the next seventy-two hours, and this weekend's horse trial.

She was removing the protective cover from her top hat when the door at her back opened and Faye Gentry strolled through.

"Your ride times are tight," Faye reported. "Only twenty minutes between preliminary tests." Leaning a hip against the scarred desk, the older woman read from one of the pocket-size notebooks she always had at hand. "Someone on the groom team'll have to warm Smooth as Silk while you present Lady Night. Lizzy, I think.''

Only half listening to her trainer's familiar preevent patter, Paige donned the hat.

"Lady's tacked," Faye went on, flipping to a fresh page. "I'll have her brought around as soon as you're ready. You'll get a decent break before testing with Kid. Intermediates begin after lunch."

Paige shifted her eyes, smiling as she focused on Faye's reflection. The woman was incredible, ageless. Fifty-two, she still had the ramrod spine and squared-shoulder stance of the professional horsewoman. Her five-foot-two frame was still subtly muscled. When she was in her twenties, catapulting to fame on the international circuit, the press had termed her handsome. She was still that, Paige decided, though she might work a bit at it now. No matter the time or place, Faye's short sable hair was expertly styled, her makeup carefully applied.

Paige had been nine years old the first time she met the legendary Faye Gentry. But long before she began training with the former Olympic hopeful, she'd read about her in the local papers. She'd never forget the day she'd accompanied her parents to Gentry Farm. It had been summer—eight months since they'd promised her the riding lessons as a Christmas gift. While Faye reviewed her program for William and Olivia, Paige had stood to one side, not quite believing she was there. To her parents, promises were merely pledges of intent—one wasn't necessarily expected to keep them. Plans to go to the zoo were dashed with an impromptu invitation to a Sunday hunt. A weekend at the shore was canceled in a wink if the mood struck Olivia to take in a Broadway play instead. One of Paige's earliest lessons in life had been to never count on them.

But on that special summer day, a young girl's deepest wish had been granted. Later Paige would remember it as the day her life had begun.

"Jack Sperry's judging prelims," Faye was saying as Paige slid her formal black cutaway from its hanger. "For him, arrogance. Lots of it. Nothing impresses Jack like a cool, classy blonde dominating twelve hundred pounds of fight."

Butterflies stirred as Paige buttoned the tailored broadcloth at her midriff. Pressing a hand to her stomach, she willed it to settle. She turned, checking her profile, then tapped her hat brim to bring it down a fraction in front. To the smallest detail, she looked as smooth and controlled as she intended the execution of her tests to be. No dangling threads. No turned seams. Beneath the silk hat, her hair was sleek against her head, not a single loose wisp to stir in the breeze.

No stray wisps, she mused. No stray thoughts.

"Get any of that?" Faye let her notebook shut with a snap.

"Sure. Jack Sperry... arrogance." Paige's tone was dry, hinting of humor. According to Faye, every judge scored up for arrogance. "Piece of cake."

Faye hummed a noncommittal sound, her discerning brown eyes sweeping over Paige. "Nice. You look nice." It was her highest form of praise. That and "You did good."

Paige waited after Faye departed. Alone, she closed her eyes, breathed in and let her mind empty. For her the competition began when she left this room. At that moment she would be totally focused, and she'd stay that way until it was over, three days from now. It was a state of mind she could achieve in the blink of an eye. Until recently, that is. She was already nine weeks into the most important season of her life, yet her concentration wasn't what it should be. There were days when absolutely nothing disrupted her focus. Then there were days when she could be distracted by a coughing spectator, a plane flying overhead. It wasn't anything she could put her finger on or a name to. Or that she would allow to continue, Paige vowed as she prepared to leave the makeshift dressing room.

Stepping outside, she drew on white cotton gloves and took a long look at her surroundings. A capacity crowd filled the sun-drenched track. Because of its proximity to Lexington, the site of next week's three-day, most of the country's top-ranked equestrians were present. The dressage ring and tiers of bleachers had been erected on the in-field. Behind-the-scenes people swarmed over the middle distance. Beyond the showgrounds an ocean of bluegrass rippled beneath a cloudless sky.

Oblivious to those she passed, Paige crossed the oval track to where Lizzy held Lady Night's reins. The black Hano-verian belonged to Tom and Lorraine Sheffield, friends of Faye's, and Paige's hosts for her two weeks in Kentucky. They also owned her second mount, Smooth as Silk—who was about as smooth in a trot as a lame donkey. Her third horse, Kidnapper, was a feisty, intermediate-level gelding out of Gentry Farm.

Paige mounted, taking a moment to settle into the thin leather saddle, then steered the mare into the practice ring. After a twenty-minute rehearsal of the preset dressage steps, Lady was on the bit—her neck gracefully arched, her moves supple and smooth, yet crisp. Her center of gravity shifted so that she carried her weight over her haunches and lifted her forelegs airily. They were, Paige knew, ready to begin.

Two thousand spectators packed the bleachers. In the holding area behind the gate, Paige blinded herself to them. Concentrating, she blocked the sounds of them, as well. She loosened her grip on the reins, allowing the mare to com-fortably canvass the ring and grow familiar with it. Short slanted rails, painted a pristine white, defined the arena's perimeter. Pots of crimson geraniums framed the eight dressage letters. The judges' stand was at the far end, shaded by a yellow-and-white striped umbrella.

Paige focused only on the sandy court. She didn't notice the sky's perfection or the sun's angle. She didn't see the busy concession stands or the milling ground crews. She visualized—some called it imagining. She pictured herself and Lady entering the ring, executing a perfect salute, beginning. In her mind's eye she saw each step of the seven-minute program, complete with brilliant *piaffes* and pir-ouettes, brisk *passages*. A ballet. Two athletes, but one harmonious unit performing a dance that was at once pow-erful, ethereal, fluid.

Imagined test completed, her vision cleared. Paige found she was staring into sapphire eyes. Hot, hot sapphire.

Something about the man's returning stare held her transfixed. He stood close enough to touch, if she'd been able to move at all. Without her gaze seeming to stray from his, Paige saw all of him. Black hair, blue eyes, bronze skin. He was lean and long and dressed like a range-grown cowboy, in leather vest and snakeskin boots. His face was arresting, sexy. Very sexy. Paige recognized male appreciation in his eyes, and arrogance. She dismissed the first, but couldn't help admiring the second. She knew scores of riders, herself included, who'd kill to be that sure of themselves.

A round of applause jolted her from the trancelike state. Oddly unsteady, she tore her gaze loose in time to hear her name announced. Good God, how had she let that happen? Concentration hours in the making had been shattered in a matter of seconds. By a pair of blue eyes!

Pull yourself together, she ordered. *Now.* With a slight press of her thighs, Paige urged the mare forward.

Seventeen years, she silently chanted to the rhythm of Lady's prancing trot. Seventeen years of long days and hard work, of training, tumbles and sweat. Seventeen years of riding in icy rain and breathless heat, of getting back in the saddle with only a roll of tape holding broken ribs together. Seventeen years of wanting one thing and one thing only, and of sacrificing whatever was necessary to get it.

With only sixteen months to go, she couldn't, *wouldn't,* start slipping.

Chapter One

Ross Tanner leaned against a corral fence in a stable yard filling with auctiongoers. Shoulders slanted to the rail at his back, black Stetson tipped low on his brow, he watched Kentucky's moneyed gentry transform a placid breeding farm into an electrically charged sales arena.

Sleek Maseratis and sumptuous Rolls-Royces whisked arrivals up the shaded gravel drive, past immaculate white-board fencing. Anticipation carried them the rest of the way. Buyers strolled sun-dappled paddocks, quiet, thoughtful. Minglers made the rounds, gathering at the skirted buffet tables positioned around the hilltop estate house. Spicy aromas drifted from silver chafing dishes, blending with those of blossoming dogwoods and premium horseflesh. The atmosphere—from red-jacketed waiters to expensive French wines—projected wealth and privilege. It was, Ross reflected, the typical setting for a Gil Brady horse sale.

They were unparalleled. Nowhere else did warmbloods go on the block with the class, quality or terrific success of a Brady auction. Here one wouldn't find the revelry of a quarter-horse sale. The audience wouldn't be flavored with the foreign accents and turbaned sheikhs of the Thorough-bred circuit. European warmbloods appealed to the sedate, drew the blue bloods.

Buffets were frequent events the weeks offered horses were on the grounds. Consignors met buyers, buyers studied prospects, prospects were tacked up, trotted out and tried. Champagne flowed. Ross skipped the presale social functions; he had neither the time nor the inclination. He made the two-thousand-mile trip if and when a particular mount interested him, timing his arrival to allow him a thorough inspection of the animal, possibly a few questions of the owner.

A month ago Gil Brady had phoned Ross about a four-year-old filly consigned to today's auction, an Irish-blood he thought warranted Ross traveling halfway across the country. Ross had known with his first look that she was everything Gil had promised. And that he was going to have her. When she was trotted into the sales arena, Ross intended the gavel to come down on his bid... assuming the damn bidding ever got started.

Banking his impatience, he shifted his weight, hooking a boot heel on the lowest fence rung, and scanned the picture-perfect view. Emerald hills, a watercolor sky, and soft sunlight. On the barn roof, a bronze weather vane shaped like a wind-whipped trotter wavered in the breeze. Spring, he mused. An uncommon season in his part of the country. Montana split the year in two—winter and summer. One cold, one hot. To Ross, the land was as beautiful as the climate was brutal. Untamed, unforgiving, it asked the most of a man, but gave back richly to those who endured.

A buzz of appreciative murmurs signaled the first sleekly groomed horse being led from his stall. The stable hand halted his charge, squaring him off in a patch of mottled sunlight. The effect was a seller's dream—artful shading enhanced the definition of form and muscle, ribbons of light licked fire over the bay's red coat. Admirers crossed to the paddock, and the yard thinned out, giving Ross an uninterrupted view of the entrance gate.

She stood there alone. Blond, beautiful and distant. His immediate thought was the same as when he'd first laid eyes on her. Ice . . . fabulous, elegant ice.

Ross didn't straighten from his comfortable slouch, though his body was no longer relaxed. Eyes narrowed beneath his hat brim, he let his gaze roam over her, lingering on her long, long legs before moving on to appreciate the rest of her. Her bearing was regal, her face exquisite. Today her hair fell free, pale champagne spilling past her shoulders. She wore pink-tinted ivory, her blouse and pleated slacks fitting loose enough to ripple in the breeze. He remembered her skin-clinging breeches of yesterday, remembered seeing her muscles flex beneath them—and remembered that his own had followed suit. Then, wearing white silk and black tails, she'd exuded cool, untouchable sex. Today she reeked of the same.

Alone, she wandered the stable yard, greeting no one, no one greeting her. Her eyes passed blindly over people, discouraging anyone from getting too close. Stopping, she glanced over her shoulder, apparently searching for someone. *Not alone.* Ross tracked the path of her gaze to the registration tables, where people stood three deep. Whoever she was waiting for would be a while yet.

Seeming to reach the same conclusion, she turned back to scan the yard. Ross saw her face in profile, full-front, in profile again. Delicate bone and flawless skin, meant for trellised verandas and Southern shade. He envisioned her astride a loping steed beneath the unrelenting sun of a Montana plain. For all her ice and restraint, he thought, she was a woman who'd be at her best when breaking free.

Instinct. Ross trusted it. Moods, undercurrents. He sensed them as one who worked with animals must. Leading a sulky broodmare to stud, driving drought-thirsty cattle over miles of dusty range, a man learned to anticipate. When Ross settled on the back of an angry Brahman in a rodeo chute, he staked his life on eight seconds of instinct. His were finely tuned. And there was something about this woman, something too disciplined about her carriage, hints of vulnerability behind the restraint. And passion, he thought. *Fire beneath the frost.*

"Nice. *Very* nice."

Ross knew the voice, so he didn't bother turning his head. "'Afternoon, Brady."

"She's got what it takes, all right." Gil clapped a friendly hand to Ross's shoulder. "Eye appeal. Sound, athletic looks. Mmm...lovely mover." He grinned, a boyish charm claiming his smooth-shaven face. Ross never forgot that behind the charm a horse trader was shrewdly calculating. "You always did have a weakness for breeding."

"Appreciation," Ross corrected.

"Weakness," Gil insisted, and jingled the change in his pocket. "Tanner, when it comes to pure-blooded fillies, you might as well hand over your wallet and let me help myself."

Ross smiled despite himself, and slipped a hand inside his jacket to lift a cigarette from the pack in his breast pocket. "Know her?"

"No." Gil squinted as if he were sizing up a prospective broodmare. "Out-of-towner," he surmised. "Didn't come to buy. Bored, maybe, with time on her hands. There's a big-deal equestrian team tearing up turf on the north side of town. She looks the type." The eyes he cut to Ross offered heartfelt pity. "Don't see her mucking out stalls on the rodeo circuit, pal."

Neither did Ross. Though it hardly taxed his imagination to come up with an alternative. He blew out a slow stream of smoke and wondered at his fascination with a perfect stranger. "Planning to hold this auction anytime today?"

"Soon, soon. Got a question for you."

"Shoot."

"See the little redhead across the way?"

The tremor of restrained laughter in Brady's voice had Ross on his guard as he looked where the other man indicated. She was petite and deliciously curved. Sunlight struck a match to her cap of tousled red-gold curls, much the way it had the bay's coat. Aware she had Ross's attention, she tipped her head to gaze back at him.

"Cute," Ross said. And young. Nineteen, twenty tops.

"She asked me if you were a genuine cowboy."

"Genuine?"

"Said I'd ask and let her know."

"You've known me for five years, Brady. What's to ask?"

To anyone with half a mind and one good eye, Ross's appearance was answer enough. As always, he'd dressed for comfort—jeans, snap-button shirt, square-toed boots with undershot heels. His hat had been saved from its share of stampedes, and looked it. Because he'd known to expect afternoon formality, he'd compromised with his aversion to "proper attire" by wearing a cream-colored jacket. But even that was cut along casual Western lines.

His looks were neither smooth nor rugged to the extreme, but an intriguing blend of both. Men trusted his face, women were drawn to it. Ross wasn't above using that to his advantage when it suited him. His eyes were blue, his gaze was incisive. By fractionally altering the arch of his brow, he could welcome or warn off. The hair flowing from under his hat was black and untamed. So, it was said, was his temper.

As with three generations of Tanner men before him, Ross was a rancher. Eight years ago, when he was twenty-five, a tragic accident had left him the oldest surviving Tanner, responsible for the family and its holdings. As a result, he had the confidence—some called it arrogance—that came of having no one but himself to fall back on, and the lean, hard body that came of long days in the saddle, riding herd and fence lines. When asked his occupation, he said he was a puncher and left it at that.

"So what do I tell her?" Gil prodded with a chuckle.

"You must be anticipating one hell of a day to waste valuable presale time on this ridiculous conversation." Ross grinned. "Tell her whatever you please."

"You might do it yourself."

"No, thanks. I don't romp with college girls."

"High school." At Ross's look of astonishment, Gil nodded.

Putting a hand to one hip, the saucy redhead extended Ross an obvious invitation. He touched the brim of his hat to acknowledge her, then turned her down by looking away. At the blonde.

"Something else on your mind, Brady?"

"Can I interest you in another look at the filly?"

"No." The bay's reserve price was high enough without Ross's enthusiasm jacking it up. "Vet reports were promising, but her breed characteristics..." He shrugged. "I've seen better."

"Like hell! Irish-bloods don't come better, and you know it. She's got everything you've been looking for."

Lazily, the blonde shook her hair back, gold and silver strands rippling with light. Something other than casual interest curled through Ross's gut. She was easily the most beautiful, most elegant, most physically perfect woman he'd ever set eyes on. "Maybe, maybe not," he murmured. "What's her place in the lineup?"

"She's listed in the sales catalog." Gil frowned at Ross's empty hands. "Hold on, I'll get you one."

"Don't bother."

"You sure? We've got plenty."

Ross cut him a look. "What's her number?"

"Twelve." Gil flashed the grin of a man mentally writing the receipt on one four-year-old warmblood filly. "Number twelve." He lifted his foot from the fence as if to leave, then hesitated. "Say, Ross, any idea when you'll wrap up your cousin's business?"

Ross felt the anger rise, but managed to push it down. He'd planned to forget about Lance, if just for this one day. "Why?"

"Horses are supposed to be vacated by Tuesday. Rumor has it there's a bank crawling all over TLD, with Lance nowhere to be found. Sounds like you'll be in town awhile." When Ross made no comment, Gil shrugged. "If you buy the filly, I'll throw in a week's board with her going price."

Ross nodded without committing himself. Gil moved on to charm a huddle of buyers gathered beneath a leafy linden.

A week. Ross suspected he'd need every day of it to, as Gil had tactfully phrased it, wrap up his cousin's business. Fresh fury balled in his stomach. Damned if he wasn't fed up with saving Lance Tanner III's ass. If the Triple T and Tanner Mines weren't so inextricably tied to Tanner Land Development, he'd have gladly let Lance fall on his pretty Mediterranean-tanned face years ago.

Lance's Louisville bank had contacted Ross a few weeks ago, the call coming on the heels of Brady's about the filly. It was time, the loan officer had said, to conduct their annual collateral review. Lance was precisely where he was every year at this time—or any other, if trouble hit: somewhere in Europe. As if he'd actually had a choice in the matter, Ross had agreed to be present, and planned the trip to coincide with today's auction.

But the mess at TLD was more serious than the usual hunt for records. This time there was talk of suspiciously shady land deals, not to mention a blemished title or two.

Yesterday, after two aggravating hours with accountants and bankers, Ross had realized he wouldn't be going home Monday, as planned. Too angry to be of help to anyone, he'd stormed out of the building, folded himself into Lance's ridiculously cramped sports car and headed for an open stretch of highway. There he'd rammed the gas pedal to the floor. He wasn't a man who sat easily in three-piece suits or boardrooms. He was a rancher—a cowpuncher at heart. He preferred wide-open plains and weeks at a stretch with hundreds of cattle and only a handful of men for company. When the weeks grew into months and the company grew stale, he hooked up with a rodeo and rode a bull or two. And he resented his cousin like hell for these periodic forays into big business and high finance.

By the time he'd cooled off, Ross had found himself on the shady roads of horse country, miles outside the city. He'd noticed the trailers first, minineighborhoods on a grassy field—horses being worked on the camp's perimeter, riders in various stages of formal dress scurrying back and forth. After a morning of brown-suited bankers, an afternoon of horses had appealed to him. Ross had stopped, looking for relaxation. Seeing the woman had been a pleasant bonus.

Now he took a last drag on his cigarette before crushing it beneath his heel. When he lifted his eyes again, the blonde's were skimming the crowd, moving unerringly in his direction. The afternoon, Ross mused, had taken an interesting turn.

She'd been manipulated. Tricked! Paige fumed. Suppressing the urge to curse out loud, she strolled the bustling stable yard. What could Faye have been thinking of, dragging her off to an auction? She'd pushed three horses through a demanding cross-country that morning. She had to push those same three exhausted horses over a jumping course tomorrow. And where was she now? At an auction!

Paige watched the steady stream of arrivals continue. Thirty minutes, Faye had said. They'd be away from the stables for only thirty minutes, an hour at the most. The breeder was just a few miles down the road from the showgrounds, and the Swedish-blood gelding was sure to be snapped up if Faye didn't immediately buy him. She'd conveniently neglected to mention there'd be hundreds of others interested in owning the Swede. Gazing over her shoulder, Paige narrowed her eyes on the jostling mob at the registration tables. *Thirty minutes, my foot.*

"So you've been manipulated," she muttered underbreath. "You're here now, and might as well enjoy it." But even as she moved deeper into the chattering crowd, she couldn't shake the feeling she belonged at the stables. Her whole being was geared to competing, to focusing on one thing and one thing only. There was too much clatter here. Too much clinking of glasses. The air, sizzling with excitement, abraded nerves riding close to the surface.

Ignore it, she told herself. Treat this as you would an event, and block everything out.

Looking past the throng, Paige scanned the wooded countryside. She didn't see it as locals or tourists might, but viewed it through the eyes of a rider. Fences and the trunks of toppled trees were translated into jumps. Hillsides were estimated for gradients, while the flats posed questions on soil quality and traction. Next Saturday's three-day cross-country would take her over similar terrain.

Feeling the familiar tension wind through her at thoughts of next week, Paige forced herself to relax. She concentrated on the sunlight, on feeling its heat penetrate her skin. *If only there weren't the waiting. If only—* Then she saw him.

The curse she'd suppressed earlier hissed out with the breath she expelled. Though his face was shadowed by the angle of his hat, Paige was certain the cowboy watching her from across the yard was the same one she'd run across entirely too often at the dressage venue. Same lean, rangy length, she decided. Same "damn the world" arrogance in his stance. And she felt the same internal magnetic pull, warring with a self-protective urge to back away and widen the distance.

It was what she wanted to do now—turn on her heels and cover ground. Lots of it. But, for the moment, the magnetic pull was winning, and her gaze remained locked with his.

She wasn't close enough to see the color of his eyes, but she recalled their sapphire heat. Her pulse skipped crazily. As it had yesterday, the jolt of attraction astonished her.

After what seemed an eternity, the cowboy tipped his hat to her. Paige nodded. An acknowledgment, she realized too late. As if, each having weighed the other, they'd agreed they were attracted. Ridiculous, she scolded herself. It was nothing. A tipped hat and a nod. No one in her right mind made something out of nothing.

Thoroughly annoyed with herself, Paige slid her hands into her pockets and was able, finally, to turn and walk away. What was there about him that made her breath catch? Her heart thud? She'd come across sexy men before. None had held her attention for more than a minute or two. Certainly none had upset her body rhythms. Yet a glance at this man—leaning against fences, hanging around the stables or behind the bleachers—and her composure disintegrated. By late afternoon yesterday, a mere suggestion of the man's shadow had been enough to enrage her.

"You're a surprise, love." The smooth voice cut through Paige's thoughts as a hand cupped her elbow.

Grateful for the distraction, if a bit lukewarm on the company, Paige smiled coolly at Travis Donahue. He was tall and gracefully slim and everything about him was pale, from his corn-silk hair to his fair skin to his ice blue eyes. Once she'd thought herself in love with him. Now she felt only regret for what should never have been.

"Shopping for a new horse, Travis?" Curious that he'd sought her out, she mused. Neither was the sort to make a friend of a past lover. They rode the same circuit, walked the same showgrounds, yet they rarely exchanged words beyond an occasional polite greeting.

"A warmblood?" His tone condemned the breed out of hand. "God, no. I'll stick with bighearted Thoroughbreds." He released her arm to lift two glasses from the tray of a passing waiter. "Busman's holiday. But what about you? Since when do you socialize once an event's begun?"

Paige shrugged and accepted a glass of champagne. "Faye was this way earlier in the week. It was love at first sight for a Swede." She let Travis take her arm and steer them again. Even as she decided she wouldn't, she sneaked a glance over her shoulder. The cowboy flashed her a smile and saluted. Paige had the distinct impression he'd known she'd turn back for one more look. *Cocky, arrogant jerk.*

Silently damning the man's ego, she sipped from her glass and concentrated on what Travis was saying.

"I saw you with the Frenchman at Badminton."

Badminton? Paige frowned. Badminton had been over a month ago. *Curiouser and curiouser.* Just what *did* Travis want?

"Jacques or Jules or whatever his name was. He was all over you at the banquet. You both called it a night at the same time."

Paige thought his summary grossly exaggerated. She and the charming Parisian had shared little more than fifteen minutes and a drink. Where he'd eventually wound up was his own business; Paige had left alone. What *was* his name? Not Jacques or Jules... His first trip to England, he'd said. His first time competing on foreign soil with his countrymen. He'd remembered Paige from the world championship in Paris two years ago, and had been effusively complimentary.

"Jean-Paul," she supplied, remembering. "Jean-Paul Dubay."

"Paige." Travis's murmur touched her like a chill wind. He'd walked them into the shadows behind the dripping branches of a willow. "Beautiful Paige." Putting a finger under her chin, he tipped her face up. Lifting a brow, she brushed his hand away. "Icy Paige," he whispered. "Don't you know, love, that your rebuffs only intrigue men? The face..." He paused to visually tour her features. "The face draws them, but it's the challenge that brings them back."

She met his eyes squarely. Hers were expressionless. "Was there something you wanted, Travis?"

"I've been watching you, love, noticing things. Little things, but I'm concerned."

"For me?" He pretended to miss her sarcasm, just as he'd pretended concern for her in the past. "I've never ridden better." That, she knew, would sting him. He'd hated that most, that she was the better rider. She'd often thought it ironic that a man who believed himself superior by virtue of his gender had chosen the one and only sport that made no distinction between the sexes. "My finishes have been exemplary."

"True, but will it last?" He sipped from his glass, considering her over the rim. "You're restless, love. Dissatisfied, perhaps?"

Paige stiffened instinctively. "Why should I be?"

Travis shrugged. "Why were you dissatisfied four years ago?"

Her fingers tightened on the fragile wineglass as she recalled that confusing, unsettling time. Then, consumed by her climb up the equestrian ladder, her life had seemed narrow. To some, riding was a sport; to Paige, it was everything. But for a time it hadn't been enough. It had seemed she wakened one morning abruptly, keenly aware of having lived twenty-two years without once having been to summer camp, a high school football game, in love. She'd wanted something else in her life, something more. She'd added Travis.

"You're wrong," Paige stated, with more certainty than she felt.

"I don't think so. You've always had the concentration of a guided missile locked on its target—blind, deaf and numb on event days. Though not recently. You really haven't been yourself, love."

"Sweet of you to worry, Travis." The cool tone belied her inner turmoil. It unnerved her to think others had seen what she was only beginning to suspect. "But quite unnecessary. I've never been better." Determined he wouldn't know he'd rattled her, she swept aside the lacy curtain of leaves.

"If you get restless, Paige . . ."

"I'll go for a long walk." She tossed the words off as she headed for the buffet. Restless. So she was feeling a bit restless. Who didn't now and then? But dissatisfied? She remembered those troubled, sleepless nights of the past, stacking the lifetime of sacrifices against a display case of trophies and trying to make them balance. No, she wouldn't allow it, not again. Not now! Preferring anger to self-doubt, she thumped her fluted glass down on one of the tables.

She was reaching blindly for a plate when she heard her name called. Turning, she saw Faye approaching at her usual hurried pace.

"Were you going to take a plate?" Faye inquired dryly. "Or throw the whole stack?"

Paige gave an indelicate snort. "Travis," she hissed. "Pompous, opinionated ass. What did I ever see in him?"

"Elegance. Sophistication. A pretty face."

"Baloney."

"Mmm . . . that's what I said. You didn't speak to me for two weeks."

"And I may not for two more," Paige threatened. "Thirty minutes, Faye?"

Faye shrugged, smiled, then turned to consider the assortment of hot and cold delicacies. "You needed a break, and you're too stubborn to listen to reason. If you'd known it was an auction, you'd have found half-a-dozen reasons not to come. Where's your plate?"

"I'm not hungry," Paige decided, and refused to be persuaded otherwise by Faye's disapproving scowl. She knew she'd lost a pound or two lately, but she didn't have much appetite during competitions, and there had been so many of them the past few months.

"Well, I am." Arms already full, Faye clumsily juggled a plate until Paige offered to take a few things off her hands.

There was a slim clutch purse made of bone-colored leather, and a ring of keys too bulky to fit in the tailored bag. Credit forms were stuffed between the pages of a glossy sales catalog, and as Paige shifted the slick brochure to one arm, a white plastic rectangle fluttered to the ground. She picked it up, recognizing it as a bid card. "Two-sixty-four?" she asked of its bold black numbers. "Are there that many bidders? How many horses?"

"Hmm?" Faye plucked strawberries from a lavish display of fresh fruits. "Horses...I don't know. Fifty?"

Paige flipped to the back of the catalog. "Fifty-six. That's a whole lot of people trying to buy only a few horses. I hope you're prepared to pay through the nose for your Swede."

"He'll be worth every penny. Wait till you see him, Paige. Proud, arrogant, handsome...God, is he handsome. Reminds me of my Arab."

"Ah, yes, I remember your Arab. Proud, arrogant—also neurotic, and mean as hell."

"A bit overbearing, perhaps. Not this guy, though. He's sensitive, eager to please."

"Which one is he?" Paige asked.

"Number forty-two."

Gray-green eyes rolled up. "My, we're going to be here a long, long time," Paige muttered. "Ah, forty-two..." She studied the warmblood's photo as Faye, with plate mounded high, turned away from the buffet. "Nice. Yeah, he's kind of handsome."

Faye laughed as they strolled along. "But if you were buying, it'd be a stallion. One with a wild streak."

"Probably. Though you know me, I'll ride any horse I can win with." Paige glanced around and saw they were walking away from the sales arena. "Where are you going?"

"To the stables. Want to come and have a look at this guy before he's led out?"

Paige considered the crowded paddock area as the auctioneer's opening spiel came over the loudspeaker. "You go ahead. I'll grab us a couple of seats before the stampede."

"All right. I won't be long."

Paige watched Faye hurry off before turning away. Responding to a force stronger than her own will, she looked down from her hilltop vantage point to the edge of the stable yard. He was gone. Sweeping a glance over acres of people, she searched in vain for a black Stetson. Gone. Forget him, she ordered herself. What do you want with a cocky cowboy who's managed to make you furious without having said a word?

The sales arena was large. Elaborate floral arrangements banked the jumps, the auctioneer's platform and the four inside corners. Bleachers flanked two sides of the corral, wooden slats sagging under the weight of a standing-room-only crowd. Forgetting that Faye would curse lustily if she had to stand in the sun instead of sitting in the shade, Paige leaned against the rails on the side where there were only a few uniformed hands manning the gate and watched the parade of warmbloods begin.

A mare with foal and carrying generated brisk bidding, selling for a whopping thirty-eight thousand dollars. That sum paled next to those she'd once watched the gavel pound up at Keeneland, a Thoroughbred racecourse across town, where Triple Crown hopefuls went for half a million to multimillions. Still, to Paige, who was constantly scrambling for her next buck, thirty-eight thousand of them was something to whistle at.

After the mare, a series of stallions under saddle were snapped up. A pair of geldings met with lukewarm interest, bids sinking. When a third failed to bring his asking price, the owner was consulted and the gray passed. A breeding crowd, Paige mused. Stallions and mares were turning over fast—in a flash if they had performance records.

A tacked-up hunter was jogged into the ring, and Paige noticed white cards flashing from the corner of her eye. Shifting her interest, she studied bidding techniques. Some were overt, others discreet. A florid-faced man in the front row had tucked his card in his hatband. The bid leapt whenever he nodded.

A mahogany bay with black stockings was offered next. The filly was put through her paces to a rapid-fire list of performance credits. Leads and diagonals were changed, jumps taken. Impressive, Paige thought. She might favor power-packed stallions, but she couldn't help appreciating a horse with this one's eventing potential.

"Magnificent, isn't she?"

His voice was deep pitched and vibrant. And much too close. Paige didn't jump, and ordered herself not to run. His hand reached from behind to curve to the rail at her left. Seeing the cream-colored jacket sleeve only confirmed what she already knew: the warm, misty breath skimming her cheek belonged to the cowboy.

For a moment, she stood utterly still. She wouldn't, she vowed, give him the satisfaction of knowing he unsettled her. Feeling the clasp of Faye's purse dig into her breast, Paige relaxed her arms. When she was sure of herself, sure her breathing was normal and her face unreadable, she turned around. His eyes stunned her—thickly lashed and shockingly blue. A smile lurked in them, urging her gaze down. The shape of his lips had her wanting to wet her own. Unless a woman had a thing for burns and blisters, Paige mused, she'd keep a thick slab of ice between herself and this man.

"Who are you?" she demanded calmly, coolly.

"Ross Tanner."

"What do you want?"

"Ten minutes." Ross watched her pupils constrict as one eyebrow slowly climbed into an arch. The purely feminine scent of her overpowered that of dust and horses. This close, he should have seen flaws, or evidence of them in artfully applied makeup. He didn't. She was, quite simply, breathtaking. "Make that twenty."

Paige refused to back up when he draped an arm along the fence. His hand, resting on the top rail, shifted so that his fingers touched the ends of her hair. Still, she stubbornly held her ground. It was one thing to maintain distance, but this close, a retreat would be running, something she would not do.

"Since I don't know you, why should I give you anything at all?"

He liked her voice. Steady, rich, and seductively throaty. Though her tone delivered a warning, her voice was liquid honey. She boldly stared back, in a silent battle of wills. God, those eyes. They were huge, a rare, unforgettable shade—not quite green, not quite gray. Once, the day before, she'd looked at him like this, straight on, her wide, unblinking stare punching the breath from his body. She'd been mounted and on deck, next to enter the ring. Then her eyes had been vacant, blinded by preoccupation. Now they narrowed to glare.

"Because I'm from out of town?" he suggested, running a lock of her hair between his thumb and forefinger. "Because I'm lonely and have no one to talk to?"

Paige pressed her lips together to stop a smile. He wasn't an easy man to discourage, she admitted. He had a way of turning icy fronts into warm puddles.

"Why don't I believe you, Mr. Tanner?"

"Because you're a cynic?"

His fingers on her hair relaxed to rest lightly on her shoulder. Paige shifted Faye's purse and the catalog to one arm and casually brushed his hand away. "Or because you look like a man who has only to choose when he's in the mood for company."

"And so I have." Not so easily discouraged, Ross touched her again, with only a fingertip that he took lightly down the side of her face. "Anything in particular you'd like to talk about?"

"Is that how it works? You pick the company, the company picks the subject?"

"Something like that."

"Sure of yourself, aren't you?" Why not? Paige asked herself. She was handling him well enough so far. And handling him, she was discovering, gave her a shot of confidence she seemed to be in need of. He was enjoyable. More, he was distracting. For the first time in too many days, her mind wasn't on a competition. "All right. What did you think of yesterday's dressage tests?"

So the eyes hadn't been blind after all, Ross mused. "You saw me."

Saw him? She'd all but tripped over him! "You'd be hard to miss." She skimmed a glance over him, from his face to the toes of his dusty boots, then back to his face. "I suspect you know that." He didn't argue the point, but kept his gaze steadily on her. "You were ringside at my events. You were everywhere I looked, in fact. You're a fan of dressage, Mr. Tanner?"

"Ross. It was my first time, actually. I had a day to fill, and an interest in horses."

"Your first." She'd figured as much. One simply didn't see cowboys hanging out at horse trials. "Did you enjoy it?"

He shrugged, then gave her a smile that she sensed was turned on himself. "It was the most senseless exercise I've ever seen a horse put through. I didn't understand any of it. Did you win?"

She might have laughed if his quick grin hadn't shot an electric current straight to her toes. "I won't know until tomorrow, when it's over." *Dangerous,* Paige decided. How could she have thought of this man in mild terms like *enjoyable* and *distracting,* when what he really was was *dangerous?* He had a way of looking at a woman that turned bones to candle wax and thoughts to smoke. He smelled of sunlight, leather and musky male skin. Paige nearly leaned forward for more of his scent. She'd flirted with the flame longer than was wise. "Well, I guess that'd be about ten minutes."

"Two and a half."

"Goodbye, Mr. Tanner.'

One step. That was all he allowed her before his hand clamped around her wrist.

"The name is Ross, Paige."

She'd never heard her name said that way, throaty and intimate. She had to swallow before she could speak again. "How do you know my name?"

"Half the state must know it by now. It was announced in quadrophonic sound every time you entered a ring."

She met his unwavering blue gaze as he resisted her efforts to free her arm. "Look, Mr. Tanner—"

"Ross."

"Okay, Ross. You gave it a shot, but I'm not interested. Let's be civil and leave it at that."

"You're interested." Her pulse tripped beneath his fingertips. Ross smiled. "I'm rarely civil."

Heat surged with her blood. Temper, Paige told herself. Not excitement. Anger. Who the hell did he think he was? "Or charming," she said. "Arrogant, provoking, but not the least bit charming."

"Or charming." It wouldn't have won her anyway, Ross decided.

Exasperated, Paige spun as far away from him as her manacled wrist allowed. She faced the arena, where the auctioneer was preparing to bang down the gavel on the bay mare. Dammit, why couldn't he simply let her go without the nuisance of an embarrassing scene?

The breeze shifted, tossing her hair into her face. Lifting her free hand, Paige held the flying strands back and debated the wisdom of grinding her heel down hard on his toes. It'd be smarter, safer, she decided, to give reasoning with him one more try.

Eyes cool, she faced him. "What will it take to get rid of you?"

He was frowning, his gaze so intense she determinedly fought a powerful urge to squirm. "Do you have twenty-three thousand dollars?"

It was such an absurd request, Paige could only gape.

"Do you?" he prodded when she remained silent.

"Why? Is that what it takes to get rid of you?"

Now, Ross thought. Now it was time to watch the ice crack. "You've bid on that horse. Twenty-three grand."

It was a moment before his words registered. "I'm not bidding."

Ross touched the card she held in her free hand, the one she'd lifted to hold back her hair. "Flash this around, the auctioneer takes it for a bid."

"But I—" Paige looked at the seemingly innocuous piece of plastic, then up at the horse flying over a fence in the arena.

"Twenty-three, twenty-three..." the auctioneer chanted. *"Do I hear twenty-four?"*

Chapter Two

"Do I hear twenty-four?"

"I don't believe you." Paige tipped her chin, hooked one eyebrow and pretended a sweat hadn't broken out on her palms.

Ross shrugged. "Suit yourself."

Though her chin stayed up, uncertainty flickered in her eyes. "Did I really?"

"You did. Really."

Paige stared hard at him, wavering between panic and disbelief. The longer she stared, the more she was convinced he'd told her the truth.

"Twenty-four? Twenty-four?"

The auctioneer's appeal threw Paige a lifeline. It slipped from her grasp when there were no immediate takers. Now what? The full impact hit; her knees nearly buckled. She knew this feeling, had felt it before—sailing into a jump and realizing once airborne that she'd set up wrong and was in for a disastrous fall; furious with herself, and frightened.

So do something! the voice of reason shouted. Do it quickly! She couldn't afford—no, *Faye* couldn't afford—to have this preposterous blunder played out. Yet, beyond that one obvious fact, Paige couldn't seem to think.

Moments ago she'd wanted nothing more than for Ross Tanner to release her wrist. Now that he had, she was oblivious of her freedom, and of her lax fingers dropping their contents. Purse, catalog and keys hit the ground with a soft thump, a jingle and a puff of dust.

How did one stop an auction? she wondered as a sickening dread rolled through her stomach. Was there a protocol? Someone to whom she appealed? Did she simply holler out at the top of her lungs?

Fighting panic, Paige cleared her throat. "How do I take it back?"

"You can't."

"Don't tell me I can't!" she snapped. "Tell me how!"

Her smooth veneer was showing a few hairline fractures. Still, Ross thought she was handling the situation amazingly well. "All bids are final, as are all sales," he explained. "It's covered in the catalog, last page. 'The highest bidder shall be the buyer.'" The breeze changed direction, lifting her hair into both their faces. It was Ross who brushed it back this time. She didn't seem to notice his fingers combing back from her temples, or his thumbs traveling slowly around the shells of her ears. "The only time Brady makes an exception is if your own vet finds..."

Paige, who rarely raised her voice above a firm command, felt a scream building in her chest. Couldn't the man see this wasn't the time for a crash course on how auctions were conducted? She'd bid twenty-three thousand dollars with Faye's card, on Faye's credit. For a horse Faye didn't want!

Ignoring Ross's calm explanation of Brady's refund policy, Paige spun on her heels to gaze hopefully at the auctioneer. She gripped the fence, her fingers whitening with her effort to will the man to look her way. It occurred to her that he might not sweep this side again. Apart from a handful of grooms chasing back and forth to fetch horses, there were only herself and Ross here.

The offered filly was trotted around again. Instinctively Paige watched and appreciated. If Faye slit her throat for this, she could at least console herself with the fact that her blood would be spilled for a magnificent animal. An all-around athlete, Paige decided, but more. A born jumper. Maybe, just maybe, she'd be forgiven...eventually.

Finally the auctioneer canvassed her side of the arena. Showing the big card, she wagged a finger back and forth to signal no.

His trained eyes skimmed over and past her. *"Twenty-three, twenty-three..."* Paige clenched her hands in frustration. He'd hardly spared her a glance. *"I've got twenty-four!"*

Twenty-four. Paige held her breath until she heard the new figure repeated. "Someone's upped the bid." She glanced at Ross for confirmation before daring to let relief flow through her. When he nodded, she exhaled and slumped against the fence. "Thank God."

A low laugh rumbled from Ross. Paige snapped straight again. She hated that he'd seen her helpless and panic-stricken. Hated herself more for coming unglued in front of him. She was a woman whose image and the importance of having it always intact had been unceasingly drummed into her; a woman of elegance and confidence before a judge, of aplomb with the press, of good sportsmanship when she was exhausted and had lost and what she really wanted to do was collapse and cry. To the best of her memory, she'd always handled stressful situations with rock-steady composure...until now.

"I amuse you, Mr. Tanner?"

"You amaze me." With his fingertip, Ross traced the haughty arch of her eyebrow. He'd wondered if she would feel as cool as she looked. She felt warm and incredibly soft. "You're the someone."

"Which someone?"

"The someone who upped the bid."

Stillness gripped Paige. He's joking, she thought. The man *has* to be joking. "That's...impossible," she countered on a weak note.

Lifting the black-and-white bid card from her numb fingers, Ross slipped it into the hip pocket of her slacks for safekeeping. "Keep that where it won't be seen, hmm?"

"But that's absurd," she retorted. "The auctioneer knows I was the last bidder. Why would he let me bid against myself?"

"Indiscriminate people, auctioneers. Offer them money, they'll take it."

"But he must know...he must... Why would I raise my own bid?"

"To edge out a second party."

"What second party?" Her voice was rising in proportion to her hysteria.

"The one you'd bluff into thinking there are three instead of two bidders for the horse."

Too stunned to speak, Paige gaped at Ross as he explained one of the psychological games played at auctions.

"If you've decided to buy at any price, why let a lukewarm customer drive it sky-high, trying to get you to fold? Unless he's equally determined, he'll drop out the minute he thinks there's a third bidder, saving you a handsome sum."

Paige turned her back on him. A lot of good he was doing her! Obeying instinct, she stepped onto the fence. The hell with pride, aplomb and image. She'd climb into the arena and stop the sale. Climbing into corrals was something she did every day. If doing so now, here, was humbling for a world-class champion, so be it. Better a tarnished image than a dead champion.

She was about to step onto the next rung when Ross circled her waist from behind and set her back down on the ground. "What do you think you're doing?"

"I'm going in there." With icy hauteur, she dared him to try stopping her. "I'll tell the auctioneer he's made a mistake. The bid is still twenty-two."

She's incredible, Ross marveled. Like no one he'd ever met. She might crack, but, by God, she was determined not to crumble. "First, you don't have to jump the fence. Use the gate. And second, it won't matter what you say when you get in there. Bids are irrevocable. Imagine the chaos—"

"Shut up!" Paige lunged for him, grabbing his shirt-front in both hands. "Just shut up!"

Ross cradled her shoulders, his brow creasing as he considered an angle he hadn't before. An oath slid out with his next breath. "You don't have the money."

She laughed, though it sounded more like a strangled hiccup. Coming undone, Paige thought. Her composure had unraveled, and she was coming undone. "How astute of you to figure that out."

"Where'd you get the bid card?" It was one thing to accidentally offer on a horse you didn't want, possibly had no use for. It was something else entirely to deal yourself into the game if you couldn't ante up. He'd assumed she came from wealth. She had a look, a way about her, inherent to women with generous daddies or large and available trust funds. It was an attitude Ross would have sworn couldn't be faked. "Your credit had to be approved."

"It isn't my card." Weariness tinged her voice. Paige heard it, and recognized the sound of defeat. "I'm holding it for a friend."

He nodded. With that, Paige accepted that her dilemma was irreversible and let go of his shirt. When she saw the wrinkles she'd caused, it seemed imperative she smooth them out, repair at least some of the damage she'd caused today.

Slowly, pressing firmly, she ran her open hands over the creased material. Once, twice, three times. Ross's muscles tightened at her touch until there was barely room in his chest for a drawn breath. Watching her face, her eyes, he decided she was oblivious of the effect her slow massage was having on him. She was aware of nothing but her own predicament.

"Twenty-four going once..."

Ross felt a twinge of guilt for letting things go so far. Dipping into his jacket pocket, he withdrew his own bid card.

"Twenty-four going twice..."

Guessing what was about to happen, Paige's eyes widened. Without taking his own off her face Ross showed his card, then tucked it away again.

*"Twenty-*five! *I've got twenty-five. Do I hear twenty-six?"*

Shocked, Paige stumbled back a step. She might have collapsed completely if his hands on her shoulders hadn't dragged her back. "You've bid on her?"

"Mmm..." Calmly, as if buying horses costing twenty-five grand were something he did every day, he smiled. "A decent filly, by the looks of her."

"I...I don't know what to say." He's crazy, Paige decided. A certifiable lunatic. Without blinking an eye, he'd risked thousands of dollars in order to save her stupid behind. And he didn't even know her. "Thanking you hardly seems adequate."

Watching her, Ross felt the stir again. "Have dinner with me and we'll call it even."

"Dinner." It was sinking in, exhausting Paige. Draining her mentally, as well as physically, so that she could hardly comprehend the invitation, much less respond to it.

She was unnaturally pale and looked suddenly fragile. Ross grimaced, feeling rotten for his role in frightening her. But dammit, unwittingly or not, she'd bid against him. He'd had to pay three thousand more for the horse. A word, a gesture, might have saved him a chunk of it, he told himself. But the chance to see her without her walls up had been too inviting.

"Sold! Number twelve, for twenty-five thousand."

The hammer slammed down close to the microphone. Paige flinched. Other sounds faded, reaching her through too many layers of disbelief—applause, the auctioneer's voice, the creak and jingle of tack as another horse was trotted by.

With his hands still on her shoulders, Ross turned her,
trapping her between the fence and his body. He's too close,
she thought vaguely. So close his hat brim shaded both their
faces. Her pulse tripped over the thrill again. A pleasant
sensation. Spending the evening with him held far more appeal than she thought wise. His hands dropped to her hips,
his fingers spread. A voice in her brain urged her to escape.
Paige had all she could do just to keep from swaying toward him.

She focused on his face, on his intense blue eyes. "Why?"
she wanted to know. "Why did you do it?"

"Does it matter?"

"Yes, it seems to." All her life she'd done for herself, by
herself. She'd asked nothing more of anyone than to be left
alone to chase her dream. Debt, she discovered now, lived
up to its reputation for being a burden. This one weighed a
ton.

"The first time I saw you, I thought you were the sort of
woman men parted with small fortunes to have...if only for
a night."

Perhaps it was those words that rushed her abruptly back
to sanity. Perhaps it was the light bump of his hips and the
tops of his thighs against hers. *If only for a night.* Indeed,
few women could boast of two or even ten hours of their
time being valued so highly. She didn't doubt there were
those who'd consider the price tag flattering. Paige wasn't
one of them.

"The first time I saw you," she returned, arching a brow,
"I thought you were arrogant."

"You're perceptive."

"You aren't." She tried to step around him, but his fingers tightened on her hips, prohibiting movement. Trapped,
Paige did the next best thing to create distance; she
straightened her spine, tipped her chin and gazed coolly at
him. "You bought a horse, Mr. Tanner. Nothing more."

No, he thought, she couldn't be bought, any more than
she could be charmed. So how did a man get to Paige Meredith?

"Hate to interrupt you, Tanner."

"Then don't," Ross warned the voice behind them. "Beat it, Brady."

Paige shifted her eyes to look over Ross's shoulder. The man standing there was grinning, his friendly brown eyes virtually dancing with mirth. She remembered seeing his picture in the catalog. Brady, Ross had said. Of Brady Auctions. Of course.

"Need your signature, pal." Gil waited, rocking patiently on his heels. The glare Ross threw over his shoulder threatened bodily harm. Gil smiled blandly and extended a document and a gold pen. "Can't proceed with the sale till we've got you on the dotted line."

"Lost track of your errand boys, Gil?" Ross backed away from Paige, not entirely comfortable with the force of will it required. Though his body obeyed, his senses wanted to cling.

Needing to steady herself before trying to walk, Paige stayed where she was and let the rails at her back take her weight. Ross took the offered paper, using Brady's back for a writing surface.

"Yours is one sale it's a pleasure seeing to personally," Gil said with an unmistakable gloating tone. Withdrawing a folded packet from his inside jacket pocket, he exchanged it for the acknowledgment of purchase Ross had signed. "Hell, Tanner, I had your name on her title this morning."

Ross sliced a quick look at Paige. She seemed not to have heard Brady's unfortunate remark. That wasn't to say she wouldn't, in the next five or ten seconds, run those words through her mind again. Gil produced a cigar and clipped the end clean, congenial, relaxed, looking as if he planned to linger. Ross thought it advisable that he linger elsewhere.

"You'll want settlement," Ross remarked.

"No hurry." Gil sucked on his cigar, squinting through thick clouds of smoke. "You know our procedure. You've got until thirty minutes after the sale's conclusion."

"And you know mine—I pay up and take off." Taking Brady by the arm, Ross turned him toward the registration tables.

Astonished, Paige watched them go. First, she thought in confusion, she hadn't been able to avoid or get rid of Ross Tanner. Now *he* couldn't seem to get away from *her* fast enough! Even Gil Brady looked baffled by Ross's strong-arming him across the stable yard.

Feeling strangely like someone who'd lost her way, Paige glanced around as if needing a familiar sight to help her get her bearings. Spectators eyed the newest prospect on the block. Hands worked the arena gates, hustling to keep things running smoothly. The sun still shone; the sky was still blue. She was still trembling. It didn't seem possible that everything had stayed the same for the rest of the world, when for her something felt irreversibly altered.

Noticing Faye's belongings strewn in the dirt, Paige stooped to pick them up. Inches from the catalog her fingers froze. *Hell, Tanner, I had your name on her title* . . . Slowly Paige stood. . . . *this morning.*

This morning! Whirling, she zeroed in on Ross's tall figure, walking beside Brady. A hot, seething anger burned in the pit of her stomach. She'd been tricked, manipulated. Twice in one day!

The two men were halfway to the registration tables when she struck out after them, her leggy stride eating up ground. She grabbed Ross's arm from behind and, with a strength born of mastering half a ton of thundering horse, pulled him around to face her. "Did he say this morning?"

With a casual flick of his thumb, Ross knocked his hat back, then had the nerve to grin at her.

"I asked you a question." She ground out the words. "Did he—" Paige flung out an arm, one finger pointing at a startled Gil Brady. "Did he put your name on the filly's papers *this morning?*"

"Tanner?" Gil wondered aloud.

Ross took in her fiery eyes and heaving breasts. There was no mistaking the white-hot intensity of her temper. Slashes of color stained her cheekbones. A vein visibly pounded at the base of her neck. God, yes, she was definitely at her best when breaking free.

"What's going on, Tanner?" Gil asked on a tentative note.

"I believe Ms. Meredith is questioning our ethics and your business practices. Thinks we struck a deal on the Irish before she went on the block." It satisfied Ross to see Brady squirm. Served him right for opening his mouth in the first place. "She was bidding against me, you see. Apparently believes she's been cheated out of a horse."

Paige glowered. "That's not what I—"

"Ms. Meredith," Gil cut in, "I run a square-dealing operation. Whatever I said to mislead or upset you, it was only in jest between friends. However, if you have the slightest doubt, I invite you to file a bid dispute with the auctioneer. He is the accepted last word."

"How about it, Paige?" Ross prodded. "Want to tell the man your story? He might agree something fishy was going on. If he decides in your favor, the rules say you get the horse for your final bid of twenty-four."

"*I* get the horse? I don't *want* the horse!" Without releasing Ross, she peered over her shoulder at Brady. "You knew he'd buy her. How?"

Gil shrugged. "When a man travels from Montana to Kentucky, leaving his ranch at roundup time, then looks at one prospect and no other, it's a safe bet she'll be going with him when he leaves."

Paige slowly brought her head back around. "Montana," she whispered as a fresh wave of anger rushed through her. "You came all the way from Montana to buy that filly?"

"To look at her."

Paige literally saw red. Ross Tanner's self-assured grin swam behind a crimson mist of fury. "Do you know what you did to me? What you put me through, letting me think I'd bid on her?"

"You did bid on her."

"No thanks to you! If you hadn't come up behind me, I'd—" Mouth open, Paige stopped. She'd what? Have had her wits about her? Have paid more attention to her actions, instead of her emotions?

"Face it," Ross murmured. "You were reckless with your friend's bid card. So I let you sweat out a few close moments." He shrugged. "Next time you'll be more careful."

"Why, you…you…" She couldn't recall deciding to slug him. Suddenly her fist was flying.

Ross intercepted the punch. There was the slap of flesh striking flesh when her wrist and his palm connected. Effortlessly he pinned her arm behind her back, then twisted the other around for good measure. He dragged her up against him, and the air rushed from Paige's lungs on impact with his body. Neither of them noticed Gil Brady cautiously backing away.

"What?" Ross softly taunted. "What am I? Go on, say it. Bet you'll feel worlds better."

Control. Paige reached deep for it. She wouldn't think of how it felt to be pressed against the length of him or of the uneven gallop of her pulse. She wouldn't think of how close his mouth was to hers, or of the heat that had nothing to do with anger spreading outward from deep inside her. She could block out anything, she told herself, anytime. Or at least bluff the best of them into thinking she had.

Instantly Paige erased all trace of emotion from her face. "'A woman men spend small fortunes to have,'" she said mockingly.

He'd planned to let her go at the first sign she'd simmered down. But when she adopted the lofty expression and condescending tone, Ross decided otherwise. She had an amazing talent for saying "Go to hell" with the simple lift of an eyebrow. Ross had never been one to back down from a challenge.

"The filly was mine for twenty-two," he told her in a deadly-soft voice. "The last bidder had dropped out when I walked up behind you." Her gaze slid away. He jerked her the tiniest bit closer, and her eyes snapped back, not quite as cool or as confident. "You cost me three thousand dollars, sweetheart. That may be a drop in the bucket by your standards. I call it a small fortune." Ross let his gaze drift down to her mouth, to her full lips, temptingly parted.

"Three grand ought to buy a man a hell of a lot better treatment than a fist flying into his face."

Paige realized his intent and struggled instinctively. He jerked her again, this time bringing her up hard against him. She held herself still while her heart raced wildly. To move at all was to stimulate the very sensations she wanted to prevent. And she *would* prevent them, she vowed.

Lips hovering above hers, Ross shifted both her wrists into the long-boned fingers of one hand, pressing them to the small of her back. His free hand tunneled into her hair to cup the back of her head. His eyes flicked up from her mouth—only once, and only for a moment. In that moment, everything changed for Paige. In that moment, she stopped resisting and started anticipating what she wanted to dread. She remembered that in one inexplicably fatuous moment yesterday she'd wondered if his mouth would feel as soft as it looked. If his body would be this hard... She heard herself moan. They both knew it wasn't in protest.

She refused to close her eyes as he touched his lips to hers, lightly, gently. Ross saw them widen at first contact, then watched them blur out of focus. She gasped, and he felt the breath snatched from his mouth into hers. His tongue stroked her lips once before slipping past them. Her lashes drifted down, and she went pliant in his arms. A mistake, he realized instantly. Having a taste of her was only going to make him want more. Much more.

Oh, yes, his mouth was soft. Soft, but hinting of power. Paige couldn't stop the sensations, the drowning waves of pleasure as he gently but thoroughly kissed her. No one should lose control so completely, she thought dimly, and losing control shouldn't feel so good. His beard was a tender rasp against her skin. From shoulders to knees, his sinewed body throbbed in unison with hers. Again Paige strained to free her wrists. Again Ross tightened his hold. With the minute particle of sanity left to her, she could be grateful he hadn't released her. Now he'd never know her futile struggle had been an involuntary urge to curl her arms around his waist and cling.

For unmeasured moments, Ross explored and enjoyed. Her mouth—warm and willing. Her taste—rich, creamy, secret. Her texture—smooth satin. Needs sprang up, unexpectedly powerful. He plunged so deep into the sheer luxury of her, he forgot they stood in the middle of a stable yard with an audience of hundreds less than fifty yards away. Never before had he wanted a woman so intensely, so quickly.

Her eyes were still closed when he lifted his head. By the time she opened them, cloudy and working to focus, Ross made sure none of his astonishment showed in his face.

"I'll let you go," he said casually as she breathed a shuddering sigh. "If you promise to keep your hands to yourself."

His bantering tone wounded, then infuriated Paige. *She* keep *her* hands to herself? And to think that for one helpless, unguarded moment she'd yielded to him, pliant, pulsing. Her gaze hardened to a glare, and she answered him through clenched teeth. "And if I don't?"

"Be warned that I hit back."

That her pulse refused to level stoked her temper. "I'll do better than that. I'll promise to never lay so much as my eyes on you again."

Gradually Ross loosened his grip on her wrists. It might be best for both of them, he decided, if she made a special effort to keep that promise.

The blood rushed back to her hands and head simultaneously. Paige wanted to massage her wrists, but refused to show the slightest sign of weakness while he was watching. He took a step back and smiled his cocky smile. She itched to curl her fingers into a fist. She might have thrown the second punch—warning or no warning—if Faye hadn't chosen that moment to make her presence known.

"And here I was worried you'd be all alone and bored to tears."

Paige whirled. Ross's deep-chested laughter at her back had the sting of sandpaper dragged over raw skin. She might have said something appropriately cutting to both of them if her own fury hadn't been in the way of her voice.

Without so much as a parting word to Paige, Ross strolled away, tipping his hat as he passed Faye. "Ma'am."

When he was gone, Paige shot Faye a warning look.

"I won't say a word," Faye promised dryly. "Not one word about stallions with wild streaks." Smiling, she looped her arm with Paige's. "So, did you save us a couple of seats?"

"Actually, no." Though it required a great deal of effort, Paige managed to smile back. "I was much too busy saving your money and my neck."

Chapter Three

Flowers and fences transformed Friday's dressage ring into a festively colorful jumping arena. There were manicured hedges, freshly painted rails, a water hazard splashing back sunlight. Riders turned out in jackets of jet, scarlet, and rich royal blue. Enthusiasm poured off the bleachers.

Astride Lady Night, Paige waited her turn in the holding area, looking cool and unflappable. Sweat trickled beneath her lipstick red coat, her eyes felt gritty, and she ached all over. Tense, tired and sore, she summed up—a prevalent condition among riders nearing the finish of a horse trial. Gritting her teeth, she stifled a yawn. God, she was tired.

She'd stumbled into the morning at five, into the stables in darkness. By sunrise she'd unwrapped her mounts' bandages, walked off their stiffness and her own, bathed and braided them for their trots before the ground jury— who'd kindly scratched Smooth as Silk—and returned them to stalls bedded with fresh hay. A strenuous morning for some, perhaps, but all in a day's work for Paige. And not one bit to blame for her fatigue. No, she had Ross Tanner to thank for that.

Cocky, arrogant jerk.

Because of him, she'd slept badly, jolting from heart-thumping dreams through most of the night. Dreams of hands pinning her down, of wonderfully clever lips taking her mouth, stealing her breath. Awake, she'd tossed and turned, unable to fathom her behavior at the auction. Had she ever in her life wanted so badly to hit someone? To kiss someone?

That kiss. She had only to close her eyes to feel again the exquisite skill of his mouth, to breathe his scent, to taste him. That kiss—powerful and weakening, yes, but just a kiss, all the same, she tried telling herself.

No, what had happened to her in those stunning seconds was too complicated for so simple a word. Its thrill lingered.

A normal response to a passionate moment, she reasoned. Nothing more. Except that she wasn't, had never been, a woman moved to passion. It was a discovery Travis had made years ago, one Paige had secretly thought convenient. She hadn't the time or the energy for more than one devotion. Grand passions left little room for big dreams.

Desire? Paige tested the word, let it bounce around her brain, and approved. More complicated than a kiss, simpler than passion. There it was, then. Desire—quick, sizzling and short-lived. Safe.

Sensing her rider's attention had wandered, Lady sidled restlessly.

Damn the man. He'd blown her concentration too often during dressage. She wouldn't allow it today, particularly when he was thousands of miles away—if not already back in Montana, then at least on his way there. The last she'd seen of Ross Tanner had been his back as he left her to settle his account with Brady. "I pay up and take off," he'd said. Gone, she thought with finality. And the blasted filly with him, thank God. Paige scanned the bleachers, looking, she realized, for his black Stetson. Not because she wanted him to be there, she decided, but to be absolutely certain that he wasn't.

Lady tossed her head. Shortening the reins, Paige collected the horse and her thoughts. Banishing Ross from her mind, she watched Tippy Lipton and Jumpin' Jack take the course.

The layout was tight and twisty, guaranteed to keep riders alert and horses interested. Because the purpose of a stadium test was only to prove the horse fit for service after the strenuous demands of the previous days, the obstacles didn't have the height or difficulty of a show-jumping competition. That didn't mean a horse trial couldn't be lost in this last arena. There were penalties for crashing a jump and for finishing over the allotted time. Paige had walked the course at dawn, pleased with how well it suited Lady's short stride and ability to turn on a dime.

Jumpin' Jack grazed a seemingly harmless vertical, and an expectant buzz swelled as the rail bounced on its flat cups. Paige winced. Gasps from the audience were unsettling. Part of a fence had been left sliding or shuddering, but a rider couldn't look back, because the next obstacle was already coming up.

The fence held, and when there was quiet again, a voice called out, "Clean!" for Tippy's benefit. But at the wall, the first jump of the triple, Tippy and Jack parted company. Tippy sailed over alone. She got to her feet, spectators applauding as she brushed herself off and remounted. As the next rider prepared to take the course, Faye, who'd been watching from the sidelines, strolled over to Paige.

"The wall demands a left-angle approach," Paige said, correctly predicting Faye's advice. "It'll cost two, maybe three seconds."

"There's time. Go conservative and clean, Lady Night locks up fourth place. Respectable for a green horse."

Paige smiled. "But third or better would be remarkable." Looking past Faye, she watched Mark Harrison effortlessly gliding over obstacles. Forty-two and one of the all-time greats, Mark was a long, lanky man, hopelessly graceless on the ground, elegance personified on the back of a horse. Paige had been sixteen the winter she took his dressage clinic, and developed a classic schoolgirl crush on him. She'd even staged an intimate moment in the barn, offering him everything—her heart and soul, her undying devotion. And her body, she'd jerkily whispered, if he felt he absolutely had to have that, too. He'd blushed, scraped his feet and stammered that he was engaged to be married. Paige had been devastated.

Ten years later, she could smile at the memory. Trapped in a newly mucked stall with a breathless adolescent unabashedly, if somewhat reluctantly, offering her innocence, Mark must have wished for a great big hole to open up and drop him into blessed oblivion.

Now Paige was going into the preliminary jumping phase with a seventh to Mark's eighth. He was the man she and Kid had to beat out of a first in intermediate after the lunch break. Both were accomplished riders, experienced in taking second place behind the other. Both had ridden on the U.S. equestrian team sent to last year's world championship. And both burned for the chance to ride for an Olympic gold medal.

As Paige looked on, Mark rode conservatively, methodically, unerringly. As always. He planned ahead and was precise, selecting the most direct path and rarely veering from it once on the course. Paige, on the other hand, rode with her mind open and anything possible.

"Listen up," Faye said in her brisk trainer's tone. "Save beat-the-clock for events that count. Your competitive streak is admirable but you'd be foolish to risk injury this close to a three-day."

"I'll keep that in mind," Paige murmured. She watched for Mark's time to flash and his new standing to register.

"Sure you will," Faye muttered. "The whole time you're flying around like a bullet gone wild."

The warning bell sounded. Paige pulled down the chin strap of her velvet-covered hard hat and steered Lady Night through the in gate. Adrenaline surged, washing away weariness and tension, fueling aggression. Lady took a thorough look at the course as they cantered once around, saw what she had to do and lunged for the start line.

She's good. Seated third-row center at the far end of the arena, Ross watched Paige merge herself with the smoothly striding horse. Last Friday she'd entered the ring to the announcement of her name and those of her horses; today she made a large galloping circle to an arm's-length list of titles. If that hadn't told him she was big-time, the silence from the crowd would have. Two thousand people held a breath. Someone important, someone they'd all heard of, read about, was gearing up to do her stuff.

Ross told himself he wasn't infatuated. It wasn't the woman that had drawn him back. He'd simply decided he'd rather be bored watching a horse show than bored pacing Lance's hideous black-lacquer apartment. The bankers so desperate to get at TLD's books that they couldn't wait a month for Ross to finish spring roundup weren't so desperate that they'd work on Sunday. On the verge of going stir-crazy, he'd remembered Paige saying she wouldn't know if she'd won until today. No, it wasn't the woman, but his own curiosity to see if she was as good as his untutored eye told him she was. Ross called himself a liar in the next breath.

She took the first three fences, relatively easy jumps, to a respectful hush. The only sound was of hooves pounding the turf and a horse heaving to breathe. They sailed over the water hazard—the first of the trickier obstacles—and touched down without a splash. Clear. The crowd erupted.

Ross didn't clap, didn't move. He watched, awed by the seamless harmony between horse and rider. She was better than good. She was magnificent. Graceful, poised. She made it look easy. He'd spurred enough cow ponies over gullies in chase of a stray to know she was landing with teeth-rattling jolts. Yet she flew as smoothly as if she'd been lifted on the wind.

Approaching jump number seven, she rose up in the saddle, her face framed between the perked, alert ears of the horse. Two strides after landing, she reined in, literally spinning the mare on her haunches. The animal's muscles bunched with checked power before exploding off in a new direction. More than her strength, her courage stunned Ross.

Good God, she'd be something flying across a Montana plain.

Lady Night slipped on an approach. Breathing a curse, Paige added three critical seconds to those she'd sacrificed on the wall approach. She couldn't afford time penalties. Making the decision, she cut the last turn sharp. Lady balked, going off stride momentarily before consenting to take the final fence at an angle most horses would have refused with a skidding stop.

They cantered through the timer without faults. Paige's eyes were on the display board as she exited the ring. She'd improved her position by four places; she'd needed five to leapfrog Harrison.

"Damn." She'd been off. Just a bit, but it didn't take much. Sometimes a fraction of an inch, of a second, meant a loss...or worse.

Trotting out to the yard, she found Faye waiting with Kidnapper. Paige dismounted, and the women switched horses—Paige to take Kid to the warm-up ring, Faye to turn Lady over to a groom for a hot walk.

"Not bad," Faye remarked.

"Not good, either." Invariably Paige demanded more of herself than anyone else would.

There was a break in the action while the ground crew rebuilt the jumps for intermediates. Spectators abandoned the stands. Riders warmed horses and walked the redesigned course. Paige kept Kid in the practice ring until the last possible moment, then walked him around the back of the bleachers.

The course was only slightly altered. Heights had been elevated. The triple was now the second element. By the time Paige's turn rolled around, and with only Harrison left to follow her, it was a sure bet she and Mark would take first and second places. Which of the two would ride out with blue ribbons was still up for grabs.

Paige was the on-deck rider when Mark arrived from the practice ring. Their eyes met, and a look passed between

them, one peculiar to friends who find themselves in the odd
position of being adversaries. "Good luck to you," it said.
"Better luck to me." Paige acknowledged him with a nod,
then prepared to begin.

The sun was hotter, the crowd louder. Kidnapper tore into
the course. Paige drove him by instinct, by the seat of her
pants, as Faye often praised or complained, depending on
the outcome. The gelding's legs were shorter than was ideal
for five-foot rails, but he popped over each as if he had
springs in his shoes. Together they finished quick and clean.

Leaving the arena, Paige passed Mark at the in gate. She
wished him well, even as she hoped his horse "brailled" the
jumps, knocking a few down. He could afford a time penalty, but his lead wouldn't allow him to pull more than one
rail.

He pulled two.

Paige trotted into the ring for the presentation of awards
and left with blue satin ribbons fluttering from Kidnapper's bridle.

Fifteen minutes later she had Kid tethered to a tree and
was hosing him down. She'd removed her hat, jacket and
gloves, rolled up her sleeves and pulled her shirttails free.
She didn't care that she splashed as much water on herself
as on the horse. She didn't care that her smartly fashioned
bun was unwinding or that she stood ankle-deep in mud. It
was over—the competition, the weekend, the nerves. It felt
nearly as good to have it finished as it did to have finished
in first place. She had the rest of today and all of tomorrow
to do as she pleased. Paige vowed to be utterly virtueless and
waste every second of them.

Nosing the air, Kid asked for more of the cool spray on his
neck. Laughing, Paige obliged, aiming the hose with one
hand while treating him to a brisk rubdown with a curry
brush.

Kid spooked suddenly, backing up as far as the tether allowed. Curious, Paige looked over her shoulder. Straight
into Ross Tanner's electric blue eyes. Her smile faded as an
ice-hot current shot up her spine. She didn't bother pretending the leap in her pulse was nerves or temper or any of

the aliases she'd given it yesterday. What flashed through her was a thrill. A *thrill*, dammit!

In one continuous movement, she drew back her shoulders, placed her fists on her hips and turned to face him. He leaned against the watershed wall, looking infuriatingly at ease. His legs were crossed at the ankles, his hands tucked in the pockets of dark brown cords. The sleeves of his lightweight beige sweater were shoved up on his arms, its softness calling attention to the hard body beneath. No hat. If he'd worn the hat, Paige thought resentfully, she might have had some warning. And if she'd known to expect him, what then?

"Well, look who's here," she said blandly. She almost asked him why he was still in Kentucky, then decided she didn't want him believing she'd wasted a single minute of the past twenty-four hours thinking about him, not even of his whereabouts. "Another day to fill, Ross?"

His smile was lazy, intimate. "Mmm...another night, too."

Ross looked her over while she gave him one of those long, direct stares that both fascinated and frustrated him for its ability to mask her thoughts. He'd liked to have gone undetected a while longer. There had been different qualities to her a moment ago, soft, appealing qualities he hadn't seen before. Another five minutes of watching her might have been enlightening. A pleasure, anyway. Now he could only look at her face as she stared at him, water shooting off to one side from the hose she held.

Sunlight filtered through the leaves to glint in her hair. The pale mass was pinned loosely, stray wisps clinging to her face and neck. On a whim, she'd fastened the blue ribbons to her slipping bun. Satin streamers hung halfway down her back, fluttering in the faint breeze. While he watched, she drew the back of her wrist across her brow. Like the flip side of a coin, everything about her was in contrast to the other times he'd seen her. She was loose and happy, dirty, drenched, not a whisper of dignity or glamour. Yet she still exuded that cool sexuality.

His quiet stare was mesmerizing. Paige ordered her bones to solidify and narrowed her eyes. "You'll understand if I don't die with delight at the sight of you. Last time we met it nearly cost me twenty-five grand."

"Today won't be that expensive. Twelve, maybe fifteen hundred bucks." As her frown formed Ross inclined his head, indicating the water spouting from the hose. "I figure that's what you paid for the saddle."

Paige snapped her head to one side and yelped. For as long as she'd been facing him, she'd been flooding the ground around Kid's tack. Her custom-made saddle was tipped on its side in three inches of mud.

"Damn you, Tanner!" Oh, he's going to be sorry, she fumed. This time he's going to pay. Sliding her thumb over part of the nozzle, she intensified the spray's pressure and aimed. Though she moved fast, the hissing stream collapsed, vanishing only inches short of its target. Paige found herself pointing a dry hose at Ross's maddeningly smug grin.

His hand still on the spigot, he tipped his head. "Close."

"Close doesn't count." She threw down the hose in frustration and stomped through the mire to her saddle. "Look what you've done!"

"What I've done?"

"Yes, you!" she fired back. Glove-soft leather squashed, giving up water like a filled sponge. She hauled the saddle to dry ground and stared down at it. Ruined. Four months for it to be delivered from England; five more to break it in. Now it was one more piece of workout tack. "If you hadn't come sneaking up behind me, I'd—"

"Uh-uh. You tried that one yesterday. It didn't wash then, and it won't now. Anyone ever tell you you've got dangerous hands?"

"A perfectly good show saddle— *Dangerous hands?*"

"With the way you handle bid cards and hoses, it's a wonder you can be trusted with a set of reins."

Leading with her chin, Paige took two indignant steps forward. "For your information, I have *great* hands."

Mud-spattered and bedraggled, she could still be the regal ice queen with the lift of an eyebrow. "I'll bet you do, honey," Ross murmured. "When you control them."

"Control! Look, you...you..." Making more splash than necessary, Paige advanced to stand toe-to-toe with him. "I've got the steadiest, quietest— I've got the best damned hands on the circuit! Judges praise them. Other riders *wish* they had— What the hell are you laughing at?"

"I stand corrected." Without warning, he tugged her into his arms. Still laughing, he dropped his head to her shoulder. "Somebody oughta give those hands a trophy. Call it The Best Damned Hands Award."

She wouldn't laugh, too, she vowed. Struggling not to, Paige drew a deep breath. Her knees liquefied. With her face pressed to the curve of his neck she'd filled herself with the heady, weakening scent of him. If he hadn't already been holding her, she thought, he'd be picking her up from the ground about now.

"Damn you, Tanner." She worked her arms between them and levered back. "It's only when you pop up that I make an ass of myself."

"Naw." Keeping one arm around her waist, Ross plucked a dangling bobby pin from her hair. He let it drop to the ground and withdrew another. "I've been here for hours, watching you outride the lot of them. What you made, lady, was one hell of an impression."

He freed the ribbons next, and knew by the way she squeezed her eyes shut on a curse that she'd forgotten them. With exaggerated care, he fitted the rosette's hook through a buttonhole on her shirt, sliding a hand behind the damp material to hold it steady. The backs of his fingers pressed the soft, warm flesh above her breast. Against his knuckles he felt the thud of her heart. When he withdrew his hand, he did so slowly, dragging skin lightly over skin.

She opened her eyes. Their green color was smoky. He hadn't expected her to stand still while he let down the rest of her hair. She surprised him by not budging as it fell, tumbling freely down her back. Ross dived into it with both hands, letting his fingers comb slowly down to the tips.

"How soon can you be ready for dinner?"

"Dinner." Paige hadn't moved because her body had stopped listening to her brain. "I don't recall dinner plans with you."

"No victory is official until the cork pops." Whatever reaction Ross might have expected, he hadn't been prepared for her mouth to soften and her eyes to grow wistful.

"Champagne." It wasn't an answer, but a thought that had somehow found its way past her lips. Backing away, Paige picked up the curry brush she'd dropped, and applied it to Kid's hide.

He shouldn't have been able to tempt her with those few words. She shouldn't want so badly to say yes. How long had it been since she'd toasted a win? Paige wondered. How long since she'd paused long enough to acknowledge one before throwing herself into the madness of the next competition? She frowned, her brush strokes growing slower. There had been a time when winning—finishing—was special, an accomplishment. Now everything was a means to an end. And only the end was important.

"You owe me one dinner, Paige. For getting you out of your jam."

Looking at Ross from her side of a chestnut rump, Paige knew she was going to say yes, and that it might be her worst move since she'd given the key to her front door to Travis Donahue. It was saved from being flat-out self-destructive by the fact that Ross would soon be leaving the state.

"Which is it, Tanner? Celebration or debt? And what jam, I'd like to know? You wanted the filly and you got her."

The vulnerability he'd glimpsed was gone. Ross wondered what had caused it. "Afraid of spending an evening with me?"

You bet your ten-gallon hat I am! "Of course not." He didn't believe her. She saw it in the way his mouth twitched as he struggled to keep from smiling. "You want dinner, we'll go to dinner. But on one condition."

"Which is?"

"I pay. It was my jam, my debt, and it's my celebration." She was prepared to insist, but after a thoughtful moment he agreed.

"Do you have a change of clothes with you?"

Lifting an eyebrow at his question, Paige smoothed a hand over one damp, dirty hip. "This is too casual?"

Letting the smile come, Ross took his eyes from hers and ran them slowly, very slowly, down to her toes and back up. "Will an hour be enough time? Or do you need more?"

"More? You're pushing your luck, cowboy. Aren't you the guy from out of town, no one to talk to, an evening to fill?" Paige tossed the curry brush aside and untied Kid. "Half will be plenty." Turning, she made as dignified a retreat as possible through the sucking mud.

"You come here often." Paige set her glass down, and Ross poured more champagne for both of them.

"Here Kentucky or here the restaurant?"

"Both."

"You sound convinced. What makes you so sure?"

"Kentucky's simple. It's obvious you and Brady are friends of long standing. You know how he operates, and he you. The restaurant?" Paige glanced around the room. The atmosphere was casual and intimate. Candlelight fluttered on the dozen or so tables. Spices tinged the air, just enough to entice. "It's the cozy sort locals keep to themselves. Off the beaten path, no neon signs to lure tourists." Savoring a sip of sparkling wine, Paige thought a moment. "Getting here was complicated, but you didn't hesitate or read street signs. So you've been here before," she concluded. "Quite a few times, I think."

Not only does the mind work, Ross mused, it works rather well. Brains, beauty, style. What red-blooded man stood a chance? Soft light and shadows gave her skin the allure of ivory satin. Jewel green silk draped her shoulders and left her throat bare. Her scent drifted across the table, conjuring up visions of gardens at midnight...of laying her down in one.

Ross resisted the pull of desire—for now. "I didn't realize you'd paid attention. You were so quiet I thought you'd fallen asleep."

"Competition letdown."

"Even when you win?"

"Especially when I win." She laughed, surprising herself. How long had it been since she'd felt so free and easy? It was only dinner, she told herself. A few hours, a little champagne. Then she remembered that her last win had been celebrated by the chatter of cameras going off and the cover on *Horseplay*. This was better. For the first time in too many years, she felt like a woman instead of an athlete.

The waiter arrived, and Paige shifted to give him room to serve. "Oh, good. I'm starving."

Ignoring his salad for the moment, Ross watched her begin. He thought she'd pick and nibble. She dug in with relish. How the hell could she eat like a bear and be thin as a sparrow? "Serious business."

Paige speared a tomato wedge and glanced over at him. "Which? Winning or starving?"

Ross grinned. "Both."

His lean cheeks creased with the flash of white teeth. The blue of his eyes deepened. Paige worked past the power of that grin and bit into the tomato. "My stomach rolls at the mere thought of food during events. This is my first real meal in three days."

"Nerves? No one would guess. You don't look nervous. You look..." He thought back to the first day. *Rigid. Too rigid.*

"What?" Fork poised in midair, Paige waited. "Don't leave me hanging. I look what?"

"Controlled. Very controlled."

"Good." Her stomach relaxed and accepted her last mouthful. For a moment she'd thought he was going to say "restless" or "dissatisfied."

"And thin," he added. "You could stand to gain a few pounds."

"Please, I get enough nagging on that subject from Faye."

"Faye?"

"Gentry. A friend, my trainer. You met her—saw her, I mean. Yesterday at the auction. Short, fiftyish, dark hair."

"Beady brown eyes?"

Paige laughed. Her recollection of Faye's eyes was of them narrowed, not in suspicion, but in curiosity. One Paige had refused to satisfy, much to Faye's displeasure. "She thought you were assaulting me."

"What did you tell her?"

"That you were dangerous and ought to be locked up."

Ross chuckled as salad plates were exchanged for side orders of pasta. It didn't make sense, he thought. The lady had more than looks going for her. She was bright, talented and fun to be with. So why was she always alone? Not always, he amended. There'd been Faye and another.

"Who was the blond guy at the auction?" Casually Ross tore off a chunk of thick-crusted bread.

Paige had to think a minute. Then her smile slid behind a thin veil of ice. "Travis Donahue."

Undaunted by her chilly warning to back off, Ross probed further. "So who's Travis Donahue?"

"A world-class eventer," she replied with practiced coolness. "And none of your business."

"I wasn't prying, Paige." *Like hell.* "This is a date—a man and woman sharing trivialities, tidbits, getting better acquainted."

"Emily Post?"

Ross shook his head. "Aunt Mary. So. How long has the affair with Travis been over?"

Dumbstruck, Paige sat back and crossed her arms. She couldn't say which stunned her more, his audacity or his perception. "You call that a tidbit?"

"Triviality?"

"I call it presumptuous."

He lifted her glass and passed it across the table. "I saw you together. There are ways men touch women. Then there are ways men touch their lovers, even ex-lovers." Thin crystal changed hands with a brush of fingers. "We've got to start somewhere. Would you rather it was with Faye?"

She'd rather it wasn't at all. "Why not with Aunt Mary?"

"All right." He smiled at her scowl, then waved a finger at the entrée placed before her. "You eat, I'll talk. Mary Tanner has been mother to me since my own died, when I was eight. We're not blood—she was married to my uncle Jake, the youngest of my father's two brothers. The other was Matt, who never married. Jake was the finance man. He took the ranch's year-end profits and invested them. In land, mostly. Sometimes in a rancher on hard times. Once in a coal mine that Matt eventually took on. Matt didn't fancy punching any more than he did romance."

Without consciously allowing it, Paige was captivated. Through the entrée, dessert and coffee being poured, she learned of the Tanner brothers and how they'd built "a couple of acres of Montana plain and a fair-to-middling herd of cattle" into a conglomerate made up of the Triple T Ranch, Tanner Land Development and Tanner Mines.

Ross described each man so clearly, Paige imagined she knew them. Jake the speculator, with a nose for sweet deals and a penchant for silk shirts and Cuban cigars. Matt the miner, a closemouthed loner, happiest in dark, cool places. Aaron the rancher, oldest brother, adviser, guardian.

Paige was stirring cream into her coffee when Ross stopped talking long enough to light a cigarette. "Well, she sounds fascinating."

"Who?"

"Aunt Mary."

Ross sat back and chuckled. "That's right, I was going to tell you about her. Still interested?"

"Order me a brandy and I'm all ears."

Ross signaled the waiter, then leaned forward. "Few people would find Mary fascinating. She's lived in the same corner of Montana all of her life, married at the age women were expected to thirty-some years ago, bore Jake a son, as he'd hoped she would, and named him after our grandfather. A conventional woman. And really quite wonderful.

"My mother died in childbirth, delivering my sister Cat—Catherine. Mary would drive out to the ranch from town every couple of days to make sure we were getting along. She did all the things mothers do and fathers forget need doing. Dragged us to the dentist, planned our birthday parties." His eyes narrowed, his mouth curving with a smile of tenderness. "She taught me to waltz the night before a big school dance . . . in the fruit cellar, so no one would find me out. I was sixteen."

Paige cupped her chin in one hand. Ross skimmed his fingertips lightly over the other, resting on the table. Despite an inner warning, she let herself stir to his touch.

"Eight years ago, the ranch's scout plane went down. My father and uncles were on board. I was twenty-five, Cat seventeen." Ross paused. Time had dulled the pain, but there would always be sadness when he thought of the men he'd loved, of the memories that would never be made.

Paige gasped. Because he'd used the past tense when talking of them, she'd realized they were dead. But the three of them together, in the same instant. It must have been devastating.

"Mary sold the house in town," Ross went on. "She and my cousin Lance moved to the Triple T. The four of us needed each other, and Cat had long been in need of a woman in the house. One who'd be there when teenage girls want to talk, which I've discovered, was two o'clock in the morning. And Mary wanted a daughter as much as Cat wanted a mother."

Paige thought of Faye and smiled.

"Cat's twenty-five now, and manages Tanner Mines. Moved to her own place three years ago. Lance . . ." Again Ross hesitated. Again he felt sadness. Beneath the frustration and the sometimes overwhelming urge to throttle his cousin, Ross mourned the relationship that might have been. "Lance left the ranch six years ago. When he isn't off jetsetting he drops in at TLD long enough to make a mess of things. So—" throwing off the mood, Ross smiled "—there's just Mary and me now. She moved back to town shortly after Cat left, but she still drives out two or three times a week. She fusses over me. I give her a hard time. It suits us.''

"Faye and I are like that."

"Tell me." He traced the fine bones on the back of her hand. Her lashes lowered fractionally in response. "Are you related?"

"No, though it doesn't seem to matter. To me she's family. I've trained with her since I was nine. Before that, I'd known of her. When she opened her schooling farm it made headlines in both weeklies.''

"Big news."

"Small town," she countered dryly. "Actually, it was big news. She'd been in seclusion for a number of years, following an accident."

Skillfully, so that she hardly noticed, Ross turned her hand over. "What sort of accident?"

"Steeplechase." Paige frowned into her brandy. The danger was always there. Riders acknowledged it, but didn't dwell on it—not the good ones, anyway. "She'd been named to the Olympic team...then the fall. Her legs and pelvis were broken. Her dreams. She can't sit a saddle for long without pain. She'll limp if she overdoes." Looking up, Paige found a smile. "But she's one of the best ground coaches in the country. She can see a turned-out toe at a hundred yards, and hurl her voice that far to make sure you know about it. I can't count the Sunday mornings I cooked breakfast to repent for turned-out toes.''

Beneath the laughter, Ross heard love. "You lived with her."

"Mmm..." His touch played at her wrist, then at the center of her palm. Automatically her fingers curled inward and linked their hands. "When I was in my teens. Poor Faye. Teenage girls are cranky at best. When one isn't your own daughter..."

Hearing herself, Paige let her voice trail away. She'd said more than she'd intended. Champagne and candlelight helped create a mood in which secrets were given. She eased her hand out from under his, hoping to dispel whatever magic had allowed her to open up.

Ross watched her withdraw. "What about your family?"

"I'm an only child."

"But you didn't live with your parents."

"Yes and no." It wasn't easy to explain. It wasn't his business, either. "They travel a lot."

Present tense, Ross noted. For a moment he'd thought she'd been orphaned. Perhaps in a way, she had. "Where do you live now?"

"Gentry Farm. There's a groom's apartment above the barn. Faye lets me have it in exchange for teaching clinics." What Paige didn't tell him was how strongly Faye had resisted Paige's move from the main house. But she couldn't have survived the constant pressure without a place to go where she could be alone.

"And tomorrow?" he prodded. "Back to Maryland?"

She shook her head, soft hair falling forward on her shoulders. "No. I have a three-day event next weekend in Lexington. The horse trial we just finished was only—"

"Whoa, whoa . . . Back up." So she's going to be in town for another week, Ross mused. And so was he. "What's a three-day event?"

"A three-day is . . . an event that takes place over three days. Actually, the big ones take as many as six, if the field is large and the courses tough." Paige crossed her arms on the table and leaned forward. "They're what's called all-around campaigns, designed to test the fitness and mental discipline of both horse and rider. The first day's test is dressage. It's—"

"Dancing with a horse," Ross interjected.

"You call that dancing?" she returned, her eyes full of laughter and candlelight. "You should see a freestyler work to music."

"I'll pass. What's on for the second day?"

"Cross-country. There are four phases—two of roads and track, one of steeplechase, then the obstacle course. If the rider is still alive and kicking on the third day," she quipped. "And if the horse wasn't retired on course, spun out in the vet box or given thumbs-down at the morning inspection, you finish with show jumping. There've been times that, come day three, the last thing I wanted to do was climb back into a saddle. Even a smooth endurance test leaves you pretty bruised.''

"What's the difference between that and a horse trial?"

"Difficulty. Magnitude. The horse trial has both dressage and stadium jumping, but the endurance factor is dropped from cross-country and only the obstacle course run. In short, horse trials are the training ground for three-days.''

"How often do you do them?"

Paige grimaced. "It's beginning to feel like every day. The closer we get to the Olympics, the more insane the schedule.''

Olympics. Ross turned the word over in his mind. Of course she'd be a contender. One hell of a goal, though. "You're training for the Olympics?"

"Not yet, not officially. First I have to make the squad." Paige tasted her brandy, letting it quiet the nerves she'd come to expect at the mere mention of the word. "Selection trials begin after the Pan-Am Games, in August. Making the Pan-Am team depends on next weekend.''

"So you're going for gold."

"Of course. I wouldn't have given so much to settle for less.''

Between champagne and victory, Paige floated into the night. The air wore a splash of azalea-scented perfume. Its warmth was soft, a caress, a whisper. As a rule, she was more attuned to internal sensations—elevated pulse rates, cramped muscles. But tonight her skin was made of a thousand sensors. Night was a brush of velvet. Ross's hand, at the small of her back, burned its imprint through the thin silk of her blouse. The car they walked to was candy-apple red and built low to the ground. Butter-soft upholstery sighed around her. Turned low, the music from the radio had a throbbing beat.

Ross pulled out of the restaurant's parking lot onto a narrow country road. "Where are you staying?"

"At the Sheffields'.''

He frowned, then shook his head. "Don't know it. A hotel?"

"Private home." She turned on the front seat and let down the window. Wind whipped through her hair, the rush of fresh air helping to clear a fog from her brain that had nothing to do with the drinks she'd consumed. "If you take us back to the racetrack, I can direct you."

Ross let out the clutch and turned onto the highway. For a long time, neither of them spoke. She noticed that he drove at a slower, easier speed heading back to the showgrounds than when he'd left them earlier. She wondered if he was as reluctant as she to see the evening end.

"What are your plans for the filly?" she asked.

Ross took his eyes off the road to glance over. "Breed her."

Paige frowned. "Isn't the Triple T a cattle ranch?"

"Mmm... We breed quarter horses to work them."

"But you have a warmblood stud for her."

"No," he said thoughtfully. "I have a quarter-horse stud. Four, actually, but I know the one I'll put her to."

Paige sat straighter. "She's warmblood. Irish." When he only nodded, she understood, and gasped. "You'll retire her. Pull her off the circuit and turn her into a broodmare."

"I sure as hell don't plan on dancing with her."

Openmouthed, Paige searched for words. Several rushed to mind. *Impossible. Abhorrent. Wrong.* "You obviously know nothing of breeding."

"The distinction or the activity?"

"Take your pick," she snapped. "An Irish-blood to a quarter horse, it's... it's inconceivable."

"Not for a couple of warmblood mares in Montana. They've conceived just fine." Answering her under-breath growl with laughter, Ross pulled off the road near the racetrack's entrance. "You don't approve of mixing blood and brawn."

"What an interesting way of putting it," Paige drawled. "But if you think you can label me a pedigree snob, think again. Eventing's full of Thoroughbreds and Arabians pumping a pint or two of quarter-horse blood. Warm-bloods are different. Pure. Her foals won't be. Besides, I'd always heard the cowboy was the bigger snob in that area, thumbing his nose at anything but a mustang or quarter horse for moving cows around.''

"Cattle. Cattle are moved, cows are milked.''

"And cowboys?''

"They saddle up whatever horse gets the job done. Don't you?''

Forced to concede the point, Paige shrugged one shoulder. "What's your reason for crossbreeding them? What are you trying to do?''

"Breed warmblood intelligence to quarter-horse instinct.''

Paige wasn't buying it. An exquisite filly reduced to serving as broodmare to cow ponies. "Why that one? She's got tremendous talent, and enough training behind her for it to show. All of which you've paid for, I might add. You could have gotten a green Irish-blood for less than half her price tag.''

"But she's the one I want.''

"A born performer, retired before her time,'' she said in an accusatory tone.

"A line of thinking cow ponies,'' Ross countered. Moonlight lent her skin an alabaster glow. Fascinated, he took his thumb down the side of her face. "With the way I pamper my fillies, Paige, she'll never miss the arena.'' Amusement glimmered from his eyes in the darkness. "Where do we go from here?''

Nowhere, she thought. Absolutely nowhere. Paige shook her head one last time, considered their surroundings and said, "Turn left at the little church up ahead, go a mile or so and turn left again.''

As they pulled up the Sheffields' tree-lined drive, Paige felt her spirits deflate, her mood flatten. Ross braked in front of the majestic white house. Even by moonlight the gardens were vivid with red and hot pink azaleas. Dogwoods in full blossom edged the clipped lawns.

Ross circled the car and, with her right hand folded in his, Paige stepped out. He didn't move back to give her room, and so she stood with her back pressed lightly against the car and Ross's body brushing against hers. He shut the door gently, then lifted her clutch purse from her hand, setting it on the hood. Her breathing grew shallow as he raised her hands to shoulder level.

Slowly Ross eased himself against her. Her breath caught, then ruffled out. "You feel good." He skimmed her lips lightly with his. "I'd forgotten how much I wanted to feel you this close to me again."

When his mouth didn't immediately take hers, but instead trailed soft kisses along her jaw to her throat, Paige felt her bones dissolve. She dropped her head back, giving his mouth freedom to touch, taste, and move on. Through half-lowered lashes, she watched the stars blur on their bed of black velvet. With gentle nips, he teased the sensitive cord at the base of her neck and along her shoulder, easing her blouse aside.

Desire was a white-hot spear. Paige gasped, stiffened, and thought about running. But it was body ruling mind now. She melted, moaned, and shifted her fingers to lace them tightly with his. He nibbled his way to her other shoulder, the crinkly softness of his hair whispering over her skin. He smelled of sunlight and smoke, like a warm autumn day. With his tongue he touched her ear, traced it. Night air chilled the wet heat so that she shivered, first from fire, then from ice. Needs raced with her blood, quicker than his lips moving leisurely on her hair.

A rose, Ross thought. She made him think of a rose. Long, slender, elegant. An exquisitely formed bud unfolding, perfect petals opening. Lush, intoxicating. Ross held himself back until he throbbed with wanting more, until need surpassed control. Drawing away, he unlaced their fingers, and with an arm around her waist, dragged her closer. His other hand tunneled into her hair as both of hers crept up his back.

Paige watched his mouth lower to hers, and her eyes closed at the moment of contact. Soft, warm. Something

lazy and thick moved through her. Not needs or wants. Not
desire or even passion. Pleasure, she realized, pure and so,
so sweet. She'd known a feeling such as this existed. It was
the secret behind the smiles shared by lovers. The breathy
laughter that sometimes whispered from shadows on hot,
still nights. She'd known it existed, but it had never been
hers . . . until now.

Ross was losing himself to her. She strained in his arms,
a tethered filly fighting to snap the thin cord of restraint.
Wanting to break free. Her scent was drugging, her taste
addictive. She pressed into the kiss, totally involved. She
pulled feelings from him no woman had come close to tugging at. Because she did so without trying, Ross found the
sensation more terrifying than thrilling. He had to free
himself, he thought dizzily, before he was beyond finding his
way back.

This was not a woman a man had only for a night. This
was a woman a man took to his bed and kept there, dug
moats around, went to the preacher with. This was a
woman, he thought with a surprising stab of regret, who had
other plans for her life.

"I have to go." He formed the words against her mouth.
"Now."

"You have to go." But her lips clung to his. "Now." Her
fingers were still tangled in his hair.

Taking her face in his hands, Ross forced a space between them. Because he couldn't walk away from those
swimming jade eyes, he closed them with light kisses.

Paige reached deep and pulled up a smile—a weak one,
but a smile nonetheless. *Let go,* she ordered herself. *Open
your hands and let go.* She did. Ross pressed a kiss to her
forehead, retrieved her purse and handed it to her, then
walked away.

Too aroused to move, she watched him go. Something—
a new instinct, a new need—hammered at her to call him
back. But the clearer voice of reason interceded. He's a man
you don't walk away from in a day, a week. You've no time,
no energy, for a grand passion. *But . . .*

Chapter Four

Paige woke slowly, clinging to dreams as she drifted. *Nowhere to go*. Snuggled up to a pillow, she smiled. *Nothing to do*.

It was the first morning in weeks she'd been allowed a leisurely float to the surface. Still, she thought groggily, she ought to at least think about getting up. It was late—wonderfully, shamefully late. Instead of dawn's chill, she felt hot sunlight on her skin. The scent of flowers drifting through open windows was intensified by the day's heat.

Moving lazily, Paige rolled onto her back, stretched her arms and opened her eyes. For the next twenty seconds, she lay frozen in that position. Roses, long stemmed and on the verge of unfolding, crowded the surfaces in her bedroom. Dozens of them. Each one the rich brilliant color of new gold. There was a cloisonné vase of them on the pink-veined marble mantel, another on the sill of the bayed window. A huge bouquet decorated the low coffee table snuggled between two plush pink velvet chairs. There were more on the nightstand to her left, where an embossed florist's card had been propped.

Finding roses where there had been none the night before stunned her only half as much as someone sending them ... and sending so many. The Sheffields had the sort of invisible staff who whispered about, seeing to needs you hadn't yet thought of. The second-floor maid wouldn't have neglected her duty simply because a tap on the door failed to rouse Paige. No, she'd have tiptoed in, placed the flowers, then crept away.

Paige lifted one of the elegant beauties from the vase on the nightstand and fell back on her pillows. Trailing velvet petals down her cheek, she read the card.

A "Gold" performance. You were magnificent. Ross.

Touched, she sniffed the exquisite bud. Instead of pleasure, its heady fragrance moved her to sadness. No, she wouldn't regret. The evening had ended precisely as it should have. Ross Tanner had a way of making her want what she couldn't have. Like time, she thought wistfully. And freedom. More lingering candlelit dinners, fewer daybreaks in a barn. *Romance.* No, she wouldn't regret, Paige decided as she slid the rose back into its vase. Then she swallowed past a great big lump of regret.

The bedroom door was already swinging open before she realized someone had knocked. Faye breezed through, brisk, businesslike, the ever-present notepad in one hand, a pen in the other. Stopping at the foot of the bed, she swept a glance over the flowers. "They caused quite a stir around here this morning. From your cowboy?"

Paige sat up in the wide canopy bed and pushed the hair from her face. Her other hand closed around the florist's card. "He isn't *my* cowboy."

"No?" Faye wandered from vase to vase as Paige rose and slipped into a short silky blue robe. "You haven't ... started something with him?"

Paige froze. "Are you asking if I slept with him?" Her voice was cool, her eyes cooler.

Faye tipped her head and thought for a moment before speaking. "Who you sleep with, Paige, is your business."

"I'd always thought so."

"Anything more serious becomes mine." Faye toyed with a flower, a slight frown creasing her brow. "We've been over this, more or less. Training for the games requires total commitment. Workouts and the right horse aren't enough. It takes effort, two hundred percent. Affairs of the heart are distracting, loaded with stress. You'll have all the pressure you can bear in the next year without adding a relationship to it."

"Let's see if I have this right." Paige rarely used this frigid tone with Faye. "A relationship is out, but a quick tumble is okay."

"Nothing is out. One is simply more sensible than the other. You can stop looking at me as if I'd suggested you pick out a street corner and take up a new trade. Riders have been releasing tension with quick tumbles, as you call them, for as long as there's been a circuit. As your trainer, as your friend, I'm advising you to put some things off."

Paige's anger went swiftly from cold to hot. It was completely unexpected. She swallowed the urge to snap she'd already put off enough. Don't. Do. Now. Later. *Why?* she wanted to scream. *Why not?* But she knew the answer to both questions. *Because.* Because the goal was so close. Because the goal was first and foremost and the rest of life had to be lived in the scant time left over. Because this was what they'd both worked for and wanted. *But did she?* Paige wondered. If she did, then what the hell was wrong with her lately? And if she didn't, when had she stopped?

It was all too familiar. The restlessness, the need, the ache for... for something. It was so close to how she'd felt before her affair with Travis, it was frightening. Yet the way she responded to Ross wasn't like anything she'd felt in her life. That fact frightened her more.

Anger fading as quickly as it had flashed, Paige dropped to the vanity bench. Whatever was churning inside her, Faye was the last person she should be lashing out at. Of the few people she had trusted in her lifetime, Faye was the only one who hadn't betrayed that trust. No one in the world loved her more or understood her better.

"I'm sorry I snapped." Paige picked up a shell-backed brush and dragged it through her hair. "It's been a tough couple of months."

"What will you do about him?" The rose cupped in Faye's palm made a name unnecessary.

"Nothing. He lives in Montana. He'll go back today, I imagine."

"I see." Satisfied, Faye glanced at her notes. "Can we run through a few things? I'm late getting out of here for the airport."

"Sure." Paige sighed. "I'd forgotten you were leaving today."

"I'll return Thursday evening. In the meantime, let the event organizers know when you'll arrive with the horses. I told them I thought Wednesday. They're expecting you to confirm." She made an efficient check mark and continued.

Replacing the hairbrush, Paige turned on the tufted bench. She cradled her legs and propped her chin on one knee as Faye made short work of her list. She wanted to talk, but had no idea what to say. She wanted to be nine years old again, so she wouldn't feel foolish for wishing she weren't here, in this place, this position, at this time in her life.

Next Faye reviewed the clinic schedule. Paige had taught riding at Gentry Farm for nearly ten years. It had been simple enough to plan classes for her young equestrians around the circuit calendar. If now and then her commitments overlapped, Faye stepped in to pinch-hit. This time, however, Faye wouldn't be a temporary substitute. This time it would be for sixteen months. A wave of loss swept over Paige. She resisted being sucked under, telling herself there was no other way. From now on she would eat, sleep, even breathe, according to a training regimen.

It hit her then, more a shock than a thrill. The day she'd once thought would never come had somehow arrived too swiftly. *Is this what I want? Why don't I know anymore?*

"...all right?"

Paige jerked herself back. "Sorry. Is what all right?"

"You. Are you all right?"

"Yeah." Paige stood, needing to spend her restlessness. She might have walked to the bed to smooth out the covers or into the bathroom to start her shower. Instead, she went to the bay window, where sunlight was coaxing the roses open, and let her hand drift over the tops of them.

"Kid's ready for a three-day." Pressing a thumb to the middle of her forehead, Paige forced her mind to the business at hand. "Something in, um...July...see how he handles the hard road in the heat." What else? "Lady— Lady has potential. I like her. Ah...she's a bit green, but if we have her to work with through the winter, I think she can make CCI in the spring. I'll talk with Tom tonight. So, if he's agreeable, let's schedule her for a couple of horse trials in October.... No, no, world championship's in October. In, ah...sometime before the worlds."

"What's wrong, Paige?" Faye demanded. "What really happened last night?"

"Nothing's wrong." Paige laughed mirthlessly, then buried her face in the velvet petals. "Nothing happened last night." *Which is probably what's wrong.*

"I can take a later plane, if you feel like company, someone to talk it out with."

On a long breath, Paige pulled herself together. She was a big girl. Twenty-six and world traveled, for God's sake. She was mature, intelligent. Whatever was nagging at her peace of mind, she'd have to work it out for herself. So begin now, she ordered.

"You have evening classes, *my* students. Then there's your Swede. Didn't his trailer leave here last night? You should be there when he arrives, get him settled in his new home."

"If you're sure." At the door Faye hesitated. "Paige, it's okay to be uncertain once in a while."

About your whole life? About everything you've worked for and thought you wanted?

"I'm uncertain about only one thing—the best way to squander my day off. Go, Faye. I'm fine. I'll see you in four days."

Once the door shut, Paige opened her fist on the small rectangular card. Giving in to a foolish urge, she ran her fingertip over the words. Turning back to the window and the brilliant bouquet, she stared out at another new day, one that brought her that much closer to the goal.

Clouds were white billows in the sky, shifting shadows on the ground. Ross studied them from the sheet-glass windows of the executive office of Tanner Land Development. Behind him the voices of two bank officers and TLD's accountant droned on.

Rain. He sensed a storm on its way. There was nothing ominous about the airy clouds. No gray fog hovered on the horizon. Still, he thought that in a day or two the weather would take a dramatic turn. Or maybe the storm brewing was within and the dramatic turn wishful thinking. Ross shoved his balled fists into his pockets. God, what purpose was he serving here? What good was he doing TLD or Lance—or himself, for that matter—staring out a window predicting the weather?

Dropping a shoulder to the casing, he watched the street fill with lunchtime traffic. The glass he gazed through was smoked and on the outside gave back mirror images of the city. The frame he leaned against was painted a glossy salmon, the tint specially blended to complement the upholstered chairs and sofas dotting the room at his back. There were splashes of maroon, too, against walls and carpet of platinum gray. Tables were framed in chrome and topped with more smoked glass.

As if his mood weren't dark enough, Ross glanced over his shoulder at Lance's desk. There was no leather-trimmed blotter on top, no drawers below. Only a signed Steuben glass sculpture dominating one corner. It was the damnedest desk he'd ever seen. The damnedest office! Glitzy, dustless. Ross half expected party guests to pour in each time the door opened. How did a man work in a silver-and-salmon office? He considered the harried men sitting at the long conference table, open files and ledger books spread between them, and concluded that Lance, at least, didn't.

For all its light colors and transparent glass, Ross felt smothered by the room. He wanted a breath of air that hadn't been processed and recirculated. He wanted to smell sunlight and heat. A woods. The scent of Paige's skin.

Damn. If he were on a Montana plain, driving cattle, he might get her out of his mind. There, lowing cows and shouting punchers would drown out the echo of her smoky voice. Dust and a swallow of beer would be the only tastes lingering on his tongue. She moved through his mind, long and lovely. Ross bit back an oath. If only he could stop seeing her. Now. Last night, as he'd smoked in the dark. Driving to TLD that morning. Passing a florist's shop, he'd pulled over without giving it a moment's thought. Unconcerned with cost, he'd bought every gold-tinted rose in the place and had them sent.

She'll have gotten them by now, he mused. He pictured her with a few of them caught up in her hair. Saw her laid back on dew-kissed grass, with more of them strewn about her. He imagined himself skimming the unfurled petals of one over her sun-warmed skin, then letting his lips follow the same path.

Damn.

Leaving her last night had been no simple feat. Staying away, he thought now, was going to be the real test. Even as part of his mind planned the next meeting, Ross decided seeing her again would be unwise. Some women were taken to bed and worked out of the system. Each of his finely tuned instincts told him Paige wasn't one of those women. No, it wasn't as simple as scratching an itch. He sensed something stronger than desire between them. Something else, though he couldn't quite put a name to it. If he was smart, Ross decided, he'd keep it that way.

"Tanner," a weary voice called from the table.

Ross pulled his shoulder away from the wall and turned around.

"If you could locate your cousin..." the loan officer suggested hopefully.

"If I could locate my cousin," Ross returned in a low, threatening tone, "he'd be of little use to you after I'd fin-

ished with him.'' Taking a seat, Ross allowed himself to be
drawn back into the maze of Lance's affairs and away from
the madness of imagining one with Paige.

The Sheffield stable was an elegant extension jutting off
the back of the house. White-painted walls trimmed in dark
green duplicated the exterior color scheme of the main
house. There was a wash stall lined with protective rubber
padding. A tack room in meticulous order. Sixteen stalls,
eight on either side of a broad aisle, were wide and deep,
with windows cut into the back walls. At one end, sliding
Plexiglas kept out rain and winter snow while permitting
natural light to flow through. Today the panels were thrown
open. A lilac-scented breeze swirled down the long, brick-
laid corridor.

At the sound of Paige's footsteps, the innately curious
horses popped their heads into the aisle. Stroking noses, she
worked her way to the far end and the guest stalls Tom had
provided for her own horses. Absolute saw her and whin-
nied a greeting.

Crooning hello to the Thoroughbred stallion, Paige lifted
a hand to his gleaming blackish brown coat. She ran her
fingers through his raven mane and down his velvety neck.
Nuzzling up to her, Absolute caught the end of her braid in
his teeth and nibbled at the pale strands. Paige pressed her
cheek to his neck and felt wholly at peace.

She'd competed countless horses in her career. Some for
private individuals, some for syndicates. A few had been her
own. Of them all, Absolute was special. She'd bought him
on instinct six years ago, when he was a green five-year-old.
Now he was in his prime. And, in the eyes of the United
States Combined Training Association, who'd named him
Horse of the Year, the finest eventing mount in the country. To Paige, he was pet, partner and, in his own unique
way, a friend.

Growing dissatisfied with the taste of her hair, Absolute
snorted and backed away. On a laugh, Paige dug out one of
the two apples she'd tucked in her waistband. Deigning to
be coaxed from his corner, he lipped the fruit from her

palm. On cue, the ash-white gray in the neighboring stall stomped and snorted jealously.

"Babies," Paige murmured, and fed Mr. Divine the other apple. "For as bad as you boys can be, you're both just a couple of babies."

Divine bobbed his head, ever the agreeable one. Absolute, the more aloof of the pair, returned to his bucket of oats. Leaning on the bottom half of the door, Paige talked to them. Nonsense, babble, but it soothed them. Soothed her, too.

Her day off hadn't worked its usual recuperative magic. Though Tom and Lorraine were delightful hosts, Paige had fallen into bed last night tense and irritable. She told herself it was because the approaching Kentucky Three-Day was too important to allow her mind to rest. She'd stubbornly refused to dig deeper for the real reason.

Accustomed to being pampered, the other horses in the barn kicked up a fuss. More than happy to be distracted, Paige checked the pail left near the house door to see what the cook might have put out.

"Carrots!" she announced, showing them a fistful. "Who wants carrots?" Paige doled them out, saving Lady Night's for last and visiting longer with her than she had the others.

As luck would have it, Absolute's stall was directly across the aisle. He didn't care for his mistress squandering her affections. Annoyed, he kicked at his stall door, then released a whinny so strident Paige was sure jackrabbits for miles around were diving down their holes.

"Jealous, are you?" But when she crossed the aisle, Absolute gave her his rump, flicking his tail in her face while he pretended interest in the view outside his window. "Better get used to her. She's going to Florida with us for the winter. Come on, quit sulking and turn around. Vacation's over. I've had my day off. You've had a whole week. It's back to work for both of us."

Nonchalantly the stallion glanced back. Glimpsing Paige, he swung his head around and pushed it farther out the window. On the outside chance she thought him the least bit interested in anything she had to say, he released a long, bored snuffle.

"Last chance." Paige rattled his halter, which was hanging beside the doorframe. "About-face, or Divine goes for his run first." Absolute continued lazily canvassing the countryside. "Have it your way, then."

Exceedingly more cooperative, Divine pushed his long white face into the halter Paige held up. She unlatched the door and led him out, his hooves making a pleasant clip-clop sound on the bricks.

Cross ties hung from bolts high on the walls at evenly spaced intervals. Standing Divine between a pair of them, she clipped one of the long chains to the left side of his halter, another to the right. She dragged off his day rug and stowed it in the tack room. Locating his bridle and cinch, she slung one over each shoulder, tossed a saddle pad onto his workout saddle and hefted that into her arms. Laden with tack, Paige walked into the corridor facing the open end of the stable. What she saw there stopped her in her tracks.

Ross stood on the threshold. Backlit by the sun, he was a tall silhouette, his features indiscernible. Paige didn't need to see his face. The wide-brimmed Stetson was a dead give-away, but it was his long, tapering body she instantly, instinctively recognized. Like a brand, she'd worn the memory of his broad chest and slim hips for two days and nights.

Oh, God, it felt too good to see him. Paige strove for a casual demeanor, while a self-protective fear curled through her stomach. If she could fool dressage judges into thinking she was cool and confident, surely she could pull off this casual routine for Ross. "What are you doing here?"

"Watching you."

He strolled forward, out of the sun, into the cool shadows of the stable. She could see his eyes now, their color and intensity, and wished there were a way to look unapproachably elegant while wearing old clothes and thirty pounds of tack.

"How long have you been standing there?"

"Not long."

Though long enough, Ross mused, to think giving in to the urge to see her again might have carried him into the danger zone. She'd stirred him, more than he'd thought possible. She'd gotten under his skin and poked something to life. *Need.* No woman had moved him to it. It was one thing to want. Ross had wanted and enjoyed his share of women. But need—for one, to the exclusion of any other—was something else entirely.

Equestrians, he'd decided, even those Olympic-bound, had lives off the circuit. They had homes, hobbies, friends. Lovers. Why not Paige? he'd asked himself.

Yes, why not? he wondered again as he looked her over. She'd rolled up the sleeves on a cotton blouse that a few too many washings had nearly bleached the yellow tint from. Rust-colored working breeches were tucked into a pair of old riding boots. With her hair scraped back and braided, her eyes looked huge.

Rooted to the spot, Paige watched Ross pass Divine in the aisle, duck under a cross tie and close the distance. What was happening to her? She couldn't seem to move, or even think straight. And what was he doing here? "Why aren't you in Montana?" she demanded.

Smiling, he pulled his thumbs from his pockets and removed his hat. "I've unfinished business here." His hips made contact with the saddle as he caught her face in his free hand, thumb and fingers spread on either side of her jaw. Gentle. His touch was infinitely gentle, tipping her mouth up.

"What sort of business?" she breathed out.

"This, for one."

The kiss was chaste, but more intimate than any Paige had ever known. She did nothing to stanch the rush of pleasure, not one damn sensible thing to push it back. Beneath the saddle, her hands curled, as if that would let her hold on to the moment.

When Ross leaned away again, she drew a breath. It was shallow, and trembled. Weak. Weak and vulnerable and uncertain. No, she couldn't let him do this to her. She wouldn't. Determinedly Paige drew back her overburdened shoulders. "That's hardly an answer."

Ross watched her features subtly change as she went from heated and shaky to cool and steady. He couldn't help admiring her control, though he suspected it would hurt her more in the long run than it could possibly help her right now. "What did you want to know?"

"When you'll pop up again would be helpful."

"You don't like surprises?"

"There are surprises and there are—" *Roses.* Suddenly Paige remembered them. "The flowers," she murmured, her shoulders slowly relaxing. "Thank you, Ross. They're lovely...extravagant, but lovely."

"Then you do like surprises." He took a fingertip down the side of her face and neck to trace the V opening of her blouse.

Because her arms were full, Paige couldn't brush his hand away. She took a backward step and broke the contact. The man had an incredible knack for catching her at a disadvantage. "Are you *ever* going back to Montana?"

"Next week."

"Next—" Stunned, Paige dropped the saddle. "Week?" Five more days of international three-day pressure *and* Ross Tanner? One was hard enough on her nerves. Both... "Why next week?"

"That's when the collateral review of TLD will finally wrap up."

She hadn't a clue what he was talking about. "TLD is here? In Louisville? I thought you were in Kentucky for the auction."

"One trip lined up nicely with the other." He kissed her again, quickly, then dropped his Stetson onto her head and picked up the saddle. "Going riding?"

"Yeah," she muttered as he turned to walk back down the aisle. "Going riding."

The hat held traces of him. A hint of his scent, earthy, intimate, very male. His closet would smell like that, she mused. His cl   His pillow. Against her forehead, the leather sweatband was warm from his skin, and slightly damp. If she closed her eyes—

"New horse," Ross called back. "How many do you have?"

His voice shattered the fantasy before it could form. Shaken, Paige started down the aisle after him. "The horses I rode last weekend weren't mine." Eyeing a halter hook, she considered tossing his hat on it. She didn't, then cursed herself for feeling as giddy as a teenage girl testing the unfamiliar weight of a boy's class ring on her finger. "Two belong to the Sheffields. Lady Night—" she pointed out the mare's stall, then another, three doors down "—and Smooth as Silk." Ross approached Divine on the left. Opting for a barrier, Paige kept the horse between them and faced Ross from the gray's right. "Kid is Faye's horse. He and the one she bought at the auction have been returned to Maryland."

"And him?" Lifting his chin, Ross indicated Divine. "Yours?"

"Yes...no. Well, sort of." *Oh, good, Paige. So poised today.*

"I see."

"Dammit, Ross, what are you doing here? Where's the filly? Don't you have to take her to Montana or something?"

"I hired a carrier." Amusement tugged at his mouth. "You thought I'd gone? Counted on it, maybe?" He shook his head, the amusement growing into a full-fledged grin. "Now, what about this gray? Is he or isn't he yours?"

Ignoring the laughter in his eyes, Paige reached across Divine's back for the saddle pad. "He's a USET horse."

"Which is?"

"United States Equestrian Team. Horses are donated to them by supporters and syndicates. Resident riders take them up to intermediate level, then they're farmed out to competitors who've applied for one." Ross slung the saddle onto Divine's back. Paige pulled the cinch from her shoulder. "I've had him just over a year." Threading leather tabs into steel buckles, she fastened cinch to saddle.

From down the corridor came the sound of a hoof smacking wood. Lifting a quizzical brow, Ross glanced toward the sounds as three more reports reverberated from the last stall.

"Ignore him," Paige said. "He's having a tantrum."

She stooped and passed the cinch to Ross under Divine's belly. They straightened together. Something happened when their eyes connected again. Surprise. Awareness. As if neither had been quite prepared to find the other standing there. So close. So easy to reach out and touch.

"Oh, yeah..." Ross murmured.

Watching the lazy way his mouth moved with the smile, Paige could only swallow and stare at him.

"You are stunning," he said. "I like you in the hat. Think maybe I'll buy you one." He tugged hard on the cinch and buckled it down. "Not black, though. Buff. One the color of Montana wheat ripening in the sun. The color of your hair."

As Paige saw it, she had two choices. She could melt on the spot, or she could go on tacking, pretend he hadn't spoken to her in a voice that should have burned down the barn.

"His name's Divine." Her diversionary tactic drew a knowing grin from Ross. "Mr. Divine, if you want to be formal about it."

"Well, he's got one hell of a divine temper."

"No, not that one. This one." Paige indicated the right horse by running her hand down the gelding's sleek white neck. "One-quarter Arab, three-parts Thoroughbred. Seven years old. Sixteen hands. I'm counting on him to be a top-ten intermediate finisher at Lexington. If he is, I'll campaign him in his first international event in the fall. He's a super horse—" Furious whinnies joined the hoof banging. Paige shouted to be heard. "I'm short on reserve mounts for the coming year. I'd like Divine to be one. He'll qualify once he finishes an international CCI. As long as—" It was suddenly quiet, and she lowered her voice. "As long as USET's satisfied with our pairing, he's mine to compete."

"You have your own horse, or do you always ride for others?"

"I have my own." The wall banging started again. Paige and Ross both turned to stare. It grew less enthusiastic, subsiding to a mopey plea. When it stopped, Paige met Ross's eyes, a wry smile curving her mouth. "That's my horse."

"Why doesn't it surprise me to learn that?" he drawled.

Paige hooked a coolly curious brow. "Because you've decided the persistent, arrogant type appeals to me?"

"And does it?"

"I'm beginning to think so. Do me a favor?" she added quickly, before she found herself blurting out more than she was prepared to hear herself say. "Bridle Divine while I spring his majesty? I'd planned on leaving him in his stall until his turn to run. Given his mood, I think I'll turn him out in the corral till I get back."

"What sort of run?"

"A gallop. Keeps them loose."

She'd taken a step back when Ross covered her hand still resting on Divine's saddle. "Let's run them together. I've got a morning to kill." With laughter in his eyes, he glanced toward the end stall. "Pacing a pen isn't going to satisfy him half as much as giving him his head for two miles."

Her free hand was already at her shoulder, her fingers closing around the bridle, before Paige hesitated. Gallops this close to an event were to exercise the horse, nothing more. No precision timing, no disciplined pacing. She could give her mind the same freedom to wander as she gave the horse to run. Alone, she escaped for a while.

Dropping her eyes to their joined hands, she saw proof there of the differences between Ross and herself. His was dark and broad, with a few nicks scarring the back. Hers was paler, slender and soft. But she knew they'd both have the calluses gripping a pair of reins built on the palms. They'd both have the strength to control an animal inherently more powerful than man, the skill to do so without inflicting pain. If she gave herself the chance, Paige thought, she'd find more they had in common.

Did she want to? The thought of a gallop with Ross appealed to her. That in itself was revealing. No one joined her on her runs. She'd never permitted it. Not Faye. Not Travis four years ago. They'd have been intruding on the one fraction of her life she'd kept for herself. Yet, try as she might, she couldn't cast Ross in the role of unwelcome intruder. Intruder, yes. But one her whole being seemed to welcome.

Taking the bridle from her shoulder, she offered it to him. Releasing her hand, he accepted it.

"He's got a lot of blood in him," she said by way of a warning. "He'll want his own way." She ran a hand over a well-muscled flank and laughed softly. "Most males do. Don't put up with any nonsense, but don't boss him, either. Fight him and he'll fight you back. He responds very nicely to a firm seat and a soft hand."

Ross's lips slowly curved. "Most males do."

Paige lifted an aloof brow, then turned to walk away. Her laugh as she walked down the long corridor was low and smoky.

Ross watched her the whole way, paying particular attention to her leggy gait and the subtle sway of hips. Not until she disappeared through a set of Dutch doors did he turn back to Divine.

In the next second, the air shuddered with the unmistakable sounds of muscle and metal crashing against a wall. It was coming from the stall Paige had slipped into.

Chapter Five

Ross identified the sounds and was off like a shot. Fresh blows shook the walls. As he ran, he thought of two-year-old heifers bucking the boards of a squeeze chute. He remembered Dusty Johnson toppling into one, and the broken body they'd dragged out afterward. Paige snapped a command. Ross shouted her name. He was three doors from the one she'd turned into when his hat came sailing out. Then silence, a thousand times worse than the racket.

"Scare ya?" Her voice trembled. Realizing the trembling was amusement, Ross skidded to a halt. Her laugh floated breezily into the corridor. He dragged a hand through his hair and let the fear drain. "Why, you overgrown fool! It was just a hat. I'm okay!" she finally called out. "He didn't know me under the hat. Tried to run away, with only three feet to do it in."

Breathing a curse, Ross watched Paige back into the aisle. Still shaken, he swept a thorough glance over her before turning his attention to the Thoroughbred she led from the stall.

He was awesome—in height, in build, in sheer physical presence. Pure-blood, Ross decided. To the last drop. The graceful shape of his head reflected three hundred years of breeding refinement. His near-black coat gleamed with good health and grooming. Intelligence shone from his eyes.

Wary of the approaching stranger, the stallion retreated. His nervous prancing fought Paige's efforts to stand him between cross ties. Ross stopped before reaching them and waited until she'd secured the halter.

"What's his name?"

"Absolute."

He heard pride in her voice, and a trace of wonderment. Yes, he was a horse you'd always be stunned by, a horse you'd never take for granted.

"Settle down," Paige murmured. "No one's going to hurt you." Like the seasoned mother of a temperamental child, she soothed the animal with a low-throated stream of prattle. "You ought to be ashamed, shying from a man less than half your size. You were certainly acting brave and belligerent a few minutes ago. Now look at you, a shivering coward." Her words chided and berated; her voice caressed, quieted.

"Does he take to others?"

"Oh, sure. I use him for schooling. Students love him. He's exceptionally gentle once he knows you, playful if he thinks he can get away with it. He just needs an introduction."

"Introduce us."

Paige smiled. Keeping one hand on the stallion's neck, she held out the other. "Walk up behind me and place your hand over mine."

Touching her shoulder first, Ross let his fingertips skim down her arm and across the back of her hand. The ridge of calluses on his palm aligned with her knuckles. The extension of his arm mirrored the extension of hers. He circled her waist from behind and eased her close.

Absolute waited, his eyes wide. He recognized his mistress, knew her touch on his neck. But her shape was changed, her scent altered.

"Everything's okay," Paige crooned, and wondered if it was the horse or herself she was reassuring.

Hearing her familiar voice, Absolute resisted backing away from the palm she held up. He bumped it with his nose, tentative, but curious about this other scent. Paige spread her fingers, and Ross folded his own into the spaces she created. Absolute sniffed the interlaced hands, drew back, sniffed again. Twisting her wrist, she eased Ross's skin against the velvet muzzle. Curiosity overtook caution, and the stallion scented along their arms to their shoulders, then blew out a long, relaxed snuffle.

"Have I met with his approval?" Ross's mouth was at her ear. His breath fanned her cheek, warm and slightly moist.

"You have. He knows you. If it's years before he sees you again, he'll remember." As would she, Paige knew.

It was easy, too easy, to let Ross turn her in his arms. It seemed the most natural thing in the world to offer her mouth, to thread her hands through his hair, to cling. Paige felt the steady beat of his heart against her breast, and pressed closer. Strength ebbed, and she held tighter. The thrum of need pulsed with her blood, and she moaned.

Though her brain began to cloud, her senses grew acute. The scents surrounding them were peaceful and welcoming. Warm, clean horses and fresh hay. The faint aroma of Ross's tobacco smoke, and beneath it a trace of his soap. Sounds were soft, unintrusive. Tails swishing. Hay rustling. His breath swirled out to mix with hers. His taste made her think vaguely of sinfully rich pleasures, like a piece of stolen chocolate—sweet, dark, best when savored slowly.

Pleasure flowed thickly, weighting her muscles. Arousal overwhelmed her. It was debilitating, Paige thought with the first stirrings of panic. Before she could react and draw away, the magic was shattered.

The jolt was unexpected. Together Ross and Paige lurched, instinctively clutching each other to keep from falling. Absolute butted them again, successfully claiming their attention. He'd already suffered his mistress's lavishing her affections on Lady Night. Enough was enough!

Paige moved her hands to Ross's shoulders and leaned back. "Some horses have mean streaks," she explained. "Absolute's is green."

"Jealous? You're kidding." Ross eyed the stallion pawing the brick floor. "You're not kidding. Someone ought to tell him that he's a horse and you aren't. Better yet, get the poor boy one of his own."

"Oh, no. She'd be a distraction. He'd think of her instead of working, winning." Straightening her arms, Paige pushed against Ross's shoulders. "Let me go. I have a horse to gallop."

Ross watched her slip into her look-but-don't-touch attitude. *So he was a distraction. Having trouble concentrating, was she?* The thought pleased him. For days she'd been on his mind, confounding him, driving him crazy. It seemed only fair that he'd penetrated her strongest defense and gotten under her skin.

Persistent, Absolute nudged them again.

"Okay, pal," Ross muttered to the horse. "She's all yours. For the moment." He backed away, scooped up his hat and Divine's bridle, then walked the gray out to the yard.

In the stable, Paige stood with her eyes shut and her brow pressed to comforting horseflesh. "I'm in trouble, Absolute. Really big trouble. I've come up against an obstacle I don't know the way around. I'm not sure I *want* to get around it." Lifting her head, she gazed into liquid brown eyes intent on deciphering what was expected of him. "You know me, I don't race at brick walls without first considering all the angles. I don't leap without checking to see what waits on the other side."

Absolute stared back at her, his soulful eyes confused.

"What would you know about it, right? You've never had one of your own." Paige chuckled, relieved to find she could at least laugh at herself. Ten minutes later, she and Absolute joined Ross in the yard.

"Northwest is a comfortable run," she told him as they trotted the horses away from the barn. Ross watched her pull the elastic band from her braid and drop it into her blouse pocket. "A few fences," she added. "A ditch or two. But pretty straightforward otherwise." Her movements had the natural flow of habit as she ran her fingers through her hair. Symbolic? Ross wondered. It was possible. He thought she might have already begun setting herself free.

After shaking her hair loose, Paige looked at Ross. She sobered as she considered the length of his leg. "You can't ride him like that."

"Like what?"

She grinned. "Like a cowboy, with your legs poker-straight, one foot pointing east and the other west. Shorten the stirrups, bend your knees and roll your toes in. Drop your heels."

"What the hell for?"

"It's proper English form. It's what Divine's used to. What he responds to."

"I don't ride proper. I ride, period." It was his turn to grin. "Don't worry about Divine cooperating. If there's a secret to making him respond, I'll find it."

Paige didn't doubt him. He certainly hadn't had any trouble finding the secret to making *her* respond . . . and respond and respond. "Absolute will want to stretch for the first mile. Divine hasn't the stride to keep up. We may lose you for a while."

"No problem."

At pasture's edge, Paige leaned forward in the saddle. In a voice too low to carry to Ross, she murmured to the stallion. His ears perked, swiveled; he listened to every word. One by one, his muscles grew taut. In the next second, they broke away at a gallop.

Ross followed. Not until the gelding was loping smoothly beneath him did he realize how much he'd needed this. He'd spent too many hours of the past week sitting in stiff-backed chairs, in rooms that felt as if they'd been hermetically sealed. He thought of the auditors waiting for him at TLD and nearly laughed out loud. Any schoolboy playing hooky would have understood why. Spurring Divine on, Ross let sun and sweat go to work on a week's worth of frustrations.

Lagging, riding behind and to the right of Paige and Absolute, Ross could fully appreciate the Thoroughbred in motion. Seventeen hands easy, with a spectacular ground-eating reach, Absolute had a glossy hide that rippled with the flex and release of muscle. After a mile of pouring on speed, the stallion looked as if he could go five more without slackening.

And Paige...Paige looked as if she could go forever. Face tipped up to the wind, blouse plastered to her body, she was all he'd imagined and more. He didn't have to see her eyes to know they weren't icy or shuttered. He didn't have to touch her to know she throbbed with excitement, was breathless with it. She lived for the headlong sprint. She might be perfection in her silks and velvets in a show ring, but here she was unrestrained passion, with something urgent and alive pulsing through her.

Together they flew—the stallion, chestnut coat glistening; the woman, shimmering hair flying like a banner at her back. Straining for more speed, they galloped at a seamless vein of white boundary fence. Hearts pounded. Lungs heaved. The mighty horse rose, front legs folding, and with a powerful thrust launched them.

Together they sailed—a blur of color and motion, clearing the fence with yards of pasture to spare.

Exhilaration spilled from Paige in a laugh. She stroked Absolute's neck in approval. It was rare for her to laugh or even smile when she rode. Cross-country courses demanded concentration. Dressage judges wanted style. But when speed was limitless and the path hers to choose, her reward was a thrill wholly different from ribbons or trophies. It was a thrill she'd once felt every time she hopped onto a saddle, but one that in recent years she'd had to forgo for points and prestige.

Wondering if Ross had kept up, Paige twisted her head to glance back at the same instant Divine took the fence. Her breath caught as they soared, then was stolen by that fragile moment when they seemed to hang above the ground. Two stunningly beautiful males; a contrast of black and white, a blend of power and domination. A shutter clicked in her mind, capturing the picture for all time.

Though Absolute could have kept up the pace through two more counties, the purpose of a gallop was to stretch without depleting. Paige reined in, taking him down to a trot and eventually a walk.

On her left the land dipped, forming the shore of a pond. She had discovered it last week. The distance was perfect for a conditioning run, the setting ideal for catching one's breath. Dismounting, she tethered Absolute, loosened his cinch and left him to graze.

Buttercups grew wild on the bank. Paige strode through them, ankle-high grass swishing past her boots. It was the only sound. A thriving cluster of oaks hugged the far side of the pond, purple-veined spring beauties trailing through its undergrowth. Not a leaf or flower stirred. She spotted a cardinal perched motionless on the tip of a branch. Like walking into a landscape painting, she thought.

Folding her legs, she dropped down to sit in the tall blue-grass. She inhaled, filling her lungs, yet a feeling of breathlessness persisted. Her heart raced, skipped. Her hands were no steadier than her pulse. Vibrant. She felt vibrant, more alive than she could remember having felt in years.

It wasn't long before the ground shivered with Divine's approach. Paige tensed—against what, she wasn't sure. Herself, she supposed. That part of her that was stirring beneath its blanket of dispassion. Leather creaked. Tack jingled. Without taking her eyes off the smooth expanse of water, she pictured Ross leaving the saddle, imagined his lean, muscled body and fluid movements.

Ross sensed that she wasn't calm. Even for a professional horsewoman, her shoulders were set too squarely. Between her knees, her hands were curled into loose fists. No, she wasn't calm. Neither was the air, he decided as he headed down the bank. An electric tension clung to it. He could smell the storm he'd sensed yesterday. Looking out, he saw gray-edged clouds gathering on the western horizon. Soon they'd cover the sun, rumbling and ready to burst. With a half smile forming on his mouth Ross wondered which would erupt first—the sky or the woman?

He looked down as she threw her head back to gaze up at him. Her hair tumbled down her back, tangled by the breakneck ride as if by a lover's hands. One look at her face, and his mouth went dry. This, he thought, this was how she'd look in those first moments of lovemaking. With her eyes bright and her lips parted. With a moist sheen covering her skin and high color in her cheeks.

No, she wasn't calm. And neither, Ross was forced to admit, was he. Without touching her, he lowered himself to the grass and stretched out. Not far, but not too close. He knocked his hat forward over his eyes and crossed his arms behind his head. Storms, he told himself, should be carefully considered before they were braved.

"You could have warned me about the saddle," he said casually. "I won't sit comfortably for a week."

Puzzled, Paige frowned, then slowly smiled. "I'd forgotten you cowboys strap those big padded chairs to your horses." She laughed and felt some of the tension drain. "My, my, Tanner, you're soft."

His response to that was a short, descriptive curse. "There's no reason on earth for a man to get that close to his horse."

Chuckling, Paige cradled her knees and watched as the cardinal took flight. If she glanced to her right, she'd see Ross's jean-clad legs and hips. To see the rest of him, she'd have to look over her shoulder. She determinedly stared straight ahead.

Even so, his nearness caused her thoughts to drift, weightless and fanciful. She plucked a buttercup and twirled it under her nose. She concentrated on its scent, on the purity of its yellow color, on each petal, perfectly formed. It was a familiar mental exercise. Fixing her mind on an object, she would shed every thought, every whim, until nothing existed but that one tangible item.

Ross studied her from beneath his lowered hat brim. The eyes, more green than gray at the moment. The classic features. The face, closed and unreadable. "What are you thinking?"

On a sigh, Paige tucked the flower behind her ear. *That I could stay here forever. Stay here and not think, not plan, not worry.*

"I'm not," she said instead. "I'm listening." She swept a glance from shore to shore. "To the quiet. A basic necessity, I've always thought, but hard to come by on the circuit. Noise—frantic, chaotic noise, from the time you wake till you fall into bed again. Sometimes..." A scurrying chipmunk caught her eye, and her voice trailed off.

"Sometimes..." he prodded.

Glancing back, she saw that his hat concealed his eyes. To linger on his mouth would be reckless, and so she gazed out at the pond again. "Sometimes I'll get up early and slip into the stables. Much as I detest being vertical at daybreak, stables at five in the morning are the only places I know of to find peace and a little privacy."

Ross remembered his first impression of her. Distance, the demand for it blatant. Just now he'd heard discontent in her voice, and he wondered if the need to isolate herself was ingrained in her personality or a recent development due to her environment. "Schedule getting to you?"

He's much too perceptive, Paige decided. "I've had days when I have to read a newspaper to find out what city I'm in."

"Why do you do it?"

"Why?" It was a question no one had ever asked. How, when, even where. Never why. "What do you mean?"

"Why? Why are you a world-class equestrian instead of a schoolteacher or geologist, nurse, computer-software designer?"

"Because—" That an answer didn't leap to mind disconcerted her. "I have a talent, a—an ability, call it what you will."

"I have a talent for blackjack. You don't see me dealing cards in Vegas."

"That's hardly the same." Peering back at him, she decided she didn't care for conversations with someone whose eyes she couldn't see. "Why are you a rancher?"

"Because I like it. Because I'm happier doing that than I would be doing anything else."

"That much goes without saying."

Ross freed one hand and lifted the Stetson several inches to gaze at her. "Does it?"

She felt suddenly like squirming. He'd hit a nerve. One she hadn't known was exposed. Their eyes held. His seemed to peel back a layer of her skin before he let the hat drop again.

"Do you like what you do, Paige?"

Scowling, she pulled her knees in closer and propped her chin on one. It was none of his business, really. She didn't have to answer him. She could lie if she pleased. No, she wouldn't lie. That was her first clue she was dealing with more than attraction. Feelings were creeping in. She cared what he thought of her.

"It's probably the wrong time to ask myself that question." It was, she decided, the only truthful answer she could have given.

Her hair spilled forward over her shoulders. With a fingertip, Ross traced the delicate ridge of her spine. "Doesn't your sport call time-outs now and then? Sounds like you're overdue for one."

"Yeah?" She sat straighter, her back reflexively unbowing at the light pressure of his touch. "Two weeks would be nice. Just two weeks, with nothing to do." Fat chance, she thought grimly. And end of subject. Grasping the sole of one boot, Paige started working her foot out.

Seeing her struggle with the warm leather, Ross rolled to his knees. "Let me." Before she could think to resist him, he'd placed her left foot against his thigh and was holding the other. "Pull."

Dropping back to both elbows, Paige braced herself. His fingers stayed wrapped around her ankle long after the second boot was off. Her pulse was racing, her heart thudding. Against his palm, her skin burned.

Delicate. Circling her ankle, Ross's fingers overlapped. Perhaps that was what drew him, the fascination of so many contradictions in one woman. Fragile to look at, to touch, but with the sensual power of an athlete. Gentility wearing French scent and sweat. Watching her face, Ross drew a fingertip over the tops of her toes. Her eyes softened, her mouth firmed. Fire licking at ice. When she tugged to free her foot, he hesitated only a moment before opening his hand. With a smile he sat back and watched her wage the battle for self-control.

Paige buried her feet in the deep grass, letting its coolness drain the heat from her skin. Because she was half-aroused and vibrating, she decided against sitting up. It would put his face, his mouth, too close. Thunder, a faraway rumble of it, gave her something to focus on. She cased the sky, finding the clouds that were boiling.

"Rain," she murmured, as if just now realizing the weather was changing.

"We've got time before it blows in."

"Looks nasty. Could make a mess of Saturday's obstacle course." Shoving that thought aside, Paige dropped her head back and closed her eyes, deciding to enjoy the sun while it lasted. She wouldn't talk about riding or the circuit. She wouldn't even *think* about them. "If your cousin runs TLD," she said, "why are you involved with the bank?"

Her hair fell, rippling and shimmering, to brush the ground. To keep from tearing his hands through it, Ross tapped up a cigarette. "Because the Triple T, Tanner Mines and TLD are legs of one and the same body—Tanner Corporation. Wound one, they all bleed. And because Lance is in Monaco," he drawled. "If not Monaco, then on the Riviera...or wherever it is the jet set is currently parked."

His sarcasm coaxed a wry smile from Paige. "Cannes." She thought of her parents. It was something she avoided whenever possible. Wouldn't it be ironic, she mused, if at this very moment William and Olivia Meredith were with Lance Tanner on someone's luxurious yacht? "I know the type." She thought she was beginning to know Ross's type, too. The man everyone turned to. The man they counted on because he always came through, leaned on because he was strong in every sense of the word. "What are you supposed to do during these . . . reviews?"

"Explain Lance—which I can't do. Explain Lance's business, which I can't do, either. Sign papers, rescue TLD, keep the ranch and the mines out of the bank's clutches."

Paige lifted her head and frowned. "What's he done to risk the ranch?"

"Probably nothing more serious than sloppy record keeping." It pleased Ross that her first concern had been for the Triple T. He thought he'd figured her out enough to know she wasn't emotionally attached to the place she called home. Apparently she knew him well enough to know he was. "While reviewing collateral, a bank rep came across a familiar piece of property. Turns out TLD owned it five years ago, dumped it for a sixth of what it cost to buy back. The guy Lance sold it to the first time was a developer. A friend."

"So?" Curious, Paige pushed up from her elbows to her hands. "He underestimated its potential. Shortsighted, perhaps, but suspicious?"

"Did he underestimate? Suppose the land's been falsely inflated. A few undeveloped acres in the middle of nowhere, mortgaged for half a million? What if its actual worth is only eighty or ninety grand?"

"Eighty or . . . oh, I see."

"Do you?" Keeping his touch light and easy, Ross cupped a hand around her relaxed calf.

"It's done with horses," she said as his palm moved lazily up the back of her leg. Paige's first instinct was to stretch and purr. She shifted away from him instead, breaking the contact. "Find a cheap nag and a few friends who'll agree to buy and sell it, each time at a higher price. Along comes the unsuspecting buyer. You show him the sales history and soak him. You and your friends split the profit."

Amused by her retreat, Ross stretched out on the grass beside her. "Or kill the horse and split the insurance money."

"Or that." Paige shuddered. It made her ill even to think about lovely, innocent animals being destroyed for greed. "What does this have to do with the ranch?"

"Bankers panic. It's their nature." He dragged deeply on the cigarette before flicking it away. "Flip-flopping land is illegal. They'll investigate, of course. In the meantime, having the Triple T to secure the loan will help them sleep easier. If I cooperate, they'll be nice guys and delay calling the state attorney general until Lance returns."

Rolling onto her side, Paige propped her head and met his eyes directly. "What will you do?"

Her face was bathed in the eerie light of the encroaching storm. Ross saw concern, compassion, there. The moment unsteadied him. Not because she offered, but because he seemed to need. Over the years, he'd learned to keep his own counsel. Cat had enough on her plate with the mines. Aunt Mary died a little each time Lance screwed up.

"I'm not waiting for an official investigation," he said, the steel of resolve in his voice. "And no one's slapping a lien on the Triple T. I've had a look at the files, and Lance's appointment book. I think it's time I dropped in on a few of Louisville's more illustrious businessmen. One of them knows why Lance borrowed a fortune for a plot of weeds." Ross skimmed a fingertip down her cheek, where the flower petals brushed her skin. "There's a reason, a legal one, that much I'm sure of. Lance isn't executive material, but he's no criminal, either."

Thunder rolled across the sky, shivered in the ground. Paige gazed off at the dark wall of clouds again. Ross saw her chin lift, as if to say she wouldn't be chased to shelter by a little noise and some water. A breeze rushed past them, blowing her hair back and putting her face in sharp relief against the marbleized sky. Good God, she was beautiful. Just looking at her stole his breath.

The gust died as abruptly as it had risen, leaving the air cooler and smelling of rain. They had a few minutes, Paige decided, before the storm drove them back. They were face-to-face, their breaths mingling, a veil of intimacy floating down and around them. What could possibly happen in so little time? she asked herself. Then she remembered how fast falls happened, and that they often occurred without warning.

"Tell me about Montana," she said. "And the Triple T."

Ross smiled. "Tell you what?"

"Well...how big is it?"

Lifting her hand, he brought her palm to his mouth. "Which, Montana or the ranch?"

Soft. His lips were soft on her skin. "The ranch. I already know Montana is big—big sky, wild mustangs, ghost towns and gold. One of the last frontiers of the romantic West."

"Romantic? Montana?" He chuckled, his lips curving against her fingertips. "Try droughts, killing blizzards and coal. You want romance, go to Paris."

"I've been to Paris." Her eyes narrowed as she gazed past his shoulder, remembering. "It drizzled. The city was gray. Is Montana?"

"No, it isn't gray. In summer the sky is blue, electric blue. Wheat comes up gold and ripens to flax. The sun doesn't set, it burns itself up." Could she see it? He was a man of looks and action when he had a message to convey. Now he searched for words. "Nights are deep purple."

She remembered his voice just this low, this gentle, when he'd talked of his family two nights ago. Lulled by it, she relaxed, unconsciously leaning toward him. "And winter?"

"White. When the plains are a desert of snow, you can ride for hours without seeing a single footstep."

"It must be beautiful."

"I've always thought so." Moving smoothly, fluidly, Ross rolled her onto her back. "Someone looking for peace and privacy would find miles of it in Montana." Her eyes locked on his, confused, yet full of passion. "I could show you places you've never been, might never find your way back from."

Paige thought he'd already begun. He hovered, his presence alone pinning her down. She felt the hard muscles and rippling strength of his body as clearly as if he'd already covered her. Her hands had automatically gone to his shoulders when he took her back, but she wasn't pushing him away. She was anticipating his kiss—every cell in her body opened to receive it. The heat of his lips, the heady flavor of his mouth. Slowly, so slowly she thought she might go mad, he fitted their bodies from waist to ankles. Her sigh trembled, caught, then shuddered out.

Tangling one hand in her hair, Ross traced her lips with the tip of his tongue. Her breath on his skin grew quicker. Every second he delayed taking her mouth, the need to devour her doubled. Curving his hand to the back of her neck, he lifted her head. Champagne hair flowed away from her face to pool on the grass. The first flash of lightning caught her that way, the exquisite facial bones highlighted, her eyes huge pools of longing.

His breath rushed softly over her face, spilling into her mouth. Already Paige could taste him. The flick of his tongue at her lips caused her to jolt. Instinctively the tip of her own tongue sought him. Something stunningly electric accompanied the mating. When he entered her mouth, filling her fully and sealing their lips, she tasted more than the heat and flavor of him. She tasted the power.

Pressed to the ground, she didn't fidget with restrained passion, but opened herself. Still, it wasn't enough. Ross swept a hand down her length, from shoulder to hip to long, slender thigh. On the upward journey, he found her breast. Her nipple beaded to the flick of his thumb. A shudder tore through her, then a long groan nearly lost to the thunder that came now in overlapping waves of sound. Buttons fell open beneath his fingers.

The first fat drops of rain fell, rustling in the trees, plinking on the pond. Ross hardly noticed them splashing onto his back. He noticed only that her skin was soft and silky, her body an exquisite complement to his. Her breast fit his palm perfectly.

The stirring circular stroke of Ross's hand lifted Paige on towering waves of pleasure. This kiss wasn't soft, as the others had been, but hard and demanding. This kiss wasn't warm, but hot and seething. When he released her mouth, she gasped, greedy for air. She was only vaguely aware that her blouse had fluttered open. His lips were seductive, whispering down her neck, pressed against the hollow at the base of her throat, nibbling a trail to her breasts.

Too high, now. Sensations gathered, built, crested. Paige felt the storm move into her body. Thoughts whirled. Emotions were in turmoil. His lips brushed her nipple through the thin barrier of her teddy, then closed over the hard bud, drawing her and the sheer lace into his mouth. Lightning flashes of pleasure slashed at her nerves.

She had to stop him, she thought frantically. If she didn't, the wave would break, sending her into a helpless tumble. If she didn't, she'd find herself making love with him, here, now, this minute. Like a drowning person struggling for her last breath before sinking forever, Paige fought her way to the surface. She arched her back, shoving hard against his shoulders at the same time.

They parted on a whip crack of thunder. Ross rolled onto his back. Desire seared his flesh. Need gathered into a hard, heavy ball and burned. He lit a cigarette, inhaling on a long, ragged breath. He'd come dangerously close to stripping Paige and taking her. While he had some pleasant memories of passionate romps in fields of clover, he had no intention of making love to Paige for the first time on the ground. He would have her on a bed, he vowed, on pillows as soft as her skin, on sheets as smooth.

He'd imagined it. Moments ago, with his mouth pressed to hers, with her body molded to his, he'd imagined undressing her by moonlight, until she wore nothing more than a drift of night air. With no trouble at all, he pictured laying her down on the heirloom bed that had passed through generations of Tanners. The significance of that image gave him a shock. In the eight years he'd slept in the mahogany four-poster, he'd slept there alone. Joining a woman in her bed was pleasure; inviting one into his own was intimacy—

something he'd felt little need for and so had carefully avoided. That he wanted it now gave him more than a shock—it gave him one hell of a lot to think about.

Frowning, Ross stubbed out the cigarette, then watched Paige fumble with the buttons of her blouse.

"It's started," she said, as if by ignoring what had happened she could pretend it hadn't.

"First time we saw each other."

"The rain… I meant…" Then she buried her head in her hands.

"Paige—"

"No, don't say anything. Give me a minute."

They both needed one—no, twenty, he corrected. But the storm wasn't going to give them more than two or three. She swore, a roughneck's oath delivered with her inherent class and distinction. Hearing her curse delicately drew a chuckle from Ross.

Paige scrambled to her feet, where she stood glaring down at him. "Well, at least you're dependable, Tanner. You consistently find my worst moments amusing." Whirling, she strode up the bank.

Paige was reaching for Absolute's cinch when Ross took her by one arm and turned her. Chin up, she was prepared to freeze him out. Then she saw that he was holding her boots out to her.

"You might find them useful for the trip back."

Paige snatched them from him. She had to hop on one foot to keep her balance and, much as she wished it weren't necessary, she accepted the arm he offered to steady herself.

"Eventually," he murmured, "we have to deal with this." He saw her eyes slowly close, then open, before she turned to tighten the cinch.

"Deal with what?" she asked, but there was a tremor in her voice. "That we wanted to make love with each other? Or that we wanted to make love with each other but didn't?"

"That we want to make love with each other. And will."

"No. No, we won't."

"Oh, yes, we will." The skies opened then, releasing sheets of water. Ross removed his hat and dropped it onto Paige's head for protection. Thunder exploded, shooting rays of lightning that startled both horses.

"No!" she snapped. The angry bat of her hand sent his hat sailing to the wet ground. "We won't."

Fury surged through Ross. She'd tossed her chin at him once too often. Grabbing her shoulders, he shook her once, fiercely. "Cut the Miss High-and-Mighty act. I'm the man you were just rolling on the ground with. You might convince others you're as frigid and heartless as that blind stare of yours. I know differently. We both do."

Wet, his skin glowed bronze. His shirt clung to his chest, molding his magnificent form. Fighting the weakness, Paige drew her head back. "You're in my way. I have a job to do, and you're..." She pushed sopping hair from her face and searched for a word. Faye's immediately leapt to mind. "Distracting."

"Distracting." He'd strangle her. No, he'd take her to the ground, here and now, rain or no rain, and show her just how distracting he could be when he set his mind to it. Ross checked his temper, knowing the battle she fought was with herself, and loosened his hold without completely releasing her. "What are you, somebody's trained racehorse? Why not wear blinders? Then you won't see a damn thing but the track straight ahead. No distractions. Just work and win. Is that what you are, Paige? A prizewinning filly whose life begins in the start gate and ends at the finish line? Good God, you're a woman. You have wants, needs."

Paige didn't care for the reminder. Inside she was churning with more wants and needs than she knew what to do with. "I have a lifetime invested in this race, and the finish line is a long way off." She pulled herself free and vaulted into the saddle. "What I *want* is to ride the best three-day of my life next weekend. To do that, I have to be steady and focused. What I *need* is to be left alone." She turned Absolute, then looked back one last time. "Go away, Ross. And then stay away."

Ross retrieved his hat as she kicked the stallion into a full gallop. Today the sky had erupted first, he mused. But the woman was close. Very close. When it happened, he had every intention of being caught in the maelstrom.

Chapter Six

Paige started the day out of sorts. After watching Absolute pace his new stall for thirty minutes, she was out of patience.

Chill winds and rain had forced riders inside, crowding the exclusive "big barn" in Lexington. With the start of competition still forty-eight hours away, the atmosphere was clubby and congenial. Debates sprang up—on curb bits versus snaffle, on oats over grain. The air smelled of saddle soap, freshly turned hay and witch hazel. Somewhere a portable radio was tuned to country-western.

There were new faces, Paige noted as she scanned the familiar scene. Looking closer, she was surprised at how many. One belonged to the willowy redhead massaging Jeremy Calloway's shoulders while Jeremy punched holes into a cinch strap. Paige saw the flash of shiny new wedding bands on both their hands. Jeremy with a wife?

She'd lost touch. She spent days, sometimes weeks, at close quarters with them, yet she was no longer sure who had married, moved, had a baby. Funny, she hadn't noticed it before. Not funny, she amended. She missed them. Missed the camaraderie. Missed having someone with whom to commiserate or celebrate. Once she'd spent the evenings after a show sprawled in the hay of a spare stall with two or three friends, sharing secrets and giggles. When had that changed? Why had she let it?

She had no one to blame but herself. Competition-ready, she was oblivious of her surroundings. Greetings went unnoticed, unacknowledged. Now so did Paige. Oh, she was admired, respected. When she left a start box, her peers pulled for her. But when the barn door closed for the night, she was alone. The price, she thought now, of the dream. It was one she hadn't planned on.

One by one, riders departed for the official briefings. Conversation dwindled. The radio was snapped off. Paige checked on Divine, then, with a few minutes to spare before the meeting, returned to Absolute.

He went on stalking, his eyes peeled to the walls as if he feared gremlins would pop out and bite him. "Keep it up," she chided, "you'll be worn out before the first bell." When her low voice failed to soothe him, she resorted to bribery. The apple she pulled from her pocket had Absolute planting his feet. He chomped happily on the treat, then, finished, began rocking from side to side. Paige blew out an exasperated breath. "I give up."

The barn was quiet except for the soft drumming of rain on the roof. The storm had raged through the night, its high winds and slashing pellets subsiding to a drizzle by morning. Eruptions of thunder and lightning had made sleep impossible. That she'd lain awake thinking of Ross was the fault of the storm, she'd told herself. Just as it was the dreary day that had her feeling desolate now.

Eventually she noticed she was repeatedly plucking at the ribbed cuff of her sweatshirt. Freshly irritated, she made herself stop. What was happening to her? Last week her emotions wouldn't have surfaced this way. Why couldn't she discipline her personal life as she always had the professional? But Ross, she corrected, was not part of her personal life.

The barn's outside door shot open, and Paige spun on her heels. When a small, elfin-faced woman stumbled through, Paige relaxed. If she'd had a fleeting image of a lean-hipped cowboy in a black Stetson, she decided, it wasn't wishful thinking, but only because he'd been on her mind.

The girl, tiny as Paige was tall, carried nearly half her weight in tack, which caused her to walk like a rubber-legged drunk. When she saw Paige, her weaving progress slowed and she bowed her head. There was something disturbingly familiar about her wary under-the-lashes look. Paige had a flash from her past, of herself as a child, creeping across rooms so as not to draw her mother's eyes. She'd discovered it was better to go unnoticed than to meet with Olivia's flat, indifferent gaze. It never failed to make Paige feel unworthy and utterly insignificant.

Ross's parting words rushed back to her. *That blind stare of yours... Frigid. Heartless.* It didn't help that she was neither, or that he'd said as much himself. He'd been describing the way others saw her. Dear God, was she becoming her mother? A woman who erased people with a look? A woman whose sole and consuming interest was herself? Paige didn't want that. No, she didn't want that at all.

"Annie, isn't it?" she said to the girl making her way down the aisle. "Annie Jackson?"

"Uh, yeah." The brunette managed a weak smile. "Hiya, Paige."

"Hi. Would you like some help?"

"No," Annie blurted out quickly. "No, I've got it. Um, did you come down from Maryland?"

She knows where I live, Paige marveled. I wasn't even sure of her name. "Louisville. Horse trial last weekend."

"Lucky you." Annie flashed a smile of genuine warmth this time. "I was eventing on the West Coast. I'm two days late, my head's on a clock two hours early, and my horses are quirky from a week on the road."

Paige glanced to her left. Absolute was still swaying. "Seems to be the day for quirky horses. Are you sure I can't take some of that off your hands?"

"I'm sure." Passing Paige, Annie spun on her heels to walk backward, tack jingling as it swirled around her. "Upset the balance and I'll fall flat on my face."

"You couldn't make two trips?"

"I'm sort of in a hurry. The ground jury questioned the soundness of my horses to compete so soon after the long trip. I'm to have them tacked in an hour. An hour!" she cried in despair. "They'll limp... We'll be scratched. From now on," she called back as she turned a corner, "one show a month. I swear this is the last time I make myself crazy getting to an event."

Smiling, Paige turned back to Absolute. It was always the last time for riders. The last time they'd beeline across countries or oceans. The last time they'd ride in monsoon-like rains or give up holidays with their family. Always the last time... until the next time.

Beginning to settle, Absolute whickered. The quiet seemed deeper and Paige realized the rain had stopped. "I'm late. See you boys later."

She strolled down the corridor, tracing Annie's path. She passed the stall the girl was moving gear into, and was three doors away before deciding to turn back. "Where do you live, Annie?"

"Me?" She blinked in surprise. "Vermont."

Paige nodded, uncertain why it seemed important to know. "Pretty state. I prelimed Divine there, Doornhof Farm." They exchanged smiles and Paige departed. At the same place she'd turned back the first time, she hesitated, then returned once more. "How many horses do you have?"

"Two. A pair of bay mares."

"I'll walk one, if you'd like. With both of us warming them they'll get twice the exercise. Enough to work out the stiffness and most of the swelling."

Hazel eyes widened in astonishment. "You'd miss the briefings."

Paige shrugged. "So we find someone to fill us in later."

"You mean it? You'll help me out?"

"Sure." A weight seemed to roll off Paige's shoulders. It was a moment before she realized it was her mood lifting.

Paige scribbled notes beneath a rough sketch of the obstacle. Later, the vague scrawls would help her recall the jump and her thoughts upon viewing it. She'd walked the course over and over; this was her fourth and final tour.

Tossing the pad aside, she leaned back on her arms and closed her eyes. The sun was warm and the air crisp, reminding her of springtime in Maryland. While the grass had dried, two solid days of rain had left the ground soft—ideal soil conditions for a cross-country. But another storm was predicted for the weekend, and more rain later today. She said a prayer for the weather to hold until she'd finished both her runs tomorrow.

Riders passed by periodically, too involved in their calculations to socialize. When Paige heard footsteps behind her, she didn't bother opening her eyes.

The hat was dropped onto her upturned face. She gasped, and sucked in a bone-melting concentration of Ross's scent. Something dangerously close to elation sped through her. *Two days.* Only two days since she'd stood in a downpour, ordering him out of her life. It had felt like two weeks...two months. *He's back.* Beneath the hat, she smiled.

She hadn't a clue how she was going to handle him. Until she did, Paige figured, it'd be wise to hide the pleasure. Schooling her features, she sat straight, letting the Stetson fall forward into her lap.

Ross had lowered himself to the grass and was propped on his elbows, facing her. "A freeway exit," he said without prompting.

God, he looked good. Rugged and appealing. And sexy. Very sexy. Striving for indifference, she folded her legs Indian-fashion. "Should I know what you're talking about?"

"Lance's plot of weeds. It borders land tagged for a new interstate exit. Perfect location for a food-and-gas stop. It'll be lucrative, worth ten times the mortgage." Ross pushed up on one arm and wondered if she knew her eyes shone with the smile she held back.

"I told you to stay away from me."

He ran a fingertip down her thigh, lazily tracing the seam of her jeans. "You also told me the persistent, arrogant type appealed to you."

"We were discussing horses, as I recall." Paige pulled her knees into her chest. She couldn't think with her senses stirring to his touch. "If the bank didn't know about this exit, how is it Lance did?"

Amused by her retreat, Ross rolled onto his side. Their bodies lightly brushed when either of them breathed. "He and the road commissioner are buddies. They make an annual trek to Mexico for marlin."

"Ahh . . . Always nice to have highly placed friends with inside information." For a moment they simply stared at each other. Then Paige dropped her chin to one knee. She was close enough to feel his breath fan over her lips. "Dammit, Tanner, I missed you."

"I thought you would." Before she could stop him, he pulled the elastic band from her braid. "I like it down," he murmured when she hissed a protest. With a sweep of his fingers, he combed her hair loose.

At the sound of approaching voices, Paige shaded her eyes and watched a course official lead a troop of equestrians over the rise. "Young Riders division," she told Ross. "It's their first three-day, so an official takes them on the course walk. Today's our only chance to study the obstacles. Horses aren't given a preview."

The attentive group gathered near a mountain of earth shored up by natural wood planks. The right-angle drop was sheer and steep. "This is Lexington Bank," the guide announced. "The most direct route is over the center, the peak point of the drop. If your horse is laboring, come at an angle and take it over one of the optional low slopes to either side. Jumping a low end reduces the chance your horse will refuse or buckle on the bounce. It'll cost you time, though, setting up and again bringing your mount back in line for the next obstacle."

The rapt band moved on, and Paige turned back to see Ross canvassing their surroundings. "So this is cross-country."

"The last phase of it, anyway." Without exercising a whit of discretion, she visually lapped him up.

"Looks more like a country-club golf course." Ross saw her notepad and picked it up. "What's this?"

"A sketch of that jump." She hooked a thumb over her shoulder.

"You call this a sketch?" He turned the page sideways, upside down, but couldn't make heads or tails of her scribbles. When he looked where she pointed, his brow creased with a frown. "You call that a jump?"

"The Water Hazard. It's a triple attempt. See the horizontal rails up on the bank? They're first for the jump into the water."

"Into." He didn't like the idea. The drop looked every inch of five feet. No, he didn't like it at all. "How deep is the water?"

"Two, two and a half feet. The second element is jumping from the water onto the bank. I'll take Absolute out on a straight path and immediately over the next set of rails. Divine'll need a stride." Paige gave the obstacle a final once-over. "We'll see falls here from green and fatigued horses."

"And those kids, the Young Riders?"

"They're excused from this and two other obstacles. The rest of the course is modified for them." She pushed up to her feet and brushed at the seat of her pants. "I've got to hustle, or I won't finish before the course closes. Or it rains," she added as a cloud covered the sun.

Ross slipped his hat on and fell into step beside her. She was fascinating to watch. Even when she stood still—contemplating, calculating—he sensed the busyness of her mind. When there was more than one element to a jump, she'd pace off the middle distance, make notes, then pace it again, lengthening her stride the second time. Measuring for two horses, he figured, each with a different stretch. He didn't know or care how many strides it took one of his horses to cover ten yards. Watching Paige, he decided she knew Absolute's reach at a gallop to the half inch.

Jump evaluated, she'd stroll down the straightaway. Now and then she'd stoop to pull up a chunk of grass and rub the earth clinging to its roots between her fingertips.

"The Sink Hole," he observed. "The Coffin. Who names them?"

"The designer." Paige climbed down from a complicated triple-tiered stair-step creation. "I'm never sure if the names are meant to warn or intimidate, or just plain scare the hell out of us."

From the looks of the jumps, Ross thought, it could be all three. "Judge's box?" he asked of an area set apart from the one roped off for spectators. "Isn't it enough to get over in one piece?"

"Hardly. We take penalty points for crashing a jump or falling off the horse. And for refusals—three, you're disqualified. Obstacles have approach requirements. We can't, for instance, take a fence backward. Don't laugh, it happens. The flags help keep us on course." She made a sweeping gesture at the sidelines. "Reds on the right, whites on the left. But you've only had this one day to commit it to memory. By the time you ride it you've come through eleven miles. You're tired and sore and trying to remember how you'd planned to take each, what's coming up." She shrugged. "Sometimes you find yourself heading the wrong way."

It wasn't long before Ross changed his mind about the tame appearance of a cross-country course. He'd decided her sort of riding was entertainment; he changed his mind about that, too. *These people are nuts. They jump off cliffs, into rivers.* After a while he stopped questioning Paige. She didn't seem to notice, preferring to work in silence. Ross let her have it, realizing her life could depend on it.

"It's dangerous," he said as they turned away from the twenty-fifth and final jump to begin the long walk back to the stables. He tucked her under his arm and she hooked her arm around his waist without thinking twice about it.

"So's crossing the street, if you're careless. I know what my horses are capable of. More important, I know their limitations."

"And your own?"

Paige flashed him a grin. "I don't have any."

The way she said it, Ross didn't think she was kidding. "Everyone does, Paige. Only fools would navigate this course without some good old-fashioned fear to keep them sharp."

"Nerves," she corrected. "Not fear. Anyone afraid of an obstacle course shouldn't try it. There've been courses, course designers, I didn't have confidence in, jumps I wasn't a hundred percent sure could be made. That's different. You ride those with dread, and praying you won't steer your horse into a situation that'll cause him irreparable harm. A good event horse has more than strength and stamina. He has complete, unhesitating trust in his rider. He'll do what his instincts tell him not to simply because you've asked. It's a huge responsibility."

The scent of rain in the air should have distressed her. Instead, Paige savored a rare contentment. She had a few reservations about the course, but on the whole was optimistic about pitting herself and her mounts against it. Caught close to Ross, she basked in the warmth of his body, his voice. She was, she realized, both athlete and woman, with neither having to sacrifice for the other.

"When do you start?" Ross asked into the lengthening silence.

"I did, this morning. I tested in dressage."

"How'd it go?"

"Third place with Absolute, which is super for him. He isn't the best candidate for quiet exercises. But he only fell out once. The next two phases are his strongest, so we're in good shape. Divine..." Here she snorted in disgust. "Eighth. I'd had higher hopes for him."

A pleasure new and soft moved through Ross. He enjoyed hearing about her day, the good, the not-so-good. He liked the smooth flow of honey that was her voice. "Any idea what happened?"

"Warm-up ring threw him off. Grass." She rolled her eyes heavenward. "Divine has a fixation with the ground. Change it and he acts like it's going to open up and swallow him. He spent the first minute of the test obsessively eyeing the sand surface."

He heard frustration in her voice, and a thin note of fatigue. "Why do you do it?"

"I thought we'd covered that the other day."

"It's dangerous," he persisted. "It wrings you dry, and you've given your life to it. Anyone who knows horses knows it's costing you a fortune. You're not paid, not even prize money. So why? Fame? Glory? There are easier ways to both, you know. You could sit on a flagpole and get in *The Guinness Book of World Records*."

They walked beside a hedge of tall forsythia bushes, bright yellow blossoms brushing Paige's shoulder. She stopped and pinched off one of the frail switches. "I told you I have a talent for it. You didn't accept that. But it's the answer—the most accurate one, anyway." They set off again, headed for the showground's hub, but at the leisurely pace of people who have no real destination. "At first I was just a nine-year-old kid, crazy about horses. I started with lessons once a week, then twice. Within a year it was every day. Once I got to know Faye, I went as much to be with her as to ride. She was ... supportive, nurturing. I'd needed that. I entered shows, started placing. People noticed me."

"Something else you needed?"

"Oh, yes." Perhaps by explaining it to him, she'd come across the answers to a few of her own questions. "To children, indifference equals rejection, and attention feels like approval."

"Nine years old." There was so much he didn't know about her, almost nothing of her life before last week. "Most kids that age get more attention than they can stand from their parents."

"Mine were..." What? Paige wondered, not for the first time. Too busy? Too insensitive? "Their life-style didn't accommodate a child. There were either too few or too many people around for anyone to notice me. There were houseguests the months they were in Maryland. Arriving by the dozen, staying for weeks. Posthunt breakfasts slid into afternoon garden parties. At night there were balls, to which my mother wore the gowns that required she spend several weeks of every season touring the couture houses of Paris and London. Then, suddenly, the house would be empty and my parents gone." Not once had they said goodbye. Paige would wake or return from school to silence. To no one.

"I was left with nannies, then governesses." There hadn't been so many that she couldn't recall each by name, but not one was remembered with affection. "I was sixteen before I realized it wasn't I who'd failed them, failed to be worthy of them. That it was they who'd failed me."

Ross's eyes narrowed as he listened. She'd come from wealth, all right, though to hear her tell it, it hadn't been a privilege. "What you didn't get at home you got in a show ring. Attention. Approval."

"And purpose. I *could* do something. Do it well, better than most. Faye made me believe in me."

"She's given you a lot, then."

"Everything. A home, who and what I am, my future, her love—" Paige broke off, surprised by how much she'd said. If he'd prodded, she might not have shared the rest. But he remained silent, and the past refused to. "At thirteen I was sent to boarding school in Switzerland. It was customary for my parents and their friends to stow children in exclusive European fortresses. We were educated, disciplined and supervised, and they were free to go to Rio during carnival, Cannes for the film festival, the Riviera to recuperate. They satisfied their parental responsibilities with no more sacrifice than the time it takes to select a school and pay the tuition." Paige heard sarcasm in her voice and carefully smoothed it. "I hated Switzerland, and managed to get expelled. Getting back to the States wasn't as easy. My parents were . . . somewhere."

Ross remembered her saying she knew people like Lance, though he thought the Merediths could probably teach his cousin a thing or two about self-gratification. "The school called Faye."

"She was great. She arranged my ticket, met the plane and put me up at Gentry Farm. It was two weeks before my parents bothered to phone."

He was beginning to understand her icy walls, and the ease with which she slid behind them. She'd had a lot of pain to numb. "That's it? She meets your plane, you have a new home?"

"Just about. My parents returned shortly before Christmas. I left Faye's as soon as I heard from them. It wasn't until I'd been home a few hours that I learned they'd been back for ten days."

Ross whispered a curse. It was inadequate, but so would have been words of comfort.

"After the holidays," she went on, "they began planning their next trip. I went back to Faye's. I showed up on her doorstep at dawn, bags in hand, hoping I'd be welcome. I'd needed to belong...somewhere, to someone. Since that day I've only stayed at my parents' home by invitation." She gave a dry, mirthless laugh. "There haven't been many."

"How did they explain that? To friends, relatives?"

"Said their daughter was training for the Olympics." Paige idly picked yellow buds from the branch, letting them drift to the ground. "It was an easy enough story to sell. Everyone's heard of gifted athletes leaving their families and moving across the country to live with their trainers. I doubt they mentioned that mine lived across town."

"And now?"

Paige tipped her head to look at Ross for the first time since she'd started talking. "What about now?"

"Do you see them?"

Her lips formed a chilly smile. "If the event is prestigious enough. The Kentucky Three-Day isn't. I suspect the Pan-American Games will be." The weather was undecided between fog and rain. Gazing through its fine mist, she saw the gleam of anger in Ross's eyes. Experience had taught her the uselessness of that emotion. "They aren't malicious. Whimsical, perhaps...selfish. Inept parents, certainly. But they gave me no less than they'd been given, so I don't suppose they knew any better." Having picked the branch clean, she tossed it aside. "I had Faye, and she made up for a lot."

Her face was dewy with moisture. Ross cupped her chin, running his thumb over her petal-soft skin. "So much that you owe her an Olympic medal? The one she lost out on?"

Coolness washed through Paige. She couldn't say why she resented his question, only that she did. "Faye didn't put a price on her generosity. If I ride in the Olympics, it will be because I've earned the right and because I want to." *If?* She repressed a quick surge of panic. Since when was she thinking in tentative terms? *If?*

"I'm sorry." Ross saw uncertainty in her eyes, then a flicker of fear. She was no longer sure. Of her chances? he wondered. Or of the goal? "That was stupid and callous. I'd have flattened anyone who'd said as much about Aunt Mary."

Resentment faded. Her braced muscles relaxed. She didn't think he offered half as many apologies as he owed, or that he ever gave one lightly. And he, more than anyone she knew, would understand her feelings for Faye. *Something else we have in common,* she thought to herself as he tucked her under his arm again.

They approached the nerve center of barns, stables and arenas, with the dressage rings on their left. "Ah, horse dancing is still in progress," Ross mused aloud.

"Come on." She grabbed his hand and pulled him along. "I say even a cowboy can learn to appreciate the art of dressage."

"Wanna bet?"

Between the late hour and the drizzle beginning to fall, the audience was thin. Paige dragged Ross to an empty section of the bleachers, where they sat with their feet resting on the plank in front of them and their elbows propped on the one behind.

A rider entered the arena and halted her mount for the salute to the judges. The pair had barely begun when her horse reared. "Someone," Ross whispered in an aside, "should teach that horse to appreciate the art of dressage."

"He's a bit tense, isn't he?" Paige observed, tongue in cheek. "Judges look for a straight line on the entrance," she explained. "And for the rider to keep her seat through a working trot. She's blown quietness during the salute, I'm afraid, but she seems to have him collected now." No sooner had the words left her mouth than the horse lunged into a gallop. Paige pretended not to see the smug look Ross slanted her way. "Seems in a bit of a hurry to get to the other side, doesn't he?"

The next exhibitor was exquisite. Elegant, with bursts of controlled power when bursts of controlled power were called for. A thing of beauty to watch. Paige leaned forward, admiring the brilliant, graceful movements. She'd been so involved in her own performances lately, she'd forgotten what it was to be a spectator.

"It's a reach for perfection," she murmured. "Of course, the perfection is unattainable."

It crossed Ross's mind that she'd spent most of her life reaching for the unattainable. His next thought was lost when she tipped her head to look at him. His gut curled and clenched. God, but she was a stunner. There was a fine mist in the air. She wore it in her hair, the paler strands glimmering like threads of silver. Her blouse was white, thin; he could see the lacy edge of her lingerie through it. She looked dewy and soft. He imagined gathering her close before a roaring fire.

"Hungry?" he asked, folding her hand in his.

Paige opened her mouth to say she never was when competing, then realized, to her surprise, that she was famished. "Yeah." She let him tug her to her feet. "But it'll have to be casual. I smell like a barn."

She smelled like cream-covered skin, Ross thought. With hints of the grass she'd walked through and a dash of the flowers she'd fondled. "I know just the place."

"And quick," she added. "I have two endurance runs tomorrow. Dawn comes early, and I've notes to study yet tonight."

"Quick and casual," he agreed. "No problem."

* * *

She'd assumed he'd taken a room at a hotel.

Her first inkling she'd been wrong came when Ross parked in front of a tall building clearly resembling an apartment house. She learned he was staying at Lance's penthouse when they were halfway across the luxurious lobby, immediately following the doorman's nod and just before the elevator sighed open.

Now she sat across from him at a white-veined black marble table in a raised alcove overlooking a living room the size of a large barn. "I've never seen a room quite like this one," she mused aloud. "One with all its walls and the ceiling painted black."

"I've never seen a room like this one, period," Ross muttered.

"Why do you stay here, if you hate it?" Paige pushed her chair back and curled one leg beneath her. She was barefoot, having removed her shoes the moment she confronted miles of snow-white carpet. She was pleasantly full. She was with Ross. She could think of nothing in the world she might be lacking.

"It beats plastic hotel furniture and room service." Ross topped off her wineglass, noting with satisfaction that she'd polished off the hearty steak dinner. "Lance and I are the same size, so I don't have to pack as much. And he leaves his car keys behind so I'll have free transportation."

"Mmm . . . well, it's a stunning place. Different, certainly, but slick and sophisticated." Across the wide room she saw her own reflection in the floor-to-ceiling mirrors stretched end to end, giving the illusion that the room was twice its already expansive size. Sofas were long and low and covered with black suede. There were long-stemmed lilies made of white silk sprouting from crystal vases. Color was confined to one uninterrupted wall hung with a massive canvas splashed with jewel-toned oils—startling blues and greens, vibrant reds. Instead of lamps, there were muted spotlights, dramatically aimed. Expensive, sleek. It said a lot about Lance. "I don't know that I'd want to wake up to it every day. Too many sharp corners. You'd never be able to curl up and feel cozy."

"What about your place?" Ross shoved away from the table and stretched his legs out to one side. Each time he looked at her, relaxed, smiling, with her impossibly long legs curled under her and candlelight playing on her face, he wanted more evenings like this one. "Cozy?"

"Not really. I'm always saying I'll do something with it...buy curtains that match, some squashy throw pillows." Paige sipped her wine, then smiled over the rim at him. "I never seem to find the time."

"Think you will?"

She shrugged. "I'm hardly there." It was time she thought about leaving. She had a course to map out, ride times to calculate. But, oh, it felt so good to relax and think about something other than the circuit.

Ross stood and circled the table. "The rain's stopped. Shall we finish our wine on the terrace?"

Against her better judgment, she let him take her hand and bring her to her feet. She felt his strength and wondered when she'd begun to yearn for a man like him to lean on. She felt his warmth and longed to melt with it. He leaned past her to blow out the candles on the table. She grew weak in the knees from the soft brush of his body.

They stepped outside, twenty floors above the city. The slap of cool, rain-soaked air helped steady Paige. She walked to the waist-high rail and let the breeze take her hair.

"You belong in Montana," he murmured.

"What?" Startled, she turned back to face him.

Ross was equally surprised by the words. He hadn't meant to say them, but he'd thought them so often they'd slipped out on their own. "You belong in Montana," he repeated.

"Oh?" What else could she say to a statement like that?

"You were born for it. The freedom, the challenge."

"You really think people are born for certain places?"

"Absolutely." Ross moved to stand beside her at the railing. "Take Lance. He was made for the city. For three-piece suits and horses that race around a track, not bolt after a stray. I need extremes—hot days, hard rides, no limits." He stepped closer, his hand covering hers on the rail. "So do you."

Paige shook her head. Her fingers trembled on the stem of her wineglass, and she tightened them. She sensed that he knew her, knew her better than she knew herself. She wanted to say, *Yes, yes, you're right.* "No," she whispered. He leaned closer anyway. "No."

Ross lifted the glass from her fingers and set it down beside his own. He took her face in both hands, tipping her mouth up but not kissing her yet. With his own heart thudding, he watched her lashes drift down as she looked at his mouth. He dragged a thumb across her lips. She wet them instinctively.

With a light brush of his mouth, he tasted the moisture there. "Find out for yourself," he murmured. "Come to Montana with me. Monday. When it's over, come home with me."

His voice alone was temptation. *Say something.* The words screamed through her mind. *Something to make him stop reeling you in like a fish opening wide on the bait.* "Just like that?" she whispered. "I compete in Virginia in two weeks, but I should pick up and go to Montana?"

"Come for that long." He nipped at her earlobe. She shuddered and leaned into him. "Two weeks."

"I can't." Paige struggled to remember why. "I'm in training."

"You want to."

Yes, she wanted to. His fingers slid into her hair. She wanted two weeks to discover the woman lost inside the athlete. He angled her head so that her mouth was placed submissively beneath his. She wanted days filled only with sun and sleep, and she wanted to laze them away with this man. His mouth crushed down on hers, taking her swiftly into a whirlwind of sensations. She wanted to go with him now, through the terrace doors, across the thick white carpet to the bedroom beyond, and make love with him. Yes, she wanted. So completely it terrified her.

Ross grew vaguely aware that she was fighting him. With their mouths clinging, passion mounting, he felt her hands work between them. She moaned with unmistakable pleasure, yet pushed at his shoulders. Even as she spun with the kiss, she struggled to extract herself.

"Don't," Paige gasped when she could speak again. Brow pressed to the top of her head, he breathed as unevenly as she. "Don't do this."

He could have her now. Take her now. She was aroused and throbbing. Desire glimmered in her eyes. He'd had enough women to know when one could be talked to, touched, and was past resistance. So why was he waiting? Good God, he'd wanted nothing but this—*her*—for days.

But not conquered, he realized. Not overwhelmed and, in the aftermath, regretting. She was simmering with passion; he wanted her boiling over. Letting his hands settle loosely at her waist, he drew back so that no other parts of their bodies touched.

"I won't force you. When we make love, Paige—"

"Don't say it." She stepped back quickly, out of reach. Whirling so that her back was to him, she stared out at the winking lights of the city. The heat coursing with her blood defied the cool breeze. "I really can't handle this now."

"Then you've got a problem." Ross lit a cigarette and dragged the smoke all the way in. "Because now is when this is happening."

"Well, now is not convenient."

"A good deal in life isn't." She turned back, and he saw ice. Her skin was marble, her eyes were jade. Her hand, reaching for her wineglass, was steady. Her gaze, too, as she stared at him over the rim. God, how he wanted to strip away the control and free her. "It can't all be scheduled like the events of a horse trial. Some things start without a warning bell going off."

"Not for me." But, oh, she was tempted, so tempted. "Not with you." This wasn't a man she could give herself to and expect to walk away from whole. She couldn't afford to lose bits and pieces of herself; she was already squeezing out every ounce of energy and emotion just getting through each day. "I should go. It's late."

"Nine-thirty is late?"

"If you have to be up at five to begin a day like mine. I have a lot to do yet tonight." Paige set down her wine and strolled across the terrace. "The doorman can call me a cab."

"I'll take you." Circling her wrist, Ross stopped her at the terrace door. For her sake, he wouldn't push. The course they'd walked that afternoon was all too clear in his mind. He wouldn't do anything to interfere with her being rested and mentally sharp in the morning.

Lifting her palm to his lips, he felt her pulse jerk beneath his thumb. It took only the flick of his tongue to have the ice in her eyes melting. No, he wouldn't push, just give her a nudge. "Montana, Paige. Two weeks. Think about it."

She let herself in the back door at Sheffield Farm, and crept quietly up the stairs. On the second-floor landing she turned toward the long hall of bedrooms. One door was open, a fan-shaped pool of light spilling out. Faye's room.

Paige stopped, sighed, and thought she should have expected it. When Faye wanted a word with her, she was blunt and up-front about it. But if she sensed Paige needed an ear, a shoulder, she left her door open and her light on. An invitation, nothing more.

It was that comforting light Paige had sought before countless competitions, after her first heartbreaking fight with her best friend, every time she returned from a visit with her parents. It was that same light she'd walked away from the day she had her first horse put down. Some things Paige handled alone.

She stood in the hall, debating. It was her choice. She could enter or walk past. She'd look in, she decided. If Faye had nodded off waiting, then Paige wouldn't disturb her.

Faye was awake, curled up on a mint green easy chair. Caught up in the plot of a blood-and-guts suspense novel, she didn't notice Paige standing on the threshold.

It was a talent Paige had never mastered—to clear her mind of the thousand-and-one details a three-day event entailed. A talent she was sure kept Faye sane. In addition to

Paige, Faye had three up-and-coming students competing in lesser classes this weekend—two preliminaries and a Young Rider. Such an undertaking would have had Paige tearing her hair out. It was Faye who arranged all their schedules. Faye who coordinated groom teams and riders, who orchestrated special bedding and feed requirements for their half-dozen horses, who managed the equipment, from show tack to shampoo. And it was Faye who calmed the nerves, defused the tempers and, when it was over, dried the tears.

Watching her, Paige felt a sweet stab of love. Of her twenty-six years, nearly half had been lived under Faye's roof. In that time they'd forged a unique, immutable bond—not quite mother and daughter, but as close to that magical union as either was likely to get. Eyes widening, Faye turned a page. Paige chuckled when she placed a freshly polished fingernail between her teeth.

"You'll ruin your manicure."

Faye looked up, smiling. "I wondered if you'd drop in."

"I usually do when I find the light burning." Paige entered the sea-foam green room, tossing her shoulder bag onto the turned-down bed. "It's one of the things I miss living over the barn."

"You know I'd love to have you back at the house."

"Mmm..." Now that she was here, Paige didn't know how to begin. She wasn't even sure she knew what she wanted to say. "How's the Young Rider holding up?"

"Like a seasoned pro. It's the other two that need constant gluing together." Faye folded her hands on the open book and waited.

Paige paced. Thumbs hooked in her hip pockets, she strolled the length of the room twice before coming to rest at the window. There, she stared at the eyes of her own reflection.

"It might not seem so heavy if you share it," Faye suggested.

"I'm twenty-six years old," Paige began haltingly. "And I don't know what I want to be when I grow up."

The next sound was the solemn thud of a book slammed shut. "Will I have missed the point if I say you've already grown up? And that you're an equestrian?"

"That isn't a career. It's a sport, not a profession."

"For the moment." Faye dug into a crumpled cellophane pack for a cigarette. She struck a match and studied Paige, looking for clues. She skimmed over the disciplined carriage to frown at the hands drawn into fists. "After the Olympics, when you no longer have to maintain amateur status, there are professional tours. Dressage, show jumping. The money is good for someone of your caliber. You could teach, full-time, hold clinics all over the country. You might open your own schooling farm. Or break and train event horses. There's a whole range of possibilities."

After. When. Was Faye that sure of a berth on the Olympic team? Paige wondered. Or could it be that *not* making the team was unthinkable. No. Today she'd told Ross Faye's generosity had been given freely, without the strings of an Olympic performance attached. And Paige believed that wholeheartedly. Rubbing at the beginning of a headache, she lowered herself to the window seat.

"Suppose I want to be a lawyer."

Faye drew back, her eyes expressing astonishment. "Do you?"

"I don't know. That's just it. I've never asked myself." She rose to pace again, something she rarely felt the need to do. "I was in junior high when I jumped on this road leading to the Olympics. There've been no twists or turns along the way, no forks where decisions are made, directions changed."

"One-track life," Faye summarized. "It wears thin, for everyone. But, Paige, in less than two years it will be over."

"Will it?" Paige stopped in the middle of the room and crossed her arms. "Suppose I don't make the team."

Doubts. Fear. Faye had known them, had learned they weren't groundless. She'd made her peace with fate's cruel reward for a lifetime of dedication. It hadn't come easy or fast. There had been months of pain after the fall, then years of anguish. Eventually she'd accepted the lost dream, and was able to find satisfaction in making champions rather than being one. Over the years she'd given her riders everything—the form, the precision, the expertise. Everything but the dream. Her students took trophies and advanced on the circuit, some made names for themselves. They did so with their feet firmly planted; Faye had seen to it, never letting them believe they were any better than their last sets of marks or that any laurels awaited them beyond those already sitting on their shelves.

Except for a solemn-eyed nine-year-old named Paige Meredith. A passionate young rider, if not quite polished. She'd lacked technical skills, but nothing Faye couldn't teach her. What had set her apart were those qualities that couldn't be taught—timing, affinity, instinct. And hunger. A huge, gnawing hunger to *be* somebody.

"It's normal to doubt." Faye stubbed out her cigarette and set the book aside. "Every rider fears the same, that after all the sacrifice and dreaming, they may not make the longlist, the shortlist, the squad."

"This isn't about doubt or fear, Faye. I thought so at first, but it isn't. It's about me. If I don't make the team, what will I do? Stay with it? Four more years? I'd be... thirty-two!" Paige tore a hand through her hair. "Let's say I make the team, but the team doesn't medal. Is that it? Or do I go for it one more time? Suppose, just suppose, I make the team *and* win the gold." She paused, green eyes boring into brown. "What will I do the next morning? The next week? Faye, what happens to me in sixteen months?"

"What happens to you?" Faye shrugged and shook her head at the same time. It was a gesture of bafflement.

Poor Faye, Paige thought. As if she hadn't enough on her mind, along comes her prize student—her Olympic-potential protégée—asking befuddling questions the night before a crucial cross-country. Turning back to the window, Paige stared out again.

"Paige, I'm sorry if I'm letting you down." Faye rose and crossed the room, meeting the reflection of her eyes in the window. "Patience. I've no other answer. If...whatever's troubling you hasn't worked itself out in the next sixteen months, then it will be there waiting for you. There'll be plenty of time then to look for answers."

Because she knew Faye expected it of her, Paige forced a smile she was far from feeling. The answers might wait, she thought. The need to find them wasn't likely to.

Chapter Seven

Predawn gloom acted as a muffle, muting and isolating sound—a cough, a curse, a long ruffling whicker. Riders crisscrossed the yard, tending to business in groggy silence. Grooms unpacked curries, combs and clippers. Trainers sipped weak coffee from foam cups. Leaning against an oak tree, Paige watched the showgrounds stir. Faye had dashed off to brief the groom team before moving the horses to the start box. As soon as the muzziness cleared from her brain, Paige would join them.

Through sleepy eyes, she contemplated the countryside. Dew trapped the thin wash of light to shimmer like frozen crystals in the cool air. Instead of gentle slopes slumbering beneath a shower of moonlight, the land looked as if it had been glossed by a film of ice. It was cold, dark and, she decided ruefully, too damn early. Paige shivered and thought longingly of a warm bed, a bundle of blankets...hot sunlight...Ross's arms...Montana.

Montana in May, she mused. Two weeks. The first intrigued her; the second enticed. And Ross...Ross obsessed her. He owned her thoughts, her dreams. He made her wonder, fantasize, ache. He made her want.

Obsessed, she thought again, annoyed with herself, and scanned the yard, looking for a diversion. She found one in a comically lopsided tug-of-war between a flyweight stable boy and a freshly bathed mare craving a frisky roll. The boy was green, the horse had decided. The outcome, Paige figured, was inevitable.

His eyes were wide with alarm as the untutored hand watched his charge drop to her knees. Giving a satisfied grunt, the animal gently keeled over and proceeded to squirm happily. As quickly as she'd gone down, the mare scrambled to her feet—a giant mud ball contentedly swishing her tail.

Paige bit down on her lower lip to hold back a laugh. The poor kid didn't need the added humiliation of learning he had an audience, or that his audience found his predicament amusing. Next time he'd ask if he had a roller before leading an unfamiliar horse to a bath.

A car sped into the yard, exuberant voices rushing from its open windows. Paige watched the toy-size compact miraculously discharge five lanky-legged men. Unshaven, hair tousled, not one of the five hurrying to the stables resembled equestrians of world-class stature. But then, today was not a day for elegance. Today was a day for sweat.

Two more cars unloaded passengers before Paige uncrossed her arms and ankles. Ready or not, the day was beginning.

Naked low-watt lightbulbs shed a comforting glow in the stable rows. At Annie Jackson's stall, Paige stopped and peeked in. "Hi," she called softly. "How's it going?"

Annie made a circle of her thumb and finger. "Great. You?"

"Fine."

"Good luck," Annie said.

"You, too."

Like a dozen others, Paige's team was gathered in the corridor, quietly consulting. "Where's Lizzy?" she asked, seeing only three familiar faces.

"Flu," Faye reported. "When we finish here, I'll see what locals are offering in the way of grooms." Her shrug said she wasn't overly concerned with finding a replacement. "You've drawn the ninth position with Abby, fourteen with Divine. Jimmy'll set the remote camera at The Rail, The Ditch And Wall, and monitor the video screen from The Water Hazard. This'll give us the widest coverage of the critical jumps. He'll radio to the vet box what's working and what's not as the first riders go through."

Paige couldn't have asked for better placement than ninth in the selection trial division. With twenty contenders, enough would have gone before to test-ride the course, but not so many they'd have it torn up.

"Steve," Faye went on, addressing the taller of the two men. "Tack, boots and shoes. If we have to pull this off shorthanded, I'll do cool-downs. Strip tack fast. We have only ten minutes to lower temps, respiration and pulse. Triple-check every piece before it goes back on. Be generous greasing their legs. I don't want to see a single horse hang up on a fence." Finished, Faye pocketed her notes. "Okay, boys, pack the gear and collect the horses at the other barn—Steve, you know which ones. Paige and I will bring the two here."

Jimmy and Steve departed, and Faye unlatched Divine's door. Before leading the gray out, she looked Paige over. "How do you feel?"

"Fine." Paige covered the hand Faye laid on her arm, and gave it a reassuring squeeze. "Honest. I've never felt more fit or focused."

"Good." Clucking at Divine, Faye led him away. Paige crossed her arms, dropped a shoulder to the jamb of Absolute's stall door and closed her eyes. It was a small lie, she rationalized. So maybe her focus was a bit blurred this morning. She was certainly fit, and, she told herself, she would *be* fine by the start bell.

Activity in the barn escalated. Blocking the sounds, she mentally transported herself to the start box and began the first of three preevent visualizations. She had just completed a flawless run of the eighteen-mile course when Absolute slipped his head over her shoulder. Keeping her eyes shut, she pressed her cheek to his silky coat. Warm. Familiar. Comfortable. *When had that stopped being enough?*

The stallion's welcoming whicker alerted her to a visitor. Paige opened her eyes to see Ross standing less than three feet away. Pleasure washed through her in one long, delicious wave. She'd hoped he'd come, but hadn't allowed herself to expect him.

Several seconds ticked by. Then his attention shifted from her face to her left hand clasping her right arm. A smile tugged at his mouth. "I haven't seen ballpoint on the back of a hand since final-exam week in high school."

"Ride times," she explained, when what she wanted to do was throw her arms around him. "No bonus points for coming in early."

Reaching, Ross caught her behind the neck and gave her a long, leisurely kiss that instantly liquefied her bones. As he stood away, he let his hand drop to her shoulder. There it tensed, then squeezed.

"What the hell is that?" he muttered.

"Padding." Paige saw more than passing concern in his eyes. "Bad falls are the exception, Ross, not the rule. Still, I'd be stupid not to protect myself."

"I don't mind telling you, I didn't sleep worth a damn last night. Wanting you with me was only half the reason." He held her face between his palms, commanding her gaze when it would have darted away. "Wanting you safe was the other half." It was, Ross had admitted during those long and uncomfortable hours, a novel and uncomfortable feeling.

Determined to keep a clear head, Paige swallowed the emotion climbing up her throat. "It'll be a walk in the park," she said in a bantering tone.

"Don't be flip, Paige. Not about this."

She sobered, indescribably moved by the softly spoken words. "I'll be careful," she promised.

"And I'll be twenty-five on my next birthday," Faye retorted.

Paige swung around, feeling, absurdly, like a child caught with her hand in the forbidden cookie jar. "Umm...Faye, meet—"

But Ross cut her off. "We introduced ourselves outside."

"Oh." She glanced from one to the other, unsure what she was looking for. Ross was smiling, and Faye, she thought, only pretending to.

"Ross heard we're a man short on the groom team," Faye said. "He's offered to fill in."

Ross watched Paige for her reaction. While he'd left little room for argument when he informed Faye Gentry she was stuck with his company and so might as well make use of him, he would, he'd decided, join the sidelined spectators if his presence was going to unsettle Paige. He was as prepared for her to resist as he was for her to be pleased. He didn't quite know what to make of her blank expression.

It dawned on Paige that Faye was waiting for her to comment. "Are you asking me? I've nothing to say about who's on the groom team."

"Then having him around won't...bother you?"

Paige laughed. She'd never known Faye to grope for words. "Why should it? I only see the groom team for ten minutes between phases C and D. Even then, they're with the horse and I'm with you, getting briefed on the course." The more she thought about it, the better Paige liked it. With Ross confined to the vet box, she wouldn't do something stupid and reckless—like scanning the crowds for his Stetson while galloping at a brick wall. "If you think he can do the job, it's fine with me."

Faye nodded at Ross, as if, Paige thought, she was conceding a point rather than confirming his assignment to the team. "You'll do cool-downs," she told him. "Be prepared to get good and wet. It doesn't require you know much about eventing, only that you have a basic understanding of horses. Steve can fill you in on the particulars. You'll find him in the orange-and-white van parked across the yard."

When Ross was gone, Paige lifted one eyebrow. "My, you certainly grabbed that bull by his horns."

"Last I'd heard, the bull had gone back to Montana."
Faye's unblinking gaze pinned Paige to the spot. "He won't
be a quick tumble. You know that, don't you?"

"My business."

"I wish you could see what you're letting yourself in for."

"If you dislike him so much—"

"I don't dislike him. Paige, I don't even know him."

"I'll rephrase it. If his presence disturbs you, why did you
put him on the team?"

"We're shorthanded. We need him." Faye fitted a halter
on Absolute and buckled it down. "And anyone with two
brain cells to rub together could see the man was decided."

Yes, Paige thought with equal parts pleasure and uneasi-
ness, the man *was* decided.

At the vet box, a roped-off area where phase C roads and
tracks ended and phase D cross-country began, Ross and
Steve set up camp. They emptied the van, dragging out
multiples of everything, from saddles and cinches to bits,
buckles and shoes. Steve checked and rechecked each item,
while Ross unloaded thermoses, sandwiches, fruit, bottles
of soda, buckets of ice. When the tools were organized to
Steve's satisfaction, they were draped with waterproof tarps
to protect them against the rain threatening overhead.

It was here that Paige and Absolute would rest for ten
minutes before attacking the obstacle course. Ross's duties
were simple enough. The second Paige dismounted, Steve
would strip the horse, inspecting every piece of tack before
it was put back on. In the meantime, Ross was to douse the
heated animal with water, frequently applying ice packs to
pulse points. "Look for blood in the water pouring off,"
Steve had instructed. "And get your hands all over the
horse. Feel for cuts, swelling, any injuries he might have
picked up on steeplechase, on the legs and belly, mostly." As
Steve retacked, Ross was to spread a thick coating of gel-
like grease down the fronts of all four legs, to assist the horse
in literally sliding over the jumps.

Ross lit a cigarette and scanned the assistance area. He
saw dozens more tarpaulin mounds, along with too many

people in too small an area, climbing over each other to get their work done. Golf carts and miniature vehicles buzzed in and out, most carrying trainers back and forth from the start box. He thought they looked like worker bees swarming around the hive. A huge semitrailer had been converted into a fully equipped veterinarian's emergency station. Three ambulances stood ready, doors open and engines idling.

"Is it always like this?" he asked Steve. "Like a battleground field hospital gearing up for the onslaught of wounded?"

"Yeah, it's always like this." Steve took a moment to visually tour the same area. "But we don't prepare for injuries. Hopefully, we prevent them." Jerking his head, he indicated the obstacle-course start line. "It's out there, after they leave us, that things get hairy."

"I walked it with Paige. Is it as brutal as it looks?"

"And then some," Steve said, then shook his head. "There's lots of talk about safety. Courses are mapped out on paper for approval by a TD—technical delegate—and the ground jury. Still, the last ten years or so, injuries have increased—the bad kind."

Ross felt a chill, a tightening in his gut. "How's this course?"

"As of last night, there'd been six voluntary withdrawals."

"Why?"

"Riders say some obstacles don't allow for honest mistakes." When Ross shook his head, Steve explained. "You gotta ease horses onto a course, give 'em a chance to settle in before asking tricky questions. By the end, they're used up. Not just physically, but here—" Steve pointed to his temple "—where it counts. Course designers know this, but instead of allowing for it, some take advantage of it. We call 'em 'gotcha' jumps."

Ross felt a ripple of fear, then another of helplessness. He vowed not to think in terms of wounds or injuries. Not when it was Paige he had to stand here and watch for, then send off again. Fine threads of tension curled through him. He wasn't used to waiting...to *worrying,* he corrected. Ross crushed his cigarette out beneath his heel, jammed his hands into his pockets and scowled.

Paige was up and ready at the one-minute warning bell.

She set her watch, adjusted her goggles and trotted Absolute to the start box. Today's batch of jitters had taken up residence in her stomach. Paige welcomed them. Only those who'd lost their edge—or their minds—rode carefree through a cross-country.

"Get set," Faye prompted, her eyes on a stopwatch and one foot in a cart, poised to take off the moment Absolute crossed the start. "Go!"

At the touch of Paige's heels, Absolute lunged. "Nice and easy," she murmured, holding him to a controlled canter. His pace was a few meters per minute faster than necessary. The time limit for the first 220 meters could be made at a moderate trot, but she knew that if she placed too much restraint on the eager stallion he'd only waste precious energy fighting her. "Soon," she promised when he asked for more rein than she was willing to give. "Soon you'll have your chance to break loose."

There was more mud than she'd expected, more damage to the course by previous riders. She made a mental note to recalculate Divine's ride times. Sighting the stand of oaks that was one of her checkpoints, she glanced at her hand for the estimated time, and then at her watch.

"Perfect," she purred. "We're on the money, so far."

They neared the end of phase A roads and track, Absolute eyeing the first steeplechase jump ahead. "Not yet," she ordered quietly, firmly, when she felt his muscles bunch with power.

Steeplechase was the fastest leg of the course. Paige never started the mile-and-a-half stretch without remembering it was there that Faye had lost everything. She'd be waiting at the finish, Paige knew, to check shoes and equipment and administer a quick sponge-down, before phase C roads and track. A safety measure worth the twenty seconds they'd have to pick up on the course, Faye would say. Because of the relief Paige always saw on her friend's face, she knew the real reason Faye waited at the end of phase B was to be certain Paige had come through in one piece.

"Here we are," she murmured. "Go. Stretch and fly, big boy."

It was fast and furious, dangerous, thrilling. Even so, Paige never let her concentration waver. These jumps were fixed; they didn't collapse if crashed into, but sent horse and rider into bone-breaking cartwheels. Shrubbery and spectators were indefinable blurs on the fringes of her vision. The wind slapped at her face. Absolute sailed over the tall hedges and stone walls, bobbling once on a landing halfway through.

"Everything okay?" she asked between jumps.

He blew out a fierce blast of air.

"All right, if you say so."

Paige saw Faye at the finish line and reined in. She kicked free of the stirrups and pulled her knees into her chest, allowing Faye to check hidden parts of the saddle. She was as breathless as the horse and feeling the first-stage burn of strain in her upper arms and shoulders.

"He did a funny little two-step on one landing," she reported as Faye sloshed water at the chestnut's underside. "See anything?"

"He's thrown a shoe. Left rear. We'll give him a new one at the vet box. Go!"

Ross saw Faye come over the rise that was a shortcut to the steeplechase field, and knew Paige had set off on the second phase of roads and track—this one five miles long and demanding a good clip.

Six horse-and-rider teams had completed that leg. The seventh was due any time. All around him pockets of pandemonium erupted. The waiting turned his breakfast to lead. Riders arriving at the vet box complained of mud and slippage, apparently more than they'd expected. Ross told himself Paige was good, one of the best. Then he remembered Faye had also been the best . . . once.

He stood beside Steve, both men alert to what was being done and said in other camps. The radio transmitter hanging from Steve's belt crackled to life as Faye arrived.

"First rider through the Water Hazard," Jimmy reported. "Sliding on the bank. Mud's a problem."

"How was she?" Ross asked Faye when Jimmy signed off.

"Fine. Just fine." But the worry lines in Ross's brow didn't smooth out. "Steve, Abby's thrown his left rear shoe."

By the time Paige cantered in, Steve was a prepared smithy. Paige circled Absolute for the required trot before the jury. One of the two vets assigned to the area checked the lathered stallion's vital signs, noting them beside the initial values taken the day before. The second vet would monitor the horse throughout the ten-minute rest period. If there was any doubt about his fitness to continue, he'd be spun out.

Paige was barely out of the saddle before Steve had the cinch unbuckled. She and Ross had only enough time for a wink and a smile before he turned to the brimming ice chests. "Switch his behind studs to mediums," Paige instructed Steve. "We're skating all over the place." Without missing a beat, Steve produced the pegs that would protrude a half inch from the stallion's shoes, improving his traction.

Sparing the sky a glance and a scowl, Paige strode directly to Faye for her briefing. Jimmy's reports from the field were constant now. The Water Hazard was proving to be as wicked as they'd feared.

"Swear to God!" came his static-filled voice. "Jumpin' Jack sank. Sank! Tippy sat there two, maybe three seconds. Then Jack...exploded from the water. Exploded! No other word for it."

"Change to medium road studs," Faye said.

"Steve's seeing to it." Paige popped the top on a can of soda, took a long, thirsty pull, and grinned. "Absolute's going great. He's really going great."

"Good. Sit down and let's see what Jimmy can tell us about the second half. There've been a couple of riders through by now."

Rest period over, Paige presented Absolute for his second required trot before the ground jury. All thumbs turned up, and once again Paige steered Absolute to a start box.

The minute she was off, Ross, Faye and Steve piled into the golf cart. With the way the obstacle course twisted and turned back on itself they could beat Paige to jump number ten, the diabolical Water Hazard.

Paige pressed the eager stallion into a canter, her mind leaping fifty yards ahead of the flying horse. She talked to him—of the jumps they approached, of his performance and her pleasure with him. "Nothing to it. A hill to climb, a vertical. Nothing to it. You're doing fine, just fine." The course curved, zigzagged, sloped up to drop away. Where it extended and leveled, she relaxed her grip on the reins, giving her arms and shoulders a rest and permitting Absolute's stride to lengthen.

The spectators here were more vocal than those lining the steeplechase field. They cheered a horse and rider into the jumps, shouted them over and whistled them on their way. Paige managed to distance the sounds, reducing them to ebb-and-flow murmurs, and maintain her concentration.

Adrenaline was pumping, replenishing the drain of strength from her muscles. At every twist, every turn, she faced a new challenge. Strategies were carried out, at times reconsidered and a different approach taken. Decisions were made in seconds, split seconds. Absolute never balked or refused, but willingly gave what was asked of him—power and speed. Paige savored the half thrill, half terror headiness of it.

At Jenny Lane Crossing—an obstacle comprised of three galloping rails arranged to form a giant, jagged Z—she positioned Absolute to come off the first rail set up to take the second and third in a single leap at the corner. It was a risky option, and one of the few decisions she'd left up in the air until faced with it in competition. It was a demand for hindquarters power she wouldn't make of Divine later in the day.

Absolute soared and stretched, his front legs reaching for ground well beyond the second rail. He landed cleanly. "Beautiful," she said, praising him, as he regained his rhythm. "Now, slow up, slow up. Next one's a bit trickier." The course took them into a small woods, the narrow trail snaking through trees and shrubbery. Even at a conservative pace, the serpentine path demanded quick thinking of riders and immediate responses from horses. The woods ended abruptly at the banks of a shallow pond.

"A splash coming up. Don't let the water scare you. It's hardly a puddle."

She miscalculated the final turn out of the woods—too sharp, too fast. Though she managed to stay in the saddle as Absolute maneuvered the pivot, her left foot slipped free of the stirrup. Her leg swung out, smashing against a tree, then, for a second—though it felt like longer—was crushed between hard-muscled horse and unyielding oak. White-hot pain speared into her hip. Her eyes teared and she ground her teeth to prevent a shudder running through her body. She'd make no moves Absolute might interpret as a lack of confidence or control. Injuries would be dealt with later. For now, she had the Water Hazard coming up—a nightmare of rails, water and mud; a steep uphill run, a blind leap into air.

It seemed to Ross that she came out of nowhere. One minute the field was empty, the next Paige and Absolute were thundering at the high vertical rails. They'd been here yesterday, he remembered. He and Paige, lounging on the grass. It had seemed peaceful then, harmless. Now the day was overcast, the sky a menacing shade of gray. The earth looked as if a giant paw had taken a swipe at it, claws extended.

He sucked in a breath as Absolute took to the air, Paige perched high on his neck. He didn't relax and exhale until they scrambled onto flat ground again. He'd never seen anything like it—horse and rider airborne, then falling, falling, to land finally with a tremendous splash. Absolute's fortitude, his sheer determination to pull himself out and up again in a single lunge, was staggering. More staggering was Paige's nerve. *God, she has guts.* Talent, tenacity, and one hell of a lot of guts.

As they came abreast of him, Ross heard the deep, hard heaves of Absolute's breathing. Paige, drenched, caked with mud, was looking straight ahead, her thoughts already on the next obstacle.

They flew by, and Faye and Steve set off, heading for the final jumps. Though Ross followed, he wasn't sure he'd watch the next time.

He found her sitting on the floor in the barn corridor, her back to the wall outside Absolute's stall. Her legs were folded, her arms crossed and her eyes closed. Crouching to sit on his heels, Ross gazed at her for several long seconds.

She'd changed into dry clothes, a duplicate outfit to the blouse and breeches of that morning. She'd washed away the mud, revealing scratches on the delicate ivory skin. Ross recalled watching her dismount at the cross-country finish line less than two hours ago. She'd slid from the saddle, seemingly boneless with exhaustion. When he saw her stumble before gaining her balance, he'd started to go to her, but had been stopped by Faye. He'd watched her unbuckle the cinch strap, drag the saddle from Absolute's back and dig for the strength to carry the lead-packed leather to the weighing stand.

She was a hell of a lot tougher than she looked. She was, Ross decided, one hell of a woman.

Even so, he was tempted to ease her onto his lap and let her sleep through the next start. The day wasn't half-over, and already there was a casualty list as long as his arm—breaks, sprains, and disabled horses. One rider was in the hospital with a broken collarbone, a young man who might just as easily have broken his neck in this crazy chase for a ribbon. A handsome chestnut gelding was dead—an aorta ruptured as he went over a jump.

On impulse, Ross skimmed her cheek with the backs of his fingers. Lashes fluttering, she opened sleep-fogged eyes.

"Always popping up without warning," she murmured huskily.

"It's time," he told her. "Faye sent me to fetch you for intermediate. Oh, and she said to tell you your finish with Absolute held—you've moved into first place."

She grinned and flung out her arms, untying the knots in her muscles. They rose together, Paige carefully easing her weight onto her left leg. It wasn't broken—she knew her body well enough to be certain of that—but she'd have a bruise the size of a watermelon in the morning.

She turned to look in on Absolute, as always holding her breath for fear she'd find him collapsed in the hay. But he was standing, his legs wrapped in bandages to minimize the swelling. She crooned a hello, and he greeted her with a lazy swish of his tail.

"How do you feel?" Ross asked her.

"That," she said with a smile, "is a question for tomorrow."

An hour later, Ross waited in the vet box, in a drizzle, watching more muddy riders come in.

"She's left the course."

At first Jimmy's staticky message didn't register. Ross and Steve exchanged puzzled looks. "Who?" Ross demanded. "Paige?"

"Who else?" Steve wondered aloud.

"How would he know? He's on the obstacle course. She hasn't come through roads and track."

"He can see parts of the steeplechase field from where he sits."

"Did she fall? Is she hurt? For God's sake, find out what happened!"

Steve repeated Ross's questions, then released the talk button.

"Negative on the fall. Hell if I can explain it. She slowed up and retired from the course. Maybe Divine came up lame. Paige looked okay from what I could see. I think she's riding him back to the barn.

"I better get word to Faye," Steve said. "She'll freak when Paige doesn't come through steeplechase on time."

* * *

Quit. Paige scowled. Officially it would go down as a voluntary retirement from the course. But changing the words didn't change the deed. For the first time in her professional life, she had quit.

It was quiet in the barn. Intermediates had yet to finish, and only a few advanced riders had dribbled back from cross-country headquarters. Instead of jokes or debates, they shared the silence of exhaustion as they tended their horses. Paige brushed the mud from Divine's ash white coat and figured she had an hour before all hell broke loose.

Quit. Like a pulse beat, the word repeated in her brain. She whispered a curse and wondered how she'd explain it to Faye.

Riding back to the barn, she'd felt good about retiring, relieved, almost buoyant. She'd finished the important run—the selection trial—and finished well enough to leap into first place. What difference could one retirement make? Now she wondered what she could have been thinking. She could count the times she'd retired from a course on her hands, with fingers left over. Never before had she pulled up for reasons other than an injury to her mount.

So why? Why had she done it?

Divine had been going fine, better than ever. He'd paced beautifully through roads and track, beginning steeplechase fresh and brimming over with energy. Then the rain had started.

Disgusted with herself, Paige tossed the brush into her grooming kit and rooted around for a hoof pick. She tried to imagine telling Faye she'd quit because of a little rain. But it was more than that. Running her hand down the gelding's right front leg, she raised his hoof, bracing it against her bruised thigh. She'd been cold, she recalled. Once the rain started, she'd been cold and wet. Going over the second jump, she'd admitted to herself she was miserable. She'd wondered what for, and discovered she no longer had an answer.

"Decide to take a time-out?"

Paige jolted at Ross's quiet words. She wasn't ready to see anyone, to have to explain or defend herself. Releasing Divine's leg, she let it drop, then straightened. "You got here fast."

He unlatched the half door and stepped inside. "You're okay?"

Concern, relief, traces of fear. Paige read them all in his eyes, and her heart softened, melted. When she should have been sorting out her own problems, all she could think of doing was reaching out to comfort him.

My God, I'm falling for him. Realization hit Paige like a thunderbolt. Yet how could she not have seen it? Attracted, even obsessed, was one thing. But falling in love... No, she couldn't let that happen. Not now. Next year, the year after, perhaps. But not now.

He walked toward her, hay rustling beneath his feet like a thousand twigs snapping. Paige shouldered Divine to one side to allow her room to get past him and through the door. Before she'd taken two steps, Ross had her by her arms and was turning her around.

"What's going on, Paige?"

"I don't know. Like you said, I took a time-out."

With her confidence shaky, her eyes, for once, were quite readable. Ross saw self-doubt laced with fear. "You're entitled, you know."

"Entitled." That one word had the effect of jarring a thing or two into perspective. "No, I'm not entitled. I made a spur-of-the-moment decision without a thought for the consequences. Divine is my number-two horse, my backup. He needs CCI certification, or all the training with him is wasted. Months. *Years.* The next international event's in August, in Germany. There's no way I can make room for it in my schedule at this late date. Which means Divine waits until Chesterland, in the fall."

Angry with herself, Paige jerked free of Ross's hold and strode to the far end of the stall. There she pressed her back to the wall and jammed her hands into her pockets. "You've no idea the number of people involved in getting me where I am today. Trainers, groom teams, sponsors. They believed in me. They put time and money into me. I owe them."

"How much?" he asked gently. "How much *more?*"

"You have to go." The words were out before she could think them over, yet she knew they were necessary, and long overdue. "Home, the ranch, Lance's apartment. Anywhere, so long as it's away from me."

It didn't surprise him. Ross wondered if he hadn't known all along it would turn out this way. She'd made her decision—about him, them, Montana. Presuming there'd ever been one to make. "Why?"

"Because I have a job to do this weekend. Tomorrow's stadium jumping with Absolute has to go well. No, not well, perfect. It won't be if I'm not focused. I've worked my whole life, given up so much, to get here, to this place. You're . . . I can't juggle it and you. I can't."

Ross met her eyes, direct gaze for direct gaze. "You're sure?"

"As sure as I am of anything anymore." Inside her pockets, her hands balled into fists. She wanted so badly to touch him, hold on to him, but was afraid that if she did, she'd be lost. She'd thrown something away today. It was only one phase of one event, but how close was she to tossing all the rest after it? He was the first, the only one, to make her wonder if she hadn't already paid too high a price for a dream.

Leaving her was a damn sight harder than Ross would have thought possible. They weren't finished with each other. Not by a long shot. There was Virginia in two weeks; he might be able to break away from the ranch by then. If not, he could always track her down in Maryland. "If you change your mind, you know where to find me."

He turned and left. Paige knew it was for good this time.

It was one of those perfect spring nights when the sky is clear and starlit and the air is mild, with a hint of ripe blossoming flowers. From the top row of the deserted bleachers, Paige gazed up at the stars. She'd watched the sun set and the moon rise. Still, she was no closer to sorting out the weekend, her feelings, or her future.

Yesterday, after Ross left, she'd gone to the showers, staying a long time under the pounding jets. Aches had been eased, dirt washed away, but a pervasive chill had remained long after her skin had turned red from the scalding water. Returning to the barn to begin her twenty-four-hour watch over Absolute, she'd found her gear stowed away, her groom team gone, and Faye waiting.

"Divine having a bad day?" she'd asked.

"No. I've no excuse for retiring, or not one that makes sense."

"Sense has nothing to do with it," Faye had said, without a trace of a rebuke. "If your mind isn't on the course, neither should your horse be."

Paige had waited, steeled for the detailed retrospection that was as much a part of an event's conclusion as limping—particularly of those that ended badly. But Faye hadn't whisked out her notebook, scribbled front to back with "a few observations." She hadn't lectured on concentration or motivation. She'd just patted Paige on the shoulder, then turned to give Absolute the strokes he was pestering her for.

Now Paige sighed and twirled the blue satin streamers she and Absolute had been awarded a few hours ago. Her ticket to a slot on the Pan-Am team. The selections wouldn't be made public and official for another month, but at this point the announcement would only be a formality. Paige and Absolute, along with three other horse-and-rider teams, would ride for the United States.

Why didn't she feel satisfaction? she demanded as she stared at the long-coveted ribbons. She'd aced the first major hurdle on the path to the Olympics. Where was the relief? The joy and excitement? Gone, she thought. With Ross. She'd felt no real emotion since he'd left, just this terrible aching emptiness.

He's so close. Releasing a long breath, she gazed off at the horizon, at the glow of the city lights. Tomorrow, he would head west and she east, until the better part of a continent lay between them. But for tonight, for a few more hours, he was only a ten-minute cab ride away. She hadn't known that to sit and to do nothing could require such effort.

"That you, Paige?" Searching for the voice, she saw Mark Harrison at the foot of the bleachers. "Thought those were your legs." Hands pocketed, he climbed the rows of seats. "You ever replace that stallion," he said as he approached, "I'd appreciate first crack at him."

Paige smiled, unexpectedly grateful for his company, then shook her head. "It'd be like selling my best friend."

He sprawled out beside her, his long body covering four bleacher rows. For a while they were quiet together. Other than the occasional hoot of a barn owl, no sounds disturbed the night's silence.

"Did you know," Mark said eventually, "that I was thirty before I made it onto the Olympic team?"

Paige decided his question wasn't half as casual as his delivery. "Yes, I believe I knew that."

"Yeah. Thirty years old," he said again. "Then the U.S. took a political stand and boycotted the games. Hell of a thing, huh? Next time around I made the shortlist, but before the final cuts my lead horse died. Three years later, injuries kept me out of the selection trials."

He patted at his pockets, coming up with a pack of chewing gum. Paige shook her head when he offered her one, then watched him slowly peel the foil from a stick. "There I was," he went on. "Thirty-seven years old, and nothing to show for it but a failing marriage, a mountain of bills, a dozen or so broken bones and a limp when it rained. 'Course, the rooms crammed with ribbons and trophies didn't count." He glanced over as Paige curled forward. "So I quit. Did you know that? That I'd quit?"

"No." There was that word again. Paige faced him, resting her cheek on one knee. It didn't surprise her to learn he'd once lost heart; she'd often wondered that he hadn't lost his mind. His name was etched on the bases of all the dominant trophies, on most of them several times. He'd had seasons that were pure magic, when he simply could not lose. But when it came to the Olympics, it seemed fate conspired against him. "I thought—I guess we all thought you were still recuperating."

"Nope. Sold my horses, moved to the family farm and asked Cassie to give me a chance to find out who she was, who she'd become in the years since I'd married her. I was off the circuit one year, a whole season."

"It's a long time to be away." To Paige, who'd agonized over taking two weeks, it was an eternity. "Not everyone could come back and do what you have, shoot straight to the top again."

"It was the best thing I could have done—for myself, my riding. I was burned-out. Training seven days a week, twelve hours a day. I was so obsessed, so driven, I'd sacrificed everything else. When it all came apart, I was an inch away from having no one and nothing to go home to."

Paige knew her retirement of Divine had generated speculation on her stability. She'd heard lowered voices in the women's shower room, in the barn when they didn't know she was within earshot. Yet she didn't think Mark was talking to her now because of this one incident. When, exactly, had she started unraveling? Weeks ago? She hadn't seen Mark in over six before last week in Louisville. Months ago? Faye had noticed—noticed and tricked her into going to Brady's auction, left bedroom lights on. Travis, too, with his buzzard's instinct for faltering creatures. Even Ross had sensed it after knowing her only a few days.

"You're telling me I'm having a breakdown? I'm cracking up?"

"No." Mark swung around to straddle the plank her feet were resting on. "Not yet, anyway." He folded one of her hands between both of his. "The ambition that drives us can be a dangerous force if it gets out of hand. It's like a powerful horse—point it in the right direction, stay on top of it, and it can take you wherever you want to go. Drop the reins and you're in for one nightmare of a ride."

Paige closed her eyes. Everything he said made sense. "I guess my reins could stand a little tightening, hmm?"

"What's next for you?"

"Virginia."

"Sponsored horse?"

Paige opened her eyes to frown at him. "No."

"Cancel. Take a month off and go—"

"A month!" she said in utter disbelief.

"You can take a month now, or sooner than you think you'll be taking a year. Start tomorrow, tonight. Get your butt to the airport and hop a plane to Hawaii. If you have to, get on the highway and stick out your thumb. Don't go home. I don't care what promises you make yourself, you'll be on a hacking trail by Friday. When you come back, you'll still know which foot goes in the stirrup first. You won't forget how it's done. This is your year, Paige. You don't want to miss it."

He made it sound so obvious, so simple, as if the quest of a lifetime didn't hang in the balance. "Suppose you don't make the cut?" she asked him. "The truth, Mark."

"If I don't make the cut, I'll be harvesting corn while others ride for gold." He grinned. "I hope like hell that doesn't happen. But if it does, I'll survive. I've got the farm, Cassie, and if I want it, another shot in four years. In that respect, we're lucky. Our Olympic chance doesn't run out at age eighteen or twenty, the way it does for other athletes. Gymnasts, boxers—amateur washups at twenty-one. Equestrians can take seven or eight shots at riding in the Games."

Mark stood and stretched, his body a lanky silhouette against the moon. "On the other hand, forced retirement has its advantages—those kids go on to make lives for themselves. Some of us never do." Crouching down, he placed his hand along the side of her face. "My friend, you can make it all the way to the Olympic Games start box and be thumbed out by the jury—years of preparation and dreaming, lost in a moment. If all you've ever done has revolved around that medal, that moment, I guarantee you your life's going to come to a screeching halt. Get yourself something, *someone,* to go home to when it's over. *Before* it's over."

Paige wasn't prepared for the wave of loneliness that swept over her, and had to swallow a knot of emotion. "You're a good friend, Mark."

"Be one to yourself," he advised earnestly. "And get off the merry-go-round for a few turns." With a last smile for her, he departed, ungracefully leaping from plank to plank.

Alone again, Paige thought over all Mark had said. She didn't waste time debating or refuting his observations; he'd described her too well. Which left only his proposed remedy.

A month. Just thinking the words made her tense. She'd have to be beyond cracking up and totally out of her mind to stop training that long in the middle of the season. No, a month was out of the question. By comparison, two weeks sounded harmless and wonderfully appealing. On a sigh filled with longing, she gazed once again at the haze of lights on the horizon. And they wouldn't, she knew, be spent in Hawaii.

But even two weeks meant canceling Virginia.

Undecided, torn, Paige stared down at her lap. She didn't see the ribbons spread across her knees, but saw instead a sheet of ivory parchment that at the moment was on a closet shelf at home, buried under long-forgotten clutter. Her diploma—from a high school she hadn't seen the inside of since tenth grade. Odd that she should suddenly think of it.

She'd been invited to take part in commencement exercises, she remembered, though she'd completed her junior and senior years by correspondence. Faye had encouraged her to attend. There'd be other Kentucky Three-Days, she'd said, but only one high school graduation. Eight years ago to the day, Paige realized now. On that day, her name had reverberated from two sets of loudspeakers, a thousand miles apart. When Paige straightened her shoulders to present herself, it had been in the jumping arena. Her diploma had arrived by mail several weeks later.

Regret built a new lump in her throat. At the time, there'd been no doubt in her mind which of the two events she would choose. But she thought that if she had it to do over . . .

There'll be other Virginias, she told herself. Would there be another Ross Tanner? Another man who would make her feel vital and alive, more vital and alive as a woman than she'd ever felt as an athlete? Or would she, months, possibly years, from now, think back on this weekend and wish she'd chosen differently?

Paige dropped her head in her hands, wishing she knew what the hell she wanted. Dammit, she *did* know, had known for some time. Just as she'd known what she wanted at the age of thirteen. Then, it had been to get out of Switzerland, and become the best rider the equestrian world had ever seen. She hadn't allowed her fears—of rejection, of failure, of the terrifying unknown—to trap her behind a wall of excuses.

She'd had more courage at thirteen, more faith in herself, than she had at twenty-six. There'd been no insulated world for her to go back to then, no place where she was successful if somewhere else she failed.

What she wanted now was two weeks. Two lazy, luxurious weeks of sunlight and sleep, with nowhere she had to go and nothing she had to do. She wanted to spend those two weeks with Ross, discovering the woman lost inside the athlete.

Chapter Eight

He couldn't sleep. Hours after he'd gone to bed, Ross was sprawled on his back, blindly gazing through the ceiling skylight. So that he wouldn't think of Paige, he made a mental list of things to do in the morning. Pack. Arrange for Lance's housekeeping service to come in and go over the place. Keep a final appointment at the bank, then stop by TLD with new reporting procedures for the accountant. At noon, board a plane bound for Billings.

Without her.

Cursing, her found his cigarettes on the bedside table and lit one. He fell onto his back again, and had to grab for the sheet slithering to the floor. Satin sheets—*black* satin. When he'd first discovered the slippery material under the spread and stocking the linen closet, he'd laughed and thought them ridiculous. After ten nights of pillows popping out from under his head and sheets sliding off the bed, he thought them a damned nuisance. Tonight, cocooned in fluid fabric warmed by his body, he thought of Paige's skin.

Aching, angry because he was aching, Ross flung himself out of bed. Cigarette clamped between his teeth, he found the jeans he'd dropped to the floor earlier and tugged them on. *So now what?* Frustrated, he dragged a hand through his hair and walked to the wall of sheet-glass window to stare out at the slumbering city.

He couldn't remember the last time he'd tossed and turned until two in the morning. He'd been through droughts, blizzards, the loss of valuable cattle to rampant viruses—Cat's teen years, for God's sake!—without losing a single night's sleep. Insomnia didn't solve problems. Along with a lungful of smoke, Ross released a bark of self-mocking laughter. Was that what Paige Meredith had become? Not a woman he wanted to spend hours making love to, but a problem?

"She's making you crazy," he muttered.

In the thirty-six hours since leaving her, he'd seesawed between relief and regret. Relief because he thought it high time he backed off and figured out if he was merely infatuated or sliding into something more serious. Regret because he thought that in the end, regardless of his conclusions, there would remain one basic, irrefutable fact: he was a man with roots and responsibilities; she was a woman passing through town on her way to a dream.

Ross swore and made the mistake of shutting his eyes. An image of Paige flashed on the insides of his lids. Her face— elegant bone structure, porcelain skin, and those fabulous, fathomless gray-green eyes. His own snapped back open, but the frame-by-frame filmstrip went on. Paige aloof, wearing top hat and tails, white silk clutching her long slender throat. Paige relaxed, laughing, braid falling apart, shirttail hanging out. The memory tape stopped, then started again in slow motion. Paige passionate, astride a chestnut stallion loping through a flower-strewn valley, her shimmery hair lifted on the wind.

God, why was he doing this?

The lady had said no, every time and in every possible way. She might have thought yes, but she'd said no. Ross had never chased a woman. Until this past weekend, he'd never paced over one or broken into a sweat fearing for one's life. If he wasn't careful—

The doorbell's chimes penetrated the closed-up room. Ross turned and scowled. He knew none of the building's tenants, nor why any of them would drop by in the middle of the night. Outside visitors were stopped in the lobby, the doorman checking each against a preapproved list or clearing them by phone—though anyone headed for the penthouse was simply told Lance was "not presently in residence." *Lance.* Of course. The man he'd most wanted to find last week and the last person he wanted to deal with tonight. Only Lance could have gotten by unannounced.

The bell sounded a second time. Swearing, Ross crushed out his cigarette. Only Lance could be so insensitive he'd drag someone out of bed when he could have easily obtained a spare key in the lobby.

Without turning on lights, he strode through the moonlit apartment. Chimes were pealing nonstop as he crossed the marble-floored foyer. *Don't be so damn anxious, cousin. The welcome waiting for you is far from warm.* Anticipating a fight—and the gratifying relief of unstrapping the tension—Ross yanked open the door.

Paige leaned against the jamb, her shoulder pressing the buzzer. When the door flew open, she shifted enough to stop the chiming. "Hi."

Desire replaced fury with a speed that unbalanced Ross. He wanted to step forward and pull her into his arms. He needed to step back and pull himself together. He could only stay as he was, and stare.

"I've surprised you. Good." Behind her back, Paige's hands were linked tight enough to stop the blood circulating. "I figured I owed you one for all the times you popped up on me without warning." How could she have forgotten his power to wipe her mind clean? She'd imagined this moment. As if preparing for an event, she'd visualized every step, rehearsed every word. But she was here now, her feet glued to the floor and her practiced speech evaporating. "I was beginning to think you'd changed your plans and left early."

She looked as cool and confident as the first day, Ross thought, while his own blood was running hot and his hands weren't quite steady. Even in a white cotton blouse and worn-soft jeans, there was an unmistakable air of class about her. Then her tongue darted out to wet her top lip. Not so confident. Steadier now than when he'd first opened the door, he noticed that her skin was flushed and her eyes were glittering. Not so cool.

His unwavering stare so unnerved Paige, she let her gaze skim away. To his broad shoulders, where taut skin gleamed. Light from the hall flowed through the open door, defining the ripple of muscles in his chest. Her pounding heart skipped a beat, and she dropped her gaze lower, to his trim waist and flat stomach. He hadn't bothered zipping the jeans he'd tugged on. Enough was revealed by the gaping denim for her to assume he slept naked. She had to concentrate on drawing her next breath.

"My plans haven't changed," he said at last. "Have yours?"

She managed a casual shrug. "I've some time to fill."

He might have laughed at her choice of words if he'd been able to find enough air. "How much time?"

Inside the apartment, the phone rang. "That'll be the doorman," she said. "Telling you I'm on my way up."

Ross started to reach for her, but stopped himself. If he touched her now, he'd have to touch all of her. If he pulled her over the threshold, he'd pull her to the floor the next instant. There'd be no explanations, no time for words, until later. Much later. Stepping back, he motioned her in, then turned to the living room and the ringing phone.

Paige followed the door closed, leaning against it as her eyes adjusted to the dimness. "Don't be cross with him." Ross glanced back, one eyebrow lifted, as if he were asking why not. "There's a party breaking up. He had his hands full pouring a couple of drunks into a cab. He seems like such a sweet old man. And he did ask me to wait, but I...ah..."

"Wanted to surprise me."

"Right."

"How much time?"

"Answer the phone, will you? Before he panics and calls the cops?"

When Ross was gone, Paige shut her eyes and willed the tension to drain. She'd known it wouldn't be a tumble, but she hadn't expected a headlong dive into a bottomless pit. *How much time?* She could still change her mind and tell him two hours. She could be in his bed in thirty seconds flat, in a taxi by dawn, on a plane to Hawaii by noon. She might leave with a few scrapes, but she'd walk away in one piece.

For the past few hours, as she cleared tack from the barn and clothes from the Sheffields', she'd tried to calculate the risks. But this was a course she hadn't previewed, one she was navigating blind and with little hope of maintaining control. A moment ago, Ross had shifted his weight to reach for her. She didn't know why he'd decided not to, only that if he had, if he'd touched her just then, something inside her would have exploded.

Determined to at least give the appearance that she was in control of herself, Paige pushed away from the door.

There were broad archways on the walls to either side of her. One opened on a games room, complete with big-screen TV and what looked like the latest in electronic computer games. The other led to the formal rooms. Passing this one, she heard the low drone of Ross's voice. Good. He sounded much too calm to be tearing into the poor doorman.

Straight ahead was a set of double doors that had been shut her last time here. They were partially open now. Beyond them she saw only an inky void. Pushing both doors wide, she saw a ceiling made of glass, and was enchanted.

Head tipped back, she entered the all-black bedroom and was halfway across it before noticing she was caught between two twenty-story-high views of city lights and stars. Like a mountaintop aerie. The perfect place, she thought giddily, to take a headlong dive. For a moment she was lightheaded, dizzy. Only when she saw a twin moon and her own image in one of the views did she realize it was an illusion, created by a seamless wall of mirrors facing a seamless wall of glass. Everything else in the room, from carpet and walls to lamps and even ashtrays, was black, blending with the pitch sky. The smoke-and-leather scent of Ross saturated the air, as she'd once imagined it would.

He felt it the moment he stepped over the threshold—the crackling energy and breathless anticipation; the pressure swelling, churning, building the storm. Paige stood at the center of the invisible turmoil, like the serene eye of the hurricane. Her head was tipped back, her face bathed in moonlight. There'd be no explanations, he realized—none were necessary. If they had words to say, they'd say them later. Much later.

She didn't hear him enter the room. When he circled her wrist from behind, Paige sucked in a sharp breath. They both knew it wasn't surprise at discovering him so near that had her gasping, but a reaction to the electrifying jolt his touch delivered to her senses.

Heartbeat quickening, she turned to face him. His eyes, so blue and intense, could still stun her. Caught up in them, she laid her loosely manacled hand on his bare chest. His skin was still warm from bed, hers cool from the night air and nerves. His muscles tightened under her palm, and she knew his response was to more than the shock of hot meeting cold. It was as hers had been to him. She felt the thrill of power, and felt her knees weakening.

"How much time to fill, Paige?" If she said a night, just this one night, he told himself, it would be enough.

"Two weeks." Under his thumb she felt her own pulse begin to thud. "You said you could show me places I've never been. Is the offer to take me still open?"

"I'll take you." Slowly, Ross vowed, completely, and so far beyond reason she'd never find her way back. Releasing her wrist, he framed her face with both hands.

His mouth covered hers, and thought fled. Paige responded to him as she had from the beginning—instantly, utterly. At a touch she was trembling. With a kiss she was swept up and soaring, her bones dissolving, her mind reeling. To keep from falling, she wrapped her arms around him, luxuriating in the feel of his skin. Smooth, hard, inflamed. Her own was tingling, alive to sensations as never before. The caress of his breath on her cheek. Heat wherever their bodies touched. And, inside, tiny bursts of pleasure in places she hadn't been aware of before this moment.

The kiss threatened his promise to take her slowly. Ross banked the flood of needs and concentrated only on her mouth, his hands never moving, while hers raced wildly over him. She was hungry, eager, a storm breaking. He could almost hear the thunder crack, the wind roar. One moment her fingers were tangled in his hair, the next they were digging into his back, tearing over his chest. The vibrations of a groan shivered through his body, but he wasn't sure which of them had made the sound.

"Paige—" His stomach muscles jumped when her thumbs dipped below his waistband. Her breath shuddered out, searing his flesh.

"Now," she whispered. "Take me now." She tugged on the denim at his waist only to have her hands captured and pulled away.

"Relax. There's no clock running." With his eyes locked on hers, Ross raised her hands to place a soft, lingering kiss in first one palm, then the other. It took every ounce of his control to treat her with such care, but he'd waited too long for this moment, wanted too long, to have it over in one crashing instant. "Dangerous hands," he murmured. He lowered her arms, curving them around his waist, and tucked her hands into the back pockets of his jeans. "Leave 'em there awhile, and just hold me. Tonight, I set the pace."

His voice was a stroke of velvet, soothing her, talking her off a ledge she'd been too willing to leap from. *Patience.* She hadn't expected it from him. His lips grazed her brow, just barely, as he reached around her to find the tail of her braid. *Tenderness.* She hadn't expected that, either. Leisurely he explored her face, only her face, his mouth skimming to her temple, to her cheek, to her chin. *Fury.* Checked, controlled, yet she felt it. A rage of passion, building, boiling. This she had expected, anticipated, wanted.

Inch by inch, he freed more of her hair, while his mouth teased the sensitive flesh at the curve of her shoulder. Braid unraveled, he pushed his hands through her hair, forcing her head back. With his tongue he spread fire, tracing a throbbing vein, gliding to the hollow at the base of her neck, flicking his way up again. Paige swayed, melted. With his teeth he tugged at her earlobe, and she turned her head to one side, begging him to devour her. But he only nipped, nibbled, until she was half-crazy with frustrated needs and desire too long suppressed.

Impatience had her hands curling into fists in his pockets. With an abandonment she felt no shame for, she used them to press his hips into hers, at the same time arching against him. A sharp spear of delight had her crying out for more.

"Easy." Ross stroked the length of her spine, settling his hand at the small of her back and holding her against him until her hips stopped their pulsing movement. "Nice and easy. We've a long way to go, and plenty of time."

If Paige were taking command of a stallion straining to cut loose, she'd have murmured words like those Ross whispered to her now. Gentling words. Pleasing, encouraging words. She closed her eyes on his baritone voice, so soft it shouldn't have been able to penetrate the roar of blood in her head. *Trust me*, he said. *Trust me completely, implicitly, to unleash the power and lead the way. I'll take us higher, deeper, farther.* It was what she wanted. To trust—to feel safe and unafraid, even as she grew weak and vulnerable. To give over control and be taken, driven. To let go. Without hesitation or the slightest trace of fear, Paige relaxed her hands and opened her eyes.

In the enormous mirror, she saw their reflections. Just the two of them, seemingly floating against a backdrop of stars. Entwined. Erotic. Mesmerized, she watched—Ross opening her buttons, sliding the shirt from her shoulders...his hands cupping her breasts over her thin silk camisole...his thumb dragging down one delicate strap...the other...peeling away the flimsy barrier so that it bunched around her elbows with her shirt...his skin and hair so dark, hers so much paler...his hands exploring, arousing, teasing, burning...

God, she was glorious. Ross felt her passion rise to heat her skin...her skin. Softer, creamier, than he'd remembered. Before the night was over, he would touch every inch of her. She was long and narrow, slim as a reed, but her breasts were full, firm. He bent his head to taste her, teasing her nipple with his tongue. Her small whimper had fresh desire sprinting through him. Wanting to give her more pleasure, to take more for himself, Ross drew her into his mouth and suckled. Her taste was silky, seductive. If he sipped from her for hours, he wouldn't get enough.

Need slammed into Paige, and she jerked her hands from his pockets. Her shirt and camisole fell past her wrists, baring her to her waist. With each tug of his mouth, the need hammered harder. Clumsy with desperation, she grasped his arms, fighting to pry them loose.

"Ross." Her legs wanted to buckle. Her body wanted to open and be filled with him. Tangling her fingers in his hair, she pulled his head back. "Take me to bed. Now. Take me—"

Her feverish plea was rushing from her lips when he fastened his mouth to hers. With the kiss, he took her deeper, deeper, and her grasping hands lost their strength. Using only his lips and unhurried strokes of his tongue, he made love to her mouth. When she was pliant in his arms, he bent to her again, drawing her into the wet heat of his mouth.

His teeth nipped, his tongue made slow, torturously slow swirls. Paige's world was spinning. "Ross..." Passion erupted, spilling pleasure like molten lava into her veins. "Oh, God... Ross..."

He lifted her, covering the three steps to the bed in one stride and falling with her to starlit satin. Hands grasped. Legs and arms tangled. They rolled over and over, coming together, pushing apart, tearing the last of their clothes off until finally, finally, they were naked. Damp flesh slid over damp flesh. Open mouth sought open mouth. The air filled with the sounds of their breathing—her quick, shallow pants; his hard, deep gasps. Her scent, heated, intensified, rose up to mingle with his, so that the room smelled of dark, smoldering passion.

Ross was already in a place he'd never been, and he was no longer in control. Never had he known such a primitive need to possess, to burn a woman with the brand of his body, to claim her as his own. Silver-gold hair poured over black satin. He filled his hands with it as his mouth roamed over her. Beneath the moon's light, her body was marble. Cool, white marble. Beneath his lips, she was on fire.

Paige writhed beneath him, her fingers digging into his shoulders. Never had she known such a primitive need to be taken and consumed. His mouth was everywhere, sampling, savoring, moving on. It had never been like this. She hadn't known it could be. She heard herself murmuring, but could make no sense of it. Steeped in passion, drowning in it, she let her mind go.

Featherlight, his lips brushed the insides of her thighs, parting her legs. His mouth found her, and she arched, gasping. His tongue plunged, and she jolted. She cried out when he pulled back and again when he returned, lifting her higher.

His name was a rasp, a whisper on her lips. Her name was a groan, thundering quietly from the depths of him.

Ross uncoiled to move over her. "God, I've wanted you—dreamed of you like this. Wild, burning. For me. Only for me."

Her eyes were open when he sank into her, her arms reaching. *For him.* She arched up, shuddering, driving him deeper. *Only for him.*

He watched her eyes widen with astonished pleasure as her arms and legs closed around him, the first peaking wave crashing over her. Rolling his hips forward, he buried himself, lost himself in the hot, moist heaven of her body.

Fused into one being, Ross drove them to thrilling, terrifying, mind-spinning heights until they teetered on the edge of the world. The storm within Paige pitched them over.

Dazed, drained, she floated back to reality. She'd thought she knew how it felt to be exhausted yet exhilarated, body and mind depleted, spirit fulfilled. But nothing she'd experienced had prepared her for exhaustion so deep or fulfillment so complete. Here was the satisfaction she'd expected to feel yesterday. Here was the joy. For a while, Paige simply drifted and enjoyed.

Ross hadn't moved. His hands were still tangled in her hair, while hers had immediately fallen away to lie open and strengthless at her sides. Her breast pillowed his cheek, and his head rose and fell to the rhythm of her breathing. That and her pulse were almost back to normal. She wasn't. Would never be. At the instant their bodies joined, Paige had been altered, and made into someone new. Pieces, whole chunks of herself, were missing, lost to him forever. What she hadn't given willingly, he'd taken, and then he'd poured himself into her. No, she would never again be the woman who'd walked into this bedroom an hour ago.

For the first time in her life, Paige was in love. Not interested or infatuated. In love. She didn't know if her heart had been offered or taken, only that it was lost. Irretrievably, irrevocably lost.

Suddenly she felt as if someone had thumbed the stem on a stopwatch. Two weeks. Fourteen days and counting. It wasn't enough time, she realized. Not nearly enough time to learn all there was to know about him, to discover his moods, his habits, to make and store the memories that would be all she'd take with her when she left. It's better that way, she told herself. The fewer memories to plague her, the easier returning to her own life, her real life, would be. She'd have to be careful, Paige decided. For the next two weeks, she'd have to keep her emotions on as tight a rein as possible, or pay the price for the rest of her life.

No! That single word seemed to explode inside her brain. No, she could not, would not, shut off her feelings. For too many years she'd lived for or because of the future, only to look back on a past filled with missed opportunities and regrets. Tonight, she vowed, and for as many days and nights as she and Ross had together, she would live every moment to the fullest. Beginning with this one.

Dragging her eyes open, she saw their reflected images on the mirrored wall. Man to woman, suspended in a star-studded void as if levitated by a magician's wand. Fascinated, she lifted a hand to Ross's head. Vision hazy, she watched her fingers comb leisurely through his tousled hair. Smiling, she took her hand to his shoulder, nails skimming lightly over his skin, then down his back as far as her arm would reach.

Contentment. For most of his adult life, Ross had believed himself a contented man. Only now, with his muscles loose and his body weak, only now, with Paige soft and pulsing beneath him, did he realize the true meaning of the word. He felt her heartbeat against his cheek, fainter now than when he'd first collapsed onto her. Her breath, then her fingers, moved through his hair. Without hurry, she ran a hand down his back, and released a low purr of pleasure. The sound vibrated throughout his body.

Shifting, he raised up on one arm to gaze down at her. Her face was turned to the wall, and her eyes were cloudy beneath half-lowered lids. Her lips, swollen from his, were curved with a drowsy smile. Dipping his head, he saw the reflection of his body covering hers.

Crushed beneath his weight, her mirror image looked newly fragile. Ross remembered the gripping strength in the willowy limbs she'd wrapped around him, the tireless rhythm of her narrow hips arching against his. Resettling his cheek on her breast, he watched her gentle exploration of his body.

With her hand resting lightly below the small of his back, she pointed the toes of her left foot to tease the baby-soft skin above his heel. Bending her knee slightly, she curved her arch to his calf. She stroked slowly up his leg, lifting her knee higher and exposing the back of her thigh to streaming moonlight.

It was then that he saw the bruise.

Paige had just decided she could stay as she was forever when Ross rolled away, hauling her onto her side as he went. She was still trying to orient herself when she heard his muttered curse.

"What— Ouch!" A flash of pain cut off her demand for an explanation. "Dammit, Ross, don't poke at it!"

"Hold still," he ordered when she tried to wriggle free. How in hell had he missed seeing it sooner? The bruise, a violent purplish black stain, marred her pale skin from the top of her thigh to just above her knee, as startling as burgundy wine spilled onto fine white linen.

"How did this happen?" he demanded.

"How do you think?" He shot her a look that had her rolling her eyes. "A tree . . . cross-country."

"You were X-rayed?"

"I didn't need to be."

"Right. Did a doctor decide that? Or did you?"

"Ross, we all look like this the day after." Despite the note of exasperation in her voice, she thought his concern rather sweet—even if he was overdramatizing. She couldn't remember the last time she'd been fussed over. "I'm fine. It's hardly—"

"Save it." He found a second bruise, smaller and fainter, high on her hip. Carefully he probed it with his fingertips. "That hurts?" He didn't have to ask; her whole body tensed with her wince.

"All of me hurts." Paige raised up on one arm to push away his hands. "Do you know what my body's been through in the last ten days?"

Yes, he knew, but he hadn't given it a thought. Because she curled forward to untangle the sheet at the foot of the bed, she didn't see the look of self-recrimination cross his face. He hadn't been gentle making love to her. After the first few minutes, he hadn't been careful or considerate, but demanding, at times ruthless. Cursing himself, Ross touched her shoulder, the gesture stopping her before she lay down again.

"Did I hurt you?"

Exasperation fled, and Paige melted. "No. Oh, no." She leaned closer to brush her lips over his. "You made me feel good."

She lay back, her eyes dewy and her mouth curved. Then her dreamy expression dissolved into a frown.

"What?" he demanded.

"Didn't this bed have pillows?"

Grinning, Ross leaned across her to reach over the side of the bed. "Good luck," he said, finding three of them in a heap on the floor and piling them up against the headboard. "They've got their own ideas about where they spend the night." He gathered her close on the mound of pillows, turning his head to bury his face in her hair. "If your leg looks the same in three days, you'll see a doctor."

Head nestled on his shoulder, Paige chuckled. "In three days it'll be pea green, mustard yellow and ugly as sin." Smiling, she closed her eyes. "What's tomorrow's schedule?" Her last schedule for two whole weeks, she thought happily.

"Flight's at noon."

"Mmm...we have to go early so I can buy a ticket," she murmured.

"I have appointments first thing in the morning." He stroked her hair, letting the water-soft strands sift slowly through his fingers. He could get used to this. To sleeping with her body wrapped around him, with the taste of her on his tongue, with every breath drenched in the scent of her. "I'll drop you at the Sheffields' so you can tie up loose ends, then swing by to pick you up when I'm finished."

"Uh-uh." Paige yawned and snuggled closer. "Let me sleep till you get back. I left Faye a note. She'll take care of loose ends."

A note? Ross lifted his head to look down at her. "You didn't talk to her, tell her you were leaving?"

"It was two o'clock in the morning," she reminded him.

It was more than that, he decided. Her body had tensed, and her eyes, when she opened them, were guarded. "She knew you were considering this, didn't she?"

"We hadn't discussed my going way, if that's what you're asking, though I doubt the news will come as a shock to her."

"This note," he said thoughtfully. "Does it say where you've gone? Who you've gone with?"

"It tells her enough that she won't think I've mysteriously vanished." Placing a hand on his chest, Paige forced a space between them. *Don't take over*, she wanted to say.

Don't tell me what to do or how and when to do it. "I don't need permission to take a few weeks off. I'm a big girl. I can make my own decisions."

"You don't have to convince me, Paige. It's Faye you should be saying that to."

"I will." Relaxing her arm, she let him fold her close again. "I'll call her. In a few days, I'll call her and... explain."

Puzzled by her choice of words, Ross wondered what there was to explain. Pushing the question to the back of his mind, he found her hand under the sheet and brought her fingertips to his lips. "Have you thought about clothes? Or do you plan to go without? Not that I'd object."

Paige yawned and let her lids drift down again. "My bags are out in the hall."

Ross frowned into the darkness. He didn't recall seeing luggage when he'd opened the door to her. Then, he hadn't been looking for any. "Shoved against the wall?" he speculated. "So I wouldn't see them?"

There was no mistaking the humor in his voice, and Paige wondered what on earth she'd done now to amuse him. "What if they are?"

"Was this a trial run? Check the old boy out first, see if he's up to speed?" In a smooth, unexpected move, Ross rolled her over and under him. "Took me for a test-ride, did you?"

Paige scowled up at him, ready to spout denials. Then his grin flashed. The man was entirely too cocky, she decided. Smoothing her brow, she treated him to one of her cool, utterly confident smiles. "Shall I tell you what I thought?"

"What you—" Ross dropped his head on her shoulder and laughed. The soft shudders of his body stirred both of them. "I know damn well what you thought. What you thought..." His words were murmured against her skin, his mouth seeking the sweetness of her. "What you felt..." He moved down her body, his cupped palm lifting her breast to his lips. "What you liked..." He touched his tongue to her nipple, a teasing flick that had her jolting beneath him.

"What you loved..." He drew her into his mouth at the same instant she took him into her body.

It stunned them both that desire could flare again so quickly. Within moments, the flare burst into flames, the flames consuming them.

Ross opened his eyes to murky half-light. It never mattered if he'd slept well or long enough; his brain was conditioned to wake and his body to rise at dawn.

Paige was curled up at his side, her head on his shoulder and one arm flung across his chest. The pillows had deserted the bed while they'd slept, and the top sheet, twisted around their hips, had tried to leave, as well.

In the short time it took his mind to clear, he allowed himself the enjoyment of looking at her. Just looking, he quickly discovered, would never be enough. He wanted to run his hands down her smooth, naked back, feel her sleep-warm skin grow taut with arousal, ease her over and make love to her. Focusing on her face, he saw exhaustion. He carefully removed her arm, then slid quietly out of bed. So that he wouldn't wake her, he grabbed his jeans from the floor and carried them out to the hall, stepping into them after pulling the door shut.

Halfway across the living room, he remembered her luggage and backtracked. As he'd guessed earlier, he found her bags against the wall to the left of the door. He'd expected a trunk, something big enough to hold saddles and boots, but there were only two khaki-colored duffel bags that he shoved over the threshold, into the foyer. That she was leaving her riding gear behind pleased him enormously.

In the kitchen, he started a pot of coffee. While waiting for it to perk, he smoked a cigarette and watched the sky lighten. Across town Faye Gentry would be rising. He tried to imagine Aunt Mary discovering a note from Cat saying she'd abruptly left town for parts unknown. She'd be frightened, Ross decided, not to mention baffled and hurt.

With a cup of black coffee in hand, he walked to the phone and dialed. It was answered on the first ring.

"It's Ross Tanner," he told the alert, expectant voice.

"She's with you," Faye said.

Though she'd delivered the words as a statement, Ross heard an inflection of uncertainty. "She said she left you a note."

"A note, yes. 'I'm taking two weeks off,'" Faye read in a clipped, colorless voice. "'Cancel Virginia. Don't worry.'"

Ross winced. It wouldn't win awards for eloquence. "I wanted you to know she's all right."

"She is not," Faye returned bluntly. "She's exhausted, confused, anxious about her future and struggling with the letdown of an anticlimactic win. If I know her, she's decided she should be handling the strain better, and so she's feeling like a failure, as well. For some time now she's felt confined and deprived, out of sync with the rest of the world. So she's doing what she assumes most 'normal' twenty-six-year-old women are doing—having an affair." He heard her sigh before she spoke again. "There isn't a rider on the circuit who hasn't been there, Ross. It's miserable while it lasts, but it passes."

Furious, he drew in a deep, calming breath. If he hadn't spent a day working with Faye Gentry, if he hadn't gotten to know her beyond the passing-acquaintance stage, he might believe she'd chosen her words with the express purpose of cutting him in half. *It passes.* She made it sound as if Paige had come to him for no other reason than that he was available, that if he hadn't been handy she'd have spent last night in some other man's bed—acting "normal." Nothing Faye could say would convince him of that. As for the rest of it . . . he thought she was probably right.

Ross scrubbed a hand over his face. This, he thought, feeling equal amounts of empathy and frustration, this was what Paige was planning to explain. Once she'd gotten it figured out for herself, he tacked on.

"May I speak with her?" Faye asked into the yawning silence.

"She's sleeping."

"I know. I doubt you'd have called me otherwise. Would you wake her, please?"

"She'd rather not talk to you." Damn, that was uncalled-for. He'd sounded spiteful and petty. "Not just yet," he added gently. "She plans on calling you soon."

"I see. I'd like your phone number, then, in case—"

"No, let her do it in her own time. If she hasn't phoned you by the weekend, I will. I promise you, I will. And, Faye, when you talk to her…it'd be best if you didn't pressure her into returning before the two weeks are up."

There was a tension-filled pause during which Ross lit another cigarette. He wondered if Faye's silence meant she was in the process of losing her temper or of fighting to get a grip on it. A little of both, he decided when she spoke again in a tight, quivering voice.

"I love her," Faye stated. "I couldn't love her more if she were my own flesh and blood."

"I know that, or I wouldn't have bothered calling."

"I have always and *only* wanted what was best for her. While this may come as a surprise to you, I think getting away is precisely what she needs right now. I have every intention of supporting her through this. Can you say the same?"

Much as Ross resented being asked to account for himself, he could hardly tell Faye to keep her nose out of places he'd poked his own into. "Yes, of course."

"Then you won't pressure her to stay when the two weeks are up."

Touché, he thought ruefully, then gave considerable attention to crushing out the cigarette he'd decided he didn't want after all.

"Ross."

"No," he said quietly. "I won't pressure her to stay."

Chapter Nine

"You're the pilot?" Paige swallowed—gulped, actually—as she peered into the plane through its open passenger door. The sum total of its interior was a cockpit equipped with only two seats.

"Mmm-hmm..." Ross said nothing more for a while, just sat on his heels, gazing up at the landing gear.

They'd flown commercial to Billings. Instead of heading for the terminal after landing, Ross had steered her to the private hangars, where a small red-and-white plane had been towed from its bay to sit glimmering in the sun. Without wasting a breath on explanations, he'd applied himself to a meticulous preflight inspection of the craft's exterior. Paige's own examination, though conducted from a distance, was no less thorough. *Was it legal for propeller blades to be so thin?*

"Does that worry you?" When Ross finally glanced over, it wasn't her apprehension he noticed, but how nicely her bottom shaped ⸱ ⸱ir of jeans. "That I'm the pilot?"

"No, of course not." She flashed a bold-spirited smile that vanished the moment he turned his back. "You've got something against cabs?" she muttered.

"It's eighty miles to the Triple T," he explained as he stowed their bags in a small cargo hold. The last piece loaded, he locked the hatch, then climbed into the pilot's seat.

Teeth gritted, Paige strapped herself in. It seemed even smaller on the inside. From where Ross sat, to her left, he had only to stretch out his arm to pull her door shut. She'd been in cars whose doors made heavier thunks!

Fighting for calm, she concentrated on Ross as they taxied away from the hangar. He manipulated switches and dials on the instrument panel with the efficiency born of experience. He talked to the tower over the radio, and though the jargon was meaningless to her, she heard authority and confidence in his voice. It'll be fine, she told herself, her folded hands nervously clutching and releasing. It'll be just fine.

The radio's disembodied voice directed Ross to a runway, then instructed him to hold for clearance. "It won't be long." He settled back to wait, watching Paige through half-closed eyes. She looked tense and drawn, he decided. A delayed reaction to the weekend's events? he wondered. Or was she having second thoughts?

He'd told himself to expect them. She was a woman with her life planned out, month to month, hour to hour. She knew weeks in advance where she was going, how she'd get there, and with whom. Now, and with less than twenty-four hours to get used to the idea, she found herself in a scout plane, bound for a Montana cattle ranch, with a man she'd met ten days ago. A lover she hadn't planned on. If her spontaneous withdrawal from cross-country had thrown her for a loop, Ross thought, there was a good chance dropping off the circuit could have her questioning her own sanity.

"Paige."

"What?" Nerves shot the word from her. Disgusted with herself, Paige unlaced her fingers. "What?" she repeated in a quieter, calmer tone.

Not so much tense, he decided, as terrified. Baffled, Ross reached for her hand. It was freezing. "What are you afraid of? It can't be flying. You were kicked back and sleeping like a rock before we'd left the ground in Louisville."

"That was an honest-to-God plane," she pointed out. "With overhead compartments and flight attendants. With an *aisle* for the flight attendants." Paige felt ridiculous, but no less anxious, and prayed they'd get in the air soon, so that they could get back down and be done with this. "This is a Tinkertoy powered by a house fan."

"You're perfectly safe." He rubbed his thumb over her knuckles in a gesture meant to soothe. As always, it surprised him to see her anxious or the least bit unsure of herself. "I've logged hundreds of hours of flight time. I know what I'm doing."

I wish I did. "I know, I'm overreacting." Something she'd done with frustrating regularity since meeting him, she thought ruefully. "I'll be fine once we're up."

He smiled, applauding her grit, then turned to the controls and opened the throttle. The radio crackled, a static-filled voice clearing them for takeoff. The engine roared; the cockpit shuddered. The plane lurched forward before the brakes grabbed and held. The thrill of anticipation shot through Paige. Power and speed. The combination always appealed to her.

The little plane hurtled down the paved strip, lifting from the ground with runway to spare. Ross banked smoothly, leveling again where rooftops left off and the huge wilderness began.

Pressing her face to the glass, tentatively at first, Paige watched the rugged land unfold beneath her.

Montana. It wasn't what she'd expected. It wasn't as flat, for one thing. Or as desolate. It was bigger—or seemed so from the window of a two-seater plane flying low enough to sweep the ground with its shadow. When a pair of antelopes bounded from a woods into the open, she laughed out loud. Forgetting her nerves enough to scoot forward, she kept track of them through the windshield.

Accustomed to gazing down from thirty thousand feet at the tidy patchwork of midwestern farmland, she'd imagined the great plains would resemble a bolt of deep gold cloth—carelessly unfurled, perhaps, and looking a bit rumpled. But that imagery was too tame for the scenery below. Buttes jutted abruptly. Streams, like trailing azure ribbons, cut puzzle pieces out of the land. Civilization ceased to exist.

Losing track of the antelopes, she lifted her eyes and gasped. The mountains, distant purple shadows moments ago, had materialized. Deep canyons and hollowed-out valleys cut through the rugged chain, exposing, in places, sheer granite walls. Snow glistening on jagged peaks flowed like rivers of cream into forests of pine and spruce at the timberline. Magnificent, she thought. Absolutely magnificent. Hands pressed to the window, she looked over her shoulder at Ross.

Her smile said it all. Until that moment, he hadn't known how important it was to him that she respond with her heart. He'd watched her taking it in, sensing her thoughts as clearly as if she'd spoken them. She'd gone from curious and surprised to completely captivated. Anything less would have disappointed him.

He dipped the plane's left wing—the side on which Paige was sitting—and pointed out the window. "See the stream? It marks the Triple T's south border." He throttled back and dropped to a lower elevation. "Home at last."

She saw cattle now, spots of black, brown and mahogany clustered together. A cowboy on horseback lifted his hat to the plane overhead and waved. Ross waggled the wings in salute.

"The airstrip's out of the way of the compound," he told her. "I'll buzz the house to call for transportation, then swing by the winter pastures."

Paige saw the group of buildings he called the compound, and wondered which of the many structures was his house. Corrals were everywhere, some linked by narrow fenced passages. Packed-dirt roads threaded in and around the buildings; dual-rutted lanes led out and away, seemingly forever.

Suddenly the plane tilted at a nose-to-ground angle. Unsure what was happening, Paige tugged on her seat belt. Frantic, she cast about for anything below resembling a runway, but surely as an arrow aimed at a bull's-eye, they were headed for a small, densely packed woods.

"Ross." Fear paralyzed her, numbed her brain so that no more words came.

"Relax." He heard her terror, but could only spare her a glance. "Everything's under control."

He's doing this on purpose. Paige gripped her seat cushion with both hands as the plane pulled out of the dive just above the treetops. *This is what he meant when he said he would buzz the house.* They climbed, gaining altitude, then swooped down for a second harrowing pass.

Level, gliding over pastures again, Ross looked closely at Paige. "Are you—?"

"Fine." She pried her fingers from the edge of her seat and forcibly held back a shudder. Her heart was in her throat and her stomach somewhere below her knees. "Once I realized what was happening, I was fine." She never, *never,* wanted to do that again. "I misunderstood. I thought you'd buzz them on the radio—you know, *call* for transportation."

"God, Paige, I'm sorry. You must have thought—" Saying the words wasn't going to help. Ross reached over, catching her chin and turning her face to him. "Sure you're all right?"

"Peachy. When do we land?"

"In less than ten minutes," he promised.

Witless from the dive, she saw little of the cattle-filled winter pastures and heard even less of what Ross told her about them. By the time he made his approach to a dirt path passing for a landing strip, her thoughts were solely on having both feet planted firmly on solid ground.

She saw a Jeep waiting below, looking in the vast wilderness as small and forlorn as a child's castaway toy. A ranch hand was stretched out on its hood, grabbing a bit of shut-eye.

Despite the primitive conditions, the landing was smooth and uneventful. Ross cut the engine a short distance from the Jeep, and Paige shoved open her door. She leapt to the ground on a fervent prayer of thanks, then leaned against the plane to give her knees a chance to steady. Aside from pushing her hair back from her face, she resisted the urge to fuss with her appearance. She'd slept in her clothes, and they looked it. No amount of tugging at hems and cuffs was going to repair what hours of traveling had done.

As Ross secured the plane, she shaded her eyes for a look around. New England colors were never so bold, she mused. The sky, infinite and cloudless, was an incredible shade of blue. To the west, foothills were awash with rich and various shades of green. The mountain range wasn't nearly as close as it had seemed from the air; only one of its jutting peaks could be seen in the distance. Poised above it, the late-afternoon sun was still white and bright.

Hearing the swish of footsteps in the grass, Paige turned as the approaching driver removed a pearl gray Stetson. Raven black hair tumbled down from the crown, falling past slender, feminine shoulders. Catherine Tanner, she realized as the woman drew closer.

"Your sister," she murmured. Her nerves scrambled, and she raised one hand reflexively. Before she could press it to her suddenly thudding heart, she found her composure. Fingers steady, she let them drift down the front of her blouse, as if she'd only wanted to make sure all its buttons were secure.

"Cat's nice people." Ross caught her hand as it fell and gave it a reassuring squeeze. "Coming from a brother, it's got to be true."

"I think I'd rather face a panel of international dressage judges."

"She won't judge."

Perhaps not, but it wasn't every day a woman met her lover's sister. Certainly Paige had never faced such an introduction.

Cat's resemblance to Ross ended with the mane of will-ful black hair. Her eyes were a stunning shade of green, her features an intriguing blend of luscious and delicate. She had a slim, leggy figure, an apricot tan, and a smile that turned to laughter as she launched herself at Ross.

Paige stood back as brother and sister greeted each other with a hard kiss and a hug. Watching them, she felt a twinge of envy. As a child she'd often fantasized having a brother or sister, someone she might have grabbed into her arms and held on to.

Grinning over Ross's shoulder, Cat held out a hand. "Paige. Welcome to Montana and the Triple T."

"Thank you." Paige clasped the offered hand, her clenched stomach relaxing. Apparently Ross had phoned ahead, sparing her the clumsy moments explaining her presence. "And you're Cat."

"My brother mentioned me, did he?" Cat narrowed her eyes on Ross as she unhooked her arms from his shoulders. "I won't ask what was said."

"Smart girl," he agreed.

"I deny it all," she told Paige good-naturedly. "Except the nice stuff." Looping their arms, she led Paige away from the plane, leaving Ross to bring their bags. "Oh, by the way," she called back to him, "you'll be happy to hear the trees won't need trimming this year. You just topped off all but the maple." Her black-lashed eyes swept over Paige. "You've survived the buzz admirably. You're not a bit green. Is falling out of the sky something you do often?"

"Never." Paige laughed, relieved to discover she liked Cat. "It was an experience I hope to live the rest of my life without repeating."

With a decidedly smug chuckle, Cat tightened her hold on Paige's arm. "You see, Ross? Everyone knows that's no way to fly a plane."

"My record's spotless," he said defensively, his long strides overtaking the two women's.

"Except for the wineglasses." Cat grinned as she opened the Jeep's passenger door for Paige. "He broke two of them last month."

"With a plane?"

"Amazing, isn't it?" Cat climbed in back beside the luggage as Ross folded himself behind the wheel. "He dived so low the house shook. Dishes in the china cabinet rattled, knocking a pair of perfectly good wineglasses to the floor."

"Don't believe a word of it," Ross interjected.

Contradicted, Cat lifted one silky black eyebrow. "Aunt Mary swore to it."

Ross was about to shoot several valid holes in the unlikely tale when he heard Paige laugh, really laugh, for the first time. She was turned in her seat, one leg tucked under her, looking more relaxed than he'd ever seen her. He still saw fatigue in her pale complexion and in the shadowed eyes, but the strain seemed to have melted away.

Ross allowed Cat to steer the conversation for most of the five-minute drive through unplowed fields. If he knew his sister—and he did—she'd spent the hours since his phone call that morning impatiently waiting to grill Paige as indiscreetly as he'd let her get away with.

At the outset, her questions were polite—where are you from, how long have you lived there? With typical ease and little time wasted, she moved from polite to probing—live alone? ever been married? When she stepped over the line to prying, Ross stepped in.

"How're things at the mine, Cat?"

Fully aware that she was being headed off at the pass, Cat chuckled. "Don't you suppose that could wait?" she countered. "Like maybe until after you've unpacked?"

Ross made the turn from dirt road to gravel drive before glancing briefly over his shoulder. "I won't be seeing you after I've unpacked."

Stately ponderosa pines lined each side of the drive. Too straight and evenly spaced, Paige decided, to have been placed by nature. Too full and majestically tall to have been planted in this century. The pines ended where the drive split to form a turnaround oval. Across it, she saw the Triple T's ranch house.

She hadn't expected a mansion. Made of native stone and wood allowed to weather, it had none of the imposing grandeur of her parents' estate house. Instead, there was a feeling of warmth about it, of protection and permanence. Three families could live comfortably in its center section alone, she mused, with room for two more in the single-story wings spreading out at each side. Chimneys jutting from the shake-shingle roof gave the impression every room was equipped with a fireplace. A broad sit-out-in-the-evening porch overlooked gardens of spring flowers in bloom. A pair of cane-seated rockers flanked the front door.

Ross pulled up at the steps leading to the porch and braked behind Cat's dusty white van. The three of them piled out, each grabbing a piece of luggage from the back seat.

"Aunt Mary stopped in this morning," Cat said as she bounded up the steps. "She stocked the refrigerator and fixed a stew. All it needs is reheating. Said she'd check with you later in the week."

Paige breathed a sigh of relief at the news that she wouldn't be meeting Ross's aunt weary and travel worn, then followed him through the front door into a central hall paneled in oak and smelling of lemon polish.

"I picked up your mail." Cat tossed her hat onto a peg by the door. "It's there by the phone. And a stack of messages Pete dropped off a little while ago. He asked that you phone him as soon as possible."

Standing back, Paige tucked her hands into her pockets and glanced around. The ceiling was twenty feet high and echoed the staccato raps of boot heels on the bare oak floor. An enormous brass light fixture hung from a rough-hewn beam, its dozen or so amber-tinted globes fitted with decorative flame-shaped bulbs. She imagined it hanging there in the days before electricity, shedding the warm glow and homey fragrance of beeswax candles.

A double-width staircase ranged up to overhanging balconies on the second floor, its newels thick and hand-turned, its banister polished to satin-finish luster. Generations of spur-booted feet had worn a smooth inverted arc into the center of each step.

To her right the hall opened onto a large, comfortably furnished room. Paige wandered as far as the two steps leading down to it. Light flowed in through uncurtained windows. Shelves filled with books and photographs took up all of one wall. Another was dominated by a generous stone hearth fronting a well-used fireplace of blackened brick. Forest green leather covered the sofas and chairs, and throw rugs woven of colorful Indian designs were strategically scattered. Though the floorboards, of disparate widths and noticeably warped, looked a hundred years old, they shone from a recent buffing.

She thought it the perfect sort of room for curling up with a book on a blustery, cold winter's night. When Ross slipped his arms around her shoulders from behind, Paige stopped herself from imagining she might still be here, snow banked at the windows, a fire spitting and popping in the hearth.

"You were right." Untucking her hands, she hooked them on his wrists. "Cat's nice people."

"I'm glad you like her—she's invited herself to dinner." He dropped his head, his beard softly grazing her cheek. "So much for making mad, passionate love under the table between courses."

Holding back a grin, Paige tilted her head to catch his eyes. "There aren't courses with stew. It's all in one pot."

They laughed quietly together, as lovers sometimes do over nothing in particular. Beneath his crossed arms, her breasts were soft and inviting, her heart thudding. Why, Ross wondered, when it had only been hours since he'd held her, should it feel like an eternity?

His hands tightened on her shoulders as he brought his mouth down on hers. The kiss was gentle, sweet. Paige relaxed with it, and sighed. A month ago, she hadn't known him. Now the shape of his body, the warmth of his lips, even the rhythm of his pulse, were familiar to her.

When the kiss was over, she leaned back against him. "This is a wonderful room." Looking over it again, she noticed there'd been windows on either side of the chimney at one time, before a wing had been added. Stained wooden shutters closed off one of the openings; the other overlooked an office. "It's older than the rest, isn't it?"

"This room was the original Tanner homestead. My great-grandparents' first real home. She cooked in the fireplace, and they slept in a loft overhead." He pointed to a trapdoor set between beams in the ceiling. "My bedroom used to be the one above. The door and fold-down ladder were hidden away in the closet, but still workable...until my father caught me using it to sneak out at night. Been nailed tight ever since."

Old and new, Paige thought. Permanence. Continuity.

"How does a hot shower and a change of clothes sound?"

"Heavenly," she murmured.

Ross grabbed her bags and led her up the stairs. When he opened the door to the bedroom that stretched across the back of the house, the faint perfume of roses drifted out. Paige saw why as she stepped over the threshold. Dozens of long-stemmed yellow-gold roses decorated the room. They graced a storage chest at the foot of a massive mahogany four-poster, spilled from a vase on a brass-fitted bureau, caught the late-afternoon sunlight on the sills of lace-curtained windows.

Overwhelmed, she buried her face in the velvet petals of one bouquet. "How did you know?"

"That you'd won?" He liked the look of her in this room, where his mother's needlepoint hung on the wall and his grandmother's quilt covered his great-grandmother's bed. "I had some time to fill."

"You were there?" Paige had to blink to hold back the tears.

"I wouldn't have missed it." He smiled. "You were magnificent."

She wasn't a stranger to praise. Over the years she'd been applauded by distinguished heads of states, from princes to presidents, receiving as many silkily spoken compliments as gold-plated trophies. But none had given her the joy she felt hearing those words from him. She went into his arms, immeasurably happy, and held on tight.

For a moment, Ross simply enjoyed holding her. Resting his chin on the top of her head, he glanced around the room that had remained virtually unchanged since he was a boy.

Large but comfortable, the combination sitting room/ bedroom was done in steel blue and ivory, with traces of dusty rose in the faded carpet. A pair of oversize wingback chairs were angled at either side of a deep-cushioned sofa facing the fireplace. A slab of granite served as a mantel. Every stick of wood was mahogany, pieces painstakingly crafted by his great-grandfather—the bed a gift to his bride on their wedding day, the rest worked on over the years and presented on Christmases and birthdays. Except for the cheval glass. That had been Ross's mother's. Her only family heirloom, her pride. He remembered that she had never been able to pass it without trailing her fingers over the frame's graceful carvings.

Despite the room's masculine overtones, the women each Tanner man had brought to it had left their imprints. In a day or two, he thought he would begin to see Paige's influence. Would she leave wisps of lace strewn about? he wondered. Would the dresser be scattered with perfume bottles? What sort of pocket items would collect on her side of the bed? Which side would that be?

He glanced at the bed then, smiling as his gaze traveled up one of its massive posts. "That up there's for you, too."

"What?" Following his gaze, Paige turned to see a buff-colored Stetson propped on a gleaming bedpost. "Oh...oh, Ross..." Fighting a fresh wave of tears, she remembered the day in the stable when he'd said he'd buy her one. One the color of Montana wheat ripening in the sun. One the color of her hair.

He laughed, because she looked like a little kid waiting for permission to dive into the packages under a Christmas tree. God, she was easy to please. "Go on, try it. See if it fits."

Grinning, giggling, Paige plucked the hat from the post and walked with it to the freestanding oval mirror. She finger-combed her hair, dragging it back from her face and reaching behind her neck to pull strands out from inside her collar.

"What are you doing?" he demanded. "Just put the thing on."

"It has to be done right." With as much care as she'd given to donning a dressage top hat, she placed the Stetson on her head. "What do you think?"

Her chin was tilted when she turned, her smile unexpectedly shy. A jade green feather the size of a silver dollar decorated the center of the hat's crown. Its color matched her eyes. He thought she was perfect.

"Oh, yeah. I like you in that hat."

"Me, too," she murmured. Facing the mirror again, she preened shamelessly, looking at herself in profile and full front, tugging on the brim to bring the hat down low on her brow, sliding it the opposite way so that it sat jauntily on the back of her head. "I love it. It's the best present anyone's ever given me." To see how she'd look without her hair flowing from under it, she gathered the heavy mane in one hand, holding it at the nape of her neck, and started posing all over again.

Ross chuckled on his way to the door. "Wear it in the shower, if you like. Can't do any more damage to it than a rainstorm. Bathroom's through that door."

He found Cat in the kitchen, arranging napkins at the unvarnished maple table. Catching her chin, he tipped her cheek up for his kiss. "Thanks, sis. You do nice work." He made a note to himself to pick up a bottle of her favorite perfume the next time he was in town.

"Hat fit?" she asked.

"Hat fit."

"She liked the flowers?"

"Loved the flowers."

"Good." Leaning a hip against the table, Cat crossed her arms and grinned. "'Cause you're gonna *love* the bill. Know what roses cost these days?"

"Yeah, as a matter of fact, I do." Ignoring the question in Cat's lifted brow, Ross scooped up a place setting. He returned the plate to its shelf in the cabinet, the silverware to its slotted drawer, and tossed the unused paper napkin into a wastebasket under the sink. "Was it much trouble for you?"

"Only the hat. I mean, exactly what color *is* ripe wheat? I had to drive out to a field of it and take some with me." She laughed, recalling how silly she'd looked trying to match a hat to a fistful of shedding wheat. "I left it to a florist to find roses the color of new gold," she added dryly. "I'd just finished putting them in vases when you buzzed the house." She hadn't paid much attention to Ross clearing away a place setting. Now she considered the two remaining. "Apparently I've remembered a pressing engagement."

"I'll walk you out."

"Is she in solitary confinement, or will you allow visitors?"

"Could I possibly keep you away?" He draped an arm around her shoulders as they stepped outside. "But... give her some time, a few days at least."

Cat frowned as she slipped her hat on. "Is something wrong, Ross? With Paige?"

"Nothing twenty-four hours in a coma won't cure. Remember cramming for exams when you were getting your geology degree? She's coming off a week something like it. The last thing she needs is to feel pressured to perform. She will until she knows you better."

"Then I'd advise you to have a heart-to-heart with Aunt Mary. Pronto," she warned as Ross opened her car door. "She's making lists of things to fix up around here before the wedding."

He drew back, then muttered a curse.

"Well, you can't really blame her, Ross. You've hardly made a habit of this sort of thing."

"What sort of thing?" he demanded.

"You know what sort. You don't bring women home for dinner, let alone for two weeks! What are we—is *she* supposed to think?"

Taking her elbow, he helped Cat into the car. "I explained it to you this morning. The lady's in need of some R and R. Solitude and sleep, lots of sleep. This seemed as good a place as any for her to get it." He shut her door, then leaned in through the open window. "She's here for two weeks, period. Get that through your heads, you and Aunt Mary both."

He's in love with her, Cat decided, though she wondered if he knew it yet. It was what she'd hoped for all day, that the brother who'd always been there for her, for everyone, who'd gotten them through some of the worst times imaginable, had finally found someone to be there for him.

"Well, that's a shame," she said, and sighed halfheartedly. "The dining room really could have used a new coat of paint." He tugged on her hair, and she grinned up at him before turning the ignition key. "Tell her I'll call before coming over."

Her shower was running when Ross entered the bedroom. The bathroom door was open a crack, allowing wisps of perfume-scented steam to drift out with the sound of rushing water. It had been three years since he'd heard the intimate noises made by another person living in the house, twenty-five since a woman's scents had clung to the air of this room. They were pleasures he'd missed. Not until this moment had he realized how much.

Stiff from the hours spent on planes, he rubbed at the knots in his shoulders as he walked to a fireside wing chair. He dropped to its deep cushions, pulled off his boots and stretched out his legs, then leaned back with a sigh. It felt good. Whether he'd returned from a trip out of town or a day on the range, it always felt good to come home.

Will it feel this good two weeks from now? Ross frowned with the thought. Will this room feel as peaceful and welcoming after ten hours of dusty range and bawling cattle? Or will it feel empty, abandoned? With a frustrated oath, he scrubbed a hand over his face. He couldn't allow himself to hope she might stay, to even think it was possible.

When he dropped his hand he saw her bags near the door where he'd left them earlier. Both were unzipped, one with its contents erupting. She needed closet and drawer space. Hearing the water shut off, Ross pushed up to his feet to see to it.

In the bathroom of cobalt blue tile and brass-fitted white porcelain, Paige squeezed the water out of her hair before stepping from the claw-footed tub. She didn't immediately dry herself off, but stood wet and shivering, hoping to shock some life into her system.

Her ears were ringing. Partly, she knew, from the constant drone of airplane engines, but mostly from exhaustion. At the first blast of hot water, her last bit of strength had drained away. She'd had to brace herself against the tile walls to keep from falling. Just one more hour, she promised her weary body. A little dinner, some small talk—then, finally, sleep. When her teeth started chattering, she took a towel from the rack and wrapped herself in it.

She walked into the bedroom, unprepared to see Ross. He stood at an open dresser drawer. Her bags were empty and collapsed at his feet, their contents now filling the drawer. All, that is, but a champagne-colored teddy dangling by thin straps from his fingertips. He was gazing at the sheer silk with an oddly bemused expression on his face.

Ross released the swath of silk that carried her scent, and watched it float into the drawer before glancing up. She took his breath away. Against the deep blue terry cloth, her skin was flushed and damp. A bead of water trickled from her temple down the side of her face. He watched it paint a glistening path from her jaw to the soft swell of breast above the towel. When he looked at her face again, he saw a weak smile and glassy eyes.

"You look awful."

"Gee, thanks." She tried without much success to smother a yawn. Before she could reach into the dresser for fresh clothes to put on, Ross slid the drawer shut. Frowning, she watched him cross to the bed. He pulled back quilt and sheet with one sweep of his hand.

"Get in," he ordered, "before you fall flat on your face."

"But, your sister. She's expecting us."

"Cat left." He read relief in her eyes even as she arched a brow in an unspoken question. "Hot date, slipped her mind."

"I'll bet." This time Paige gave in to the yawn. "Actually, a nap before dinner sounds pretty good."

"I'll call my foreman," Ross said. "Catch up on ranch business, then grab a shower before I wake you." He unhooked her towel and let it drop to the floor.

Paige slid gratefully between crisp, cool sheets, sighing as Ross tucked the quilt around her. The pillowcase smelled sweet and fresh, as if it had recently hung on a line snapping in the breeze. She closed her eyes and moaned. "God, this feels good." Her mind began to float, her body to sink, as exhaustion closed in. She fell asleep with his lips still warm and soft on her brow.

Ross picked up her soggy towel and tossed it into the laundry hamper in the bathroom. Returning to the bedroom, he stood with his hands shoved deep in his pockets, looking at Paige, burrowed deep in the bed. Why did watching her sleep make him feel vulnerable? What sort of heartache had he invited into his life when he'd invited her into his home? Afraid of the answers, he crossed to the windows to gaze out.

Mountains formed a dramatic backdrop to the Triple T's rolling pastures and evenly planted wheat fields. From where he stood he could see the ranch's outbuildings, the stables and barns, the bunkhouse, mess hall and half-dozen storage sheds surrounded by miles of weathered fence. It was only a short walk from the kitchen door directly below him to the first of the paddocks where horses were turned out or saddled up. The only working parts of the ranch hidden from view were the cattle chutes and branding corrals.

Putting the master bedroom at the back of the house instead of the more traditional front overlooking the lawn and gardens had been his grandfather's doing. Planting a lofty row of pines to screen the corrals, his grandmother's. While the flourishing barricade accomplished its purpose of obstructing the unholy vision of bare-chested punchers that had so offended Josephine Tanner, it couldn't shut out the piercing curses and cattle cries or defeat the smell of dust, blood and sweat that by the third day of branding permeated every room of the house. Ross smiled suddenly with memories of Josie that were surprisingly clear. Though she'd outlived her husband by twelve years, she'd died when Ross was only six.

The sound of a clock striking the hour jolted him. Good God, it wasn't like him to go wandering through the past this way. He'd thought more about his ancestors in one afternoon than in the past thirty-three years put together. What he ought to be thinking about was the future. If he didn't touch base with Peterson soon, there wouldn't be one to think about.

Paige woke to a tickle on her cheek. Eyes closed, she caught the heady scent of roses as the petals of one whispered across her lips. Her mouth curved in response. A delightful shiver skipped up her spine. She turned her head on the pillow, contentedly purring as the soft stroking continued down her neck.

Blood heating, she moved from dreamless sleep to lazy arousal without fully waking. She felt boneless, her lids heavy as she struggled to lift them. The pink haze of sunset suffused the room, its soft light flowing gently through lace. Lips parting, she gazed up at Ross. He was propped on one elbow, his chest and flat belly exposed above covers draped loosely at his hips. His hair was damp and uncombed. She smelled the tang of soap on his skin. Though he knew she was watching him, his eyes stayed on the rose he trailed lightly over her.

When he drew the sheet down to her waist, Paige dropped her gaze. Through half-lowered lashes, she saw dozens of yellow-gold rose petals scattered over the quilt. Twisting her head, she saw more of them in her hair, spread out on the pillow. Emotion swelled, the romance of it weakening her.

With a small snap, Ross separated the bud he held from its stem. Slowly he rolled the flower between his thumb and forefinger, loosening petals so that, one by one, they rained down onto her arms, shoulders and breasts.

Senses swimming, she could only watch as he lowered his head. With the tip of his tongue he flicked aside a petal resting in the curve of her elbow. When he opened his mouth on the sensitive flesh there, her hand clenched automatically, trapping a fistful of fragrant shredded roses. He shifted to her breast, where a curled petal cupped her nipple. His breath alone made it flutter and float away. He drew her into his mouth. For only a moment, a taste.

Never had Paige felt so precious. Never had she been touched in ways that made her feel so special or cherished. She'd expected his mouth to be greedy. His lips were worshipful, leaving her skin hot and wet as he ran soft kisses up to her throat. She'd expected his hands to race and ravage. His touch skimmed over her, soft as a sweet summer breeze. She murmured, half moan, half sigh, to say, what?—she wasn't sure. Before she could make sense of her thoughts, his lips covered hers in a deep, drugging kiss.

Ross didn't want to hear words, only the sound of her breathing. He didn't want to think, only to explore, discover, savor. He needed to give and to take, and to forget for a while that the day would come when she would go. There was no place in the universe but this room. No time in space but this moment—no before, no after. For now, she was here, and she was his.

Hands linked, eyes open, they kissed and kissed again. The pink light of sunset warmed, deepened to rose. Still he was content to linger over the warm-honey flavor of her mouth.

His gentleness overwhelmed her. She'd thought their first night of insatiable hunger and mindless fulfillment had shown her all that a man and woman could be to each other. He taught her there was more. Without rush, he seduced. Without urgency, she responded. No demands or desperation, just heart-wrenching patience. Passion built slowly, quietly. Pleasure deepened to intimacy, turned to yearning. Somewhere in those magical moments she knew what it meant to give everything, and by giving, to become whole.

Before need could rob him of sanity, he slipped inside her, then lay still and watched her eyes fill with the wonder of their union. On a shuddering sigh, she stirred beneath him. The sound alone nearly shredded his control.

"Don't move," he whispered.

She moaned in protest, the command impossible to obey. "I have to—"

"Don't move."

Gathering control, he caressed her with his lips, with his breath skimming over her face. Releasing her hands, he took his down the length of her. She trembled, her heartbeat quickening under his palm. Her own hands closed into fists on either side of her head, pale as porcelain in the rich gold of her hair. Lightly he touched her lips with his fingertips, his gaze trapped in the depths of her wide, unblinking eyes. Did she know he loved her? How deeply and completely he loved her? No. How could she, when he was only just realizing it himself?

Love. With no other woman had he felt so empowered and yet so weakened by something as simple as the pureness of emotion. Or so vulnerable. Loving her was going to bring more pain than joy. But he wouldn't think of that now. Not now. Tonight, just for tonight, he would imagine what could not be—a future measured in years instead of days.

Slowly, he began to move. She wrapped herself around him, breathless, clinging. One body, one heart thudding. He lifted her higher, higher, the rhythm gentle, the peak exquisite. Together they drifted down to float on a warm river of contentment.

Chapter Ten

Spring was the most hectic, most exciting, season on a ranch. It began when the first calf was born and didn't let up until the last was branded. The weeks in between were long and punishing. In addition to the usual chores, there were daily patrols to check creeks and ditches, pump houses and salt licks, grazing conditions. There were fences to ride and repair, breech births to deliver, sick calves to nurse. Before roundup could begin, horses that had been turned out for the winter had to be roped and corralled and have the buck ridden out of them.

Those horses had been running wild in the hills the day Ross left for Kentucky. Now he cantered one of them, a white-socked sorrel, over a treeless range rapidly filling with cattle.

It felt good to be back in the saddle. He might have covered more ground in less time if he'd taken one of the ranch's Jeeps, but the temptation had been too great to ride and ride hard. The sun burned with high-noon intensity in a cloudless blue sky. The air was calm and dry, blessed with the promising scent of new grass and the comfortable low-ing of cows on the move.

He'd spent the morning flying over pastures, scouting strays. He'd have preferred the canter first, but the flight had been necessary. And favorable. Despite his prolonged absence, he didn't think they were more than a few days behind schedule. The farthermost winter pastures were cleared, cows and their calves mustered from the hollows and outcroppings and gathered into bunches. Closer to the corrals, bunches had already been driven into groups and the first of the groups merged into a manageable herd. Ross had counted seventy-six strays from the air.

Four men rode with him now. Following Ross, they distanced themselves from the migrating herd, avoiding the dust and the cowboys at work.

Cattle flowed into the range from three directions, a dozen or more hands working each of the lumbering columns. Men on foot whistled and waved, hazing the agreeable beasts along at a gentle pace. Others on horseback rode flank, guiding the rivers of beef and streaking after maverick dogies, driving them back into the pack.

Ross spotted Peterson and changed direction. Without needing to be told, the small posse veered off, headed for the north pastures. Ross knew he'd see them—and the seventy-six strays—by nightfall tomorrow.

"Pete." Ross reined his horse alongside the foreman's roan gelding. The other man nodded, his squint-eyed gaze scanning the range.

His first name was Percival, though Ross was the last one living to know that, and he looked like every twelve-year-old kid's movie-version image of a cowboy. His face, lined and leathery beneath his wide-brimmed hat, testified to decades of exposure to Montana's ruthless climate. An ever-present plug of tobacco bulged out his left cheek. There was a slight bow to his back now, and more gray than black in the beard he shaved only on Sundays. But his build was still lean and wiry, and his arms were as strong as those of a man half his years. Ross didn't know his exact age, only that he and Ross's father had punched their first cows together. Had he lived, Aaron Tanner would have turned sixty-two in August.

"Heard that tin misqueeter of yours buzzing around this morning," Pete declared sourly.

Now it was Ross's turn to nod. A good deal of the time Pete griped for the pleasure of it. His quarrel with the plane, however, was stubbornly sincere. Ross no longer argued that three hours in the air saved as many days in the saddle. Pete's resistance to this particular modern-day method of ranching had lost any chance of being overcome eight years ago, in the crash that had taken the lives of the Tanner brothers.

"So what'd ya see?" Pete muttered, his gravelly tone pretending disinterest.

"Good grass and water on the summer range." Relaxing in the saddle, Ross withdrew a cigarette and lighter. "A couple of breaks in the east fence that can wait a week or two. Strays—none that seemed to be in any trouble. Cully and his boys have gone after them." Though the air barely stirred, he cupped a protective hand around the spurt of flame and red-tipped cigarette, then released a lungful of smoke. "You've done a fine job, Pete. The Triple T couldn't have been left in better hands."

"Been doing it long enough." Compliment dismissed, Pete turned his head to spit a stream of tobacco juice to the ground.

The number of cows seemed unending as Ross's glance passed over them in search of the crew bosses—the Bradley brothers, Jim and Joe, on each of the outside files; Sam Kelly driving the middle line. Backtracking, he saw Ned Foster riding flank on Sam's team, and watched with interest. He was making a respectable showing of himself, Ross thought, for a kid who wasn't born to the land. Son of the town's dentist and a recent high school graduate, he was toughing out his first season as a cowboy. Everyone in the county knew his father was furious, more determined than ever that, come fall, Ned was going to college. He'd work the boy hard for the next three months, Ross decided. Perhaps Ned would develop a sudden yearning for campus life.

By the time Ross finished his cigarette, the range was a churning sea of dusty hides. "Bigger herd than usual," he noted, a trace of concern in his voice. No other foreman in the state was as skilled as Pete at moving or managing cattle. Ross rarely questioned his judgment.

"Plenty of graze," Pete said. "Might put a couple extra hands on 'em overnight. Six oughta do it. The rest'll head back this afternoon to move the next bunch down to the piece we pushed these here off to."

And so it went. Day by day, section by section. Groups growing to bunches, bunches swelling to herds; herds shifted from pastures to cutting pens to branding chutes. And then the long, restful drive to the summer range to graze and grow fat.

With whoops and hollers, the ground crews prodded stragglers into hurrying at an ungainly trot. Hands on horseback surrounded the newly formed herd, halting its forward progress. They rode its perimeter, tightening the circle with each pass to keep the milling cows in check, while lost calves bleated and raced, frantic to find their mamas.

Satisfied the herd would settle in without incident, Ross and Pete nudged their mounts to a walk. "I'd like to start branding in three days," Ross stated, knowing they probably needed four. "These boys up to pulling off miracles?"

"Three days." It was second nature for Pete to scrutinize the sky before hazarding a guess. "Maybe. If the weather holds."

"I'll call the neighbors tonight, tell them they're welcome day after tomorrow." Despite vigilant attention to fence lines, breaks occurred and cattle strayed. The Triple T's borders touched on those of three other ranches. It was unwritten law that neighboring outfits extended each other the courtesy of viewing their herds. They'd bring their own hands to cut cows carrying their brands and ride them home.

An advancing dust whirl signaled the approach of the lunch wagon—a battered blue pickup—and an eagerly anticipated break for the men. Even as work continued, glances cut to the bouncing cook truck. Each crew boss assigned two men to the herd. The rest broke away to make camp.

Ross was tempted to join them. The food would be plain and plentiful, the talk easy. The time, however, couldn't be spared. He had yet to tour the outbuildings or see his horse breeder and stable manager. Davey Anderson, the Triple T's herdsman, was anxious to show him a pair of bull calves he'd pegged as potential breeders. Ross tipped his hat to Popeye, the ranch cook, and asked Pete to stop at the house that evening. With a boot to the sorrel's flank, he broke away at a ground-eating lope.

Paige floated toward consciousness, absorbing sensations as her mind cleared. Night air chilled the room, yet she felt warm and cozy. She was cuddled against Ross, her back to his chest, his head on her pillow. She heard the whisper of lace as curtains fluttered at a window. Downstairs, a grandfather clock struck the half hour. She hadn't a clue what time it was, or even what day. She opened her eyes to glance at her wrist, then remembered she almost never wore her watch anymore.

The room was dusky, the sky just beginning to pale. She closed her eyes again, happy to sink into dreams, but discovered she was too wide-awake to sleep. And why not? she thought with a smile. In the three—or was it four?—days since she'd arrived at the Triple T, she'd done little more than sleep. Sleep, eat, and make love with Ross.

He lay beside her, his arm hooked possessively around her waist, his deep, even breaths ruffling her hair. Turning her head on the pillow, she watched him sleep, realizing it was for the first time.

He'd been up at the crack of dawn every morning, while she'd stayed in bed till noon—except the first thirty-six hours, when she'd slept round the clock, rousing only to eat, and only because Ross insisted. He'd been angry, she recalled. At her, initially—presumably for causing her own collapse—then at himself, because he'd left her alone all day. She remembered thinking during one of her brief lucid periods how odd it was that the more she slept the more sleep she seemed to need. And each time she drifted up from the fog he'd been there, threatening her with doctors between spoonfuls of soup.

In the first blush of morning, his face was relaxed, his hair rumpled. Paige resisted the urge to brush it off his forehead. The slightest touch might wake him, robbing him of sleep he richly deserved.

He put in long, hard days, literally working from dawn to dusk. Evenings, he spent an additional hour on ledgers and paperwork. It would let up soon, he'd promised last night, then asked if she was bored.

No, she wasn't bored. Lazy, perhaps, but not bored. For the first time in thirteen years, her days were unscheduled. *Her* days, to do—or not do—whatever she pleased. She was as content to putter in Mary Tanner's vegetable patch as she was to nap in the rope hammock strung between a pair of oak trees. She might choose to spend the afternoon in front of the television, remote control in hand, cruising through talk shows, game shows and soap operas. Or she might choose to spend it in the kitchen, indulging her newfound enthusiasm for cooking.

With a smile, she recalled Ross's surprise at the elaborate dinner she'd prepared the night before. She'd cut an armful of flowers from the garden, arranging them on an ivory linen tablecloth set with china and crystal. Candlelight flickering, soft music playing in the background, she'd listened for the distinctive drum of his boot heels on the back porch. Anticipation, she'd discovered, wasn't always a prelude to stomach cramps. Last night it had made her feel giddy. The look on his face, disbelief giving way to pleasure, had been worth the two hours it took to return the kitchen to order.

Should it be this easy to move into a man's house, his life? Paige wondered. And would the fact that it was so easy make it that much harder to move out when the time came? No sooner had the question formed than she pushed it aside. She refused to waste one precious moment on regret. The present was all that mattered—the fragile dawn, the warm cocoon of their entwined bodies, and her own contentment.

As she watched him, his eyes opened, so suddenly Paige laughed. "Do you always do that? Wake up in two seconds flat?"

Startled, Ross blinked. "What's wrong?" His eyes narrowed to help bring her into focus. "Are you sick?"

"No. Do I look sick?"

"It's..." He raised up on one elbow to glance past her at the clock on the nightstand. "It's five-thirty. If you're not sick, why aren't you sleeping?"

Paige laughed again. "I'm slept out. 'Bout time, don't you think?"

Her laughter, so light and carefree, convinced Ross she was on her way to a full recovery. He'd had his doubts that first day. It had scared the hell out of him to come home and discover she hadn't budged since he'd left her that morning. His first thought was that she'd slipped into the coma he'd mentioned to Cat. Now, the eyes that had been dull and unfocused—when she'd been able to open them at all—were clear and bright. Skin bleached of all color had warmed to a healthy glow.

Satisfied, Ross lay back down, then felt the mattress give as she rolled to the edge of the bed. With one hand, he circled her wrist and tugged. She tumbled to sprawl across his chest, her silky hair spilling down to frame his face.

"Going somewhere?" he murmured, stirring to the morning-fresh scent of her skin.

"Well, I had planned on going to the kitchen." Her breath caught on a thrill as he swept an open hand over her back, her hip, her thigh. "I ran across this great omelet recipe. Thought I'd whip one up for you."

"Incredible."

"My offer or my thigh?"

"Your fondness for housekeeping." He nuzzled her neck. "And your thigh," he murmured against her skin.

"I am not fond of housekeeping," she corrected dryly. "Perhaps you hadn't noticed, but there's a week's worth of laundry piled up in that little room off the kitchen. And I haven't found your vacuum cleaner. Probably because I haven't looked for it." His hand retraced its journey, his thumb gently tracing the length of her spine. A wonderfully erotic sensation, she decided. "I take it you're not hungry."

"Starving," he groaned, rolling her onto her back. But not for omelets, Paige mused dreamily as his mouth found hers.

Making love with him was never the same. There were, she'd discovered, as many levels and textures to passion as there were ways for a man to touch a woman, a woman to touch a man. Sometimes they came together in a storm of need, sometimes with laughter. This morning they loved with whispers and sighs in the quiet enchantment of a new day.

Paige made the omelet...eventually. Wearing Ross's robe, sipping a second cup of coffee, she watched him switch his cleaned plate for the scraps left on her own. From the radio on top of the refrigerator, a grainy voice reported the previous day's commodities closings. Pork bellies and corn were up, wheat down, beef cattle unchanged. She could imagine couples across the country starting the day just this way. Radios in Chicago tuned to traffic reports instead of feed prices. Coffeepots in California just beginning to perk. Warm kitchens smelling of sunshine and breakfast.

After a glance at the wall clock, Ross shoved back from the table. "Late," he said, and leaned down to kiss her goodbye.

When the back door closed behind him, Paige pulled her knees into her chest and smiled. Odd that such an ordinary, everyday occurrence should give her such pleasure. Perhaps if she'd played with dolls when she was nine, hostessing pretend tea parties instead of learning to braid a tight mane, she wouldn't be sitting here now, getting such a kick out of playing house. Playing wife, her subconscious warned. So she allowed herself to fantasize. So what? As long as she knew it was make-believe, no more real than dolls sipping tea, what harm could it do?

Hugging her knees, she glanced around the kitchen, her smile dissolving. The sink overflowed with more bowls, plates and spoons than the making of one meal should require. Because she'd burned the butter in the first skillet, she'd had to dirty a second. There was jelly on the toaster, and there were toast crumbs on the floor. Yolk speckled the walls, because she'd taken the eggbeater out of the mix without turning it off first. In short, the place was a disaster.

Wouldn't it be nice, she mused, if she could pretend the room clean again?

The sun was peeking over the horizon when Ross reached the stable yard. Hands and horses crowded the enclosure, spilling through its gates into the rutted lane and beyond. Over the sound of roll call and team assignments, cowboys bragged of past feats and took up dares to outride and outrope. By week's end, they'd remember they were exhausted. This morning, however, the grueling spring and hard weeks of roundup were forgotten, and spirits rejuvenated in the excitement of the first day of branding.

Leaving the tack room, Ross eyed the string of horses hitched to the fence and settled on a dapple gray gelding. He was halfway across the yard when Ned Foster fell into step beside him.

"Mornin', boss."

"Ned." Tossing saddle and pad onto the gray's back, Ross joggled them into place before tightening the front cinch strap. Ned, he noticed, had slanted a shoulder to a fence post and was thoughtfully gnawing on a toothpick. Ross hoped he had the sense not to trade it for a plug of tobacco before the summer was over. "Something on your mind?"

"Pete," Ned blurted out. "He's put me on the gate."

So that's the way the wind blows. "Someone's got to do it."

"Why me?" He sounded young, Ross thought. Young and angry and bitterly disappointed. "Why'd he take me off Sam's team?"

"No one took you off Sam's team. That was roundup. This is branding. Different work, different crews."

"But the gates? Come on, anyone could do that. Let me go out with Sam, Mr. Tanner. Please."

Ross stooped to reach for the rear cinch, taking his time as he debated the best way to answer the boy. He was a hard worker, willing and eager to learn, but still nervous in the pack. In a hollow about a mile from the compound lay the first of six holding grounds, where a thousand head of cattle were massed together. Using little more than cowboy savvy and their broad-chested mounts, Sam Kelly and his crew would wade into that sea of beef, driving a third of it over the rise onto the bottleneck flat leading to the cutting pens. Riding into a herd that size was tricky business—when one cow moved, the rest tended to follow. If cows on the move turned back or the herd as a whole decided to run, men and their horses would be caught in the middle. They'd need slick skills and cool heads to get out and get out quick. Ned had neither.

"Bosses make their own assignments," Ross said finally. "I'd need a damn good reason to pull rank on one of them. Got one for me?"

The ball was back in Ned's court. Sensing defeat, he nodded, then spit the toothpick over the fence and walked away.

By ten o'clock, the first bunch of anxious calves and puzzled cows had been pushed into one end of the fenced maze of chutes and corrals and out the other to scatter and rest on a sloped pasture. Dust hovered as high as a man's shoulders. The sun climbed, and sweat rolled.

Calling for a fresh horse, Ross trotted out of the corral to join Pete at the outside rails. "How many?" he asked, handing the lathered gray over to a stable boy.

"Three hundred twenty, give or take a few."

"Give me two more hands in the cutting pen." Saddle leather groaned as Ross mounted a buckskin mare. "And tell Mike to turn down the pressure on that hose. We want to kill lice, not the cows."

By the time Ross joined Cully and the Bradley boys in the bottleneck, the next group was coming over the rise, trampling the tender spring grass. He'd lost count of the times he'd seen this sight. It never lost its power to awe and excite him.

It had the same effect on Paige as she stepped through the pine-tree barrier. For a moment she could only stare at the flood of cattle pouring over the ridge, their legs obscured by a thick cloud of ground-covering dust. Cowboys straddling horses and fence rails whooped and shouted, rousing the pack onward. She searched for Ross among the men in and around the connected pens, but the only face she recognized belonged to his foreman.

Ross sensed a change. With the tail-end cows reluctantly jogging the final yards, he saw both Bradleys turn in their saddles. It wasn't the herd they were looking at.

Then Cully was shouting. "Gate! Dammit, Ned, shut the gate!"

Ross wheeled the buckskin in time to see Ned tumble to the ground from the top of the corral fence in his haste to act on Cully's order. Ned scrambled to his feet, leaping to shut the gate, but not before three renegade cows and a terrified calf darted free of the pen.

Then Ross saw Paige.

She was strolling toward Pete, seemingly unaware of the commotion she'd caused. She moved with the classic elegance that came from having endless legs and infinite self-confidence. Unbound, her gold-shot hair spilled down her back from under the buff Stetson. She wore a hunter green T-shirt and washed-out jeans. Mouths couldn't have opened wider if she'd walked out in a beaded ball gown. Ross took one hard look around and noticed how quickly the men went back to work. Saddled hands closed rank, forming a barrier between the escaped cows and pasture beyond. The Bradley brothers went after the mavericks. Cully bore down on Ned.

"What's the matter, you never seen a girl before?" Cully said mockingly. "They've got them in town, don't they? Must have been some in that school you went to."

Much as Ned deserved a razzing, Ross sympathized. He'd been weak limbed himself the first time he laid eyes on Paige. Hell, even flint-hearted old Pete had shuffled and stuttered the night he met her. Grinning at the memory, Ross took off after the calf.

Paige joined Pete at the rails. He met with Ross at the house most nights, and he was the only ranch hand she'd met so far. He welcomed her with a grin that deepened the creases in his leathery skin.

"Should I be here?" she asked, knowing he wouldn't hesitate to tell the truth.

"You can be anywhere you want, I reckon. 'Twere me, I'd be at a swimmin' hole coolin' off."

Looking at everything at once, Paige hooked her arms over the fence of the largest pen, where cattle chased and cried. A man jumped in with them, dragging a hose that he turned on the herd. The sharp bite of chemicals cut through the earthier smell of dust and animals, the antiseptic fumes stinging Paige's nostrils.

"Lice," Pete said to her lifted brow. "Keeps flies away, too."

Ross rode into the pen then. As soon as she saw him, her pulse skipped. There was an unexpected sexuality to the sway of his hips in the saddle, to the impression of tensed muscles beneath his sweat-dampened shirt. Every eye was on them as he tipped his hat to her. Paige tipped her own back. While the subdued greeting might have disappointed their audience, Paige felt the heat of his gaze long after he turned away.

With a great deal of noise from both cowboys and cattle, the calves were separated and kept in the largest corral, while cows, heifers and steers were forced out through a series of pens ending in a chute where they were vaccinated. If a sloppy brand had grown over, the animal was sent to yet another holding area. Pungent curses flavored the cacophony of sounds. Pete lifted his hat to swipe a shirtsleeve across his brow, his cheeks flushed with embarrassment.

Paige chuckled. The time had long passed for such chivalry. Still she thought it rather sweet.

As she watched, the motherless calves huddled together on one side of the corral, bleating in confusion. Fires burned on the other side. Ross and a second man Pete identified as Cully were the only two inside the corral on horses. The rest of the men belonged to the ground crews.

"First calf goes to the lead roper," Pete told her as Ross lifted his coiled lariat from the saddle horn. He made a clean toss, roping a calf and dragging it to a fire where the ground crew took over. In under a minute, the calf had its ear clipped, received a shot and was branded. Now the smell of burned hair and seared skin mingled with those of animals, dust and antiseptic.

"They're so little to be handled that way," Paige murmured.

"Little? Why, hell, it takes a strong rope and a pair of grown men to hold one down," Pete told her. "Don't mind their bawlin'. It's just 'cause they want their mama. A good brander sticks the iron so that only the hair is burned off, the skin isn't damaged."

She watched as a fourth calf was dragged to the fire, brown-velvet eyes rolled back in terror. As with the previous calves, this one was clipped, injected and branded. At the point where the others had been released, the ground crew continued. Too late, Paige realized that, unlike the first three, this was a bull calf. First his horns were removed, then he was rolled onto his back to receive the cut that turned him into a steer. Blood spilled into the dirt, the air dripping with its sweet, sticky smell. Paige felt her knees weaken. Long after the calf had scrambled to his feet, she had a white-knuckled grip on the fence.

"Missy?" Pete said. "Something wrong?"

It didn't surprise her that he asked. When the calf's blood ran, so had her own—straight out of her head and into her feet. There were beads of sweat on her brow that had nothing to do with the heat. "I've just remembered I left something on the stove." Deciding she wasn't going to be sick or fall flat on her face, Paige let go of the fence and took a trial step backward. "I should get back, before I burn the house down."

* * *

Paige was feeling more confident about her third batch of pie dough. Refutably confident, perhaps, since she'd had to feed the first two to the garbage disposal. Consulting the cookbook, she dusted the countertop with flour.

She'd already gone through a five-pound bag of the stuff, half of which she was wearing between the neck of her red T-shirt and the hems of her cutoffs. Scaly patches of dough covered her bare arms, her face and even the tops of her thighs. She didn't let the mess she made bother her. Once— *if*—she mastered doing it right, she'd try for doing it neat.

She overturned the bowl, mealy lumps rolling onto the countertop.

"It needs more shortening."

Paige whirled at the voice and immediately recognized the slim woman with quiet hazel eyes and hair the color of polished pewter. There was a picture of her, arms around Cat, on Ross's dresser. She was taller than Paige had imagined, as youthful as Faye for fifty-something, but without Faye's dependence on cosmetics.

"Mrs. Tanner," Paige began, too flustered to think what to say next. Her hands were too sticky to extend or even stuff into her pockets.

"Mary, please...." Her voice was low and smooth, trailing off as, with eyes widening, she swept a glance over Paige. Then, pulling herself together, she smiled. "Everyone calls me Mary."

"You can laugh if you like," Paige said. "I've been teaching myself to cook for a week now. I've got a pretty good idea how I look." She shrugged and sighed. "So much for making a good first impression."

Amusement tugged at the corners of Mary's mouth. "You've made a fine first impression." Crossing to the pantry, she lifted a fresh apron from a hook, tying it at her waist as she surveyed Paige's concoction. "There's no saving it, I'm afraid."

"I thought maybe if I kneaded it..."

"Pie dough?" Now she did laugh. "Bread dough, yes. Never pie dough." She dipped a measuring cup into the sack of flour, leveling it with the blunt edge of a knife.

"I didn't do that," Paige said.

Humming in response, Mary opened a cupboard door, removing a sifter and a clean mixing bowl. She poured the flour into the sifter.

"I didn't do that, either."

Mary smiled sympathetically. "You shouldn't feel bad. Learning to cook is one thing, learning to bake something else entirely. What had you planned for a filling?"

"Apples." Paige nodded at a bushel of them. "Someone left them on the back porch yesterday."

"Martha. Martha Anderson," she explained when Paige shook her head. "She picks up a bushel for me when she goes to the fruit market. Sends them with Davey, her husband. He works here at the ranch. How many pies did you plan to make?"

"One seemed ambitious enough for a start."

Chuckling, Mary slid open a drawer and removed a device Paige assumed was the pastry blender referred to in the cookbook. Since she hadn't known what one looked like, she'd substituted a fork.

"It's as easy to make six pies as one," Mary said. "Why don't you peel the apples? With two of us, we'll have them done in no time."

"'No time,'" Paige discovered, was three and a half hours. Together they peeled, sliced, mixed, rolled and crimped. They talked about the ranch and the roundup, the house and the gardens. Not once did Mary pry or prod. Grateful, Paige was able to relax and enjoy herself.

When Ross arrived at the end of the day, he found his aunt and Paige at the kitchen table, gabbing over a pitcher of fresh-squeezed lemonade. Six apple pies were cooling on the countertops, cinnamon-scented steam rising from flaky golden crusts.

As he crossed the room, Paige lifted her face. Without hesitating, Ross leaned down to kiss her. The questions Mary had kept to herself were answered—to her satisfaction, at least—in the ease of that gesture, so natural it seemed as involuntary for both of them as breathing.

"Cat's coming for dinner," Paige said as their lips parted. "She'll be here any time now."

"Give me ten minutes to shower." He turned to Mary and gave her a wink. "Hello, stranger." He pressed a kiss to her forehead, at the same time folding one of her hands in his. "Took you long enough."

"It's been an unusually busy week." She squeezed the hand he held, relaying a message meant only for him. He squeezed back.

"Ten minutes," he promised as he left the kitchen.

Dinner was a long, relaxed affair, with none of the stifling conversation Paige associated with family gatherings. It was the first time all three Tanners had been together in nearly a month. In their enthusiasm to catch up, they bounced from one subject to another, laughing nearly as much as they talked. Every now and then one of them thought to draw her into the conversation, but for the most part she watched and listened and thoroughly enjoyed them.

Cat was as witty and forthright as Paige remembered. There didn't seem to be a topic on which she hadn't formed an opinion, nor an opinion she could be swayed from. Mary, in her calm, efficient way, limited her input to advice and support—whether or not it was asked for. Ross adored them. It was obvious in the softness of his smile, the fondness of his gaze. So much love, Paige thought with a twinge of envy.

Though the days were at their longest, it was already dark when the four of them walked out the front door. From the porch, Ross and Paige watched Cat's van and Mary's smaller sedan maneuver the oval turnaround. When the last set of taillights winked out, Ross took her hand, linking their fingers and leading her to one of the rocking chairs. He dropped to its seat, tugging her down onto his lap. She giggled at first, then draped her legs over the chair arm and nestled her head on his shoulder.

"Nice," she murmured.

"Very nice," he agreed, and set the chair rocking.

The air smelled of flowers ripe from the day's heat, even though the mercury had already begun its nightly plunge. It still surprised Paige that temperatures could fluctuate by as much as forty degrees in a twenty-four-hour period. An owl hooted, scaring a hawk from the trees. She could hear its wings flap over the steady rhythm of the chair's rockers rolling on the floorboards.

"You had the plane up today," she murmured.

"Mmm..."

"Cat's right, you know."

He laughed, the sound a soft rumble in his chest beneath her ear. He curved one hand around her thigh, while the other began loosening her braid. "Are you going to tell me I broke more glasses?"

"No, but it's a miracle you didn't break windows, with the way they rattled." She shifted so that she could see his face. Her lips brushed his chin, then were captured by his mouth. For countless moments, they kissed and rocked, until her mind clouded over. "Are you trying to shut me up?" she asked at last, resettling her head on his shoulder.

"Was there more you wanted to say?"

"You have to stop flying like that."

"Come on, Paige. I—'

"It upsets your aunt. It terrifies her, in fact." He stopped the chair's movement. Every part of his body that touched hers grew tense. "I think it reminds her of...you know, the accident."

"Why do you think that?"

"I saw her. Today, when I thought you were going to come through the roof any minute. She turned ash white, closed her eyes and just stood there, frozen. Except for her hands. They trembled. It's as if she's paralyzed, until you get far enough away that she can't hear the engine."

He stared out at the night, then breathed a curse. Why had it never occurred to him? Ross silently rebuked himself. Mary was the last person on earth he would hurt. The accident that had taken her husband the last thing in the world he wanted to remind her of.

"Couldn't you invest in a radio?" Paige said into the heavy silence. "Or leave a Jeep or pickup at the landing strip, so you wouldn't need anyone to go out for you?"

"Sure," he said in a distant voice. "I had no idea. I didn't even think!"

Paige hated the grim look on his face, the self-loathing in his eyes. "So now you know." It wouldn't, she knew, happen again. She nipped playfully on his lower lip, lifting a hand to his head to bury her fingers in his thick, unruly hair. She was rewarded with a groan of pleasure when she took his mouth in a hot, urgent kiss.

She was trying to distract him, Ross realized as she pressed herself into the kiss. Doing an expert job of it, too. He pushed up to his feet while he still had the strength to stand and, with Paige in his arms, carried her through the door.

Ross knew the house was empty the moment he let himself in the back door. He'd gotten used to coming home to pots bubbling on the stove, music playing on the radio or the distant drone of television voices. If Paige wasn't in the kitchen when he came through the door, she'd call out from the den or down from the second-floor landing.

Today the kitchen was neat as a pin, the house silent. The only smell was a faint drift of furniture polish. He had a moment of panic before remembering she'd made plans to go shopping with Cat.

This is how it will be when she's gone, he thought. No, worse. Much worse. There won't be recipe cards taped to the refrigerator after she leaves, or cheerful bowls of daisies in the front hall. Her hat won't be hanging from its peg by the door. He walked into the bedroom, a room he used to think of as his but now considered theirs. It still surprised and pleased him to see her watch beside his pocket change on the bedside table, her blouses mixed with his shirts in the closet.

As he had the first day he brought her to the ranch, Ross dropped to a wing chair and stretched out his legs. Her perfume lingered in the air, a subtle blend of spice and roses. How long before it fades? A day? A week? He listened to the quiet and wondered how he'd stood it month after month these past three years. All too soon he'd have to listen to it again. For an eternity.

* * *

At branding's end, the hands and their families gathered at the Triple T for a celebration picnic, a carefree holiday dedicated to the enjoyment of good food, good fun and good friends.

There were games and prizes for the youngsters; calf roping and tug-of-war for the adults. The smell of grilling beef wafted from the barbecue fires where Popeye single-handedly sauced ribs, turned steaks and chased teens from the beer kegs. An extra buffet table was needed to hold the variety of dishes each family contributed to the feast. The desserts alone could have fed a small army.

At sundown there'd be fiddle music, sing-alongs, and dancing under the stars.

Escaping the crowds, Paige headed for the tempting shade of an oak tree, where Cat was already lying on her stomach, her head pillowed on her crossed arms. The festivities had been going on for some time, the interest in Paige finally abating. Though the talk and speculation, she suspected, would continue for weeks. Sinking down to the cool grass, she folded her legs and leaned back against the oak's trunk. The clank of metal against metal rang out from the horseshoe pit.

"How's that arm?" Cat asked without lifting her head.

"What arm?"

"The one everybody's been pumping. I thought old Carson was going to keep at it till he got you to spit water."

Paige laughed. One of the nicest things that had happened to her in the past ten days was her friendship with Cat. She liked having a friend her own age, one with whom there was no rivalry.

"Uh-oh," Cat grunted.

Paige looked up to see a straw-haired toddler heading her way at a teetering run. Giggling, he dumped himself into her lap.

"That's what you get for sneaking him treats," Cat told her.

Paige stiffened, unacquainted with the care and handling of babies, though that didn't seem to matter to the tyke. He squirmed in her lap, making a comfortable niche for his diaper-padded bottom, then laid his head on her breast and promptly went to sleep. Despite feeling awkward, she curved her arms around him.

"I'm so sorry." Because the woman rushing over bore a striking resemblance to the toddler, Paige assumed she was his mother. "You won't remember me, you've met so many people today. I'm—"

"Martha Anderson," Paige finished. It was hard to forget someone who'd been responsible for an afternoon peeling apples.

"I apologize for Cody. He doesn't usually go to strangers."

"She was feeding him Popsicles, Marty," Cat announced.

"Oh, well, for Popsicles he'd let you adopt him," Martha said fondly. "Here, let me take him."

"I don't mind," Paige assured her. She rather liked it, in fact. "It seems a shame to wake him. Go on, have some fun. He'll be fine."

"You're sure?" She was already backing away, eager to retreat before the offer was withdrawn. "Holler if he gives you any trouble."

"Bet you don't see her again till sundown," Cat predicted as Martha lost herself in the crowd.

Unconcerned, Paige leaned back and scanned the guests spread over the grounds. Beyond the corrals, teenage boys strutted and flexed, to the breathless delight of teenage girls. Children dived for pennies hidden in a mound of sawdust, mothers coaching from the sidelines. One of the buffet tables had been cleared, and a hot poker game was under way. Behind his grill, Popeye made his anchor tattoos bump and shiver for a fascinated eight-year-old.

In her lap, Cody heaved a dreamless sigh, his little body growing limper as he slipped deeper into sleep. Such a sweet baby face, she mused. So small and perfectly formed. Gently she touched his hair, marveling at how silky it felt.

"Who's this?"

Paige glanced over her shoulder as Ross rounded the tree. "Shh. Cody Anderson. And he's sound asleep."

"I'd be, too, if my head were laying where his is."

"That's my cue," Cat mumbled, and rolled to her feet. "Catch you guys later."

Ross gave his sister a wink as she strolled off, then stretched out on his back. The combination of cold beer and hot sun made a nap in the shade appealing. He gazed at Paige through lowered lids, the vision of her cradling the baby blurry at the edges. With one hand, he reached out, running his fingers along the hem of her white shorts, lightly skimming the warm skin beneath.

"People are watching," she warned when his stroking ventured higher on her leg.

"Yeah?" He raised up on one arm to sweep a glance over the grounds. "So they are. Ought to give them something worth watching." Before she could react, he took her mouth in a long, thorough kiss that provoked an approving scream of whistles.

Released, she slanted him a cool look. "Now we know what they'll be dishing up for breakfast tomorrow."

There was no apology in the grin he shot her. He plucked a blade of grass and stuck it between his teeth, then lay back and closed his eyes. "Meet everyone?"

"Mmm... I had no idea you employed so many people."

"Only half of them year-round. The rest sign on for spring and fall roundups. They'll take off tomorrow, day after. Some to their own farms and ranches, most to catch up with a rodeo."

"And you? Pete said you 'rodeo' for a week or two every summer."

"Yeah, if I can get away."

"Would I be in the way if I tagged along?"

Ross opened one eye, squinting as he considered her. By his calculations, her two weeks would be up in three days. Surely she knew that. He couldn't be the only one keeping track of the time. "I won't go right away. Ten days at the earliest."

"I'm in no hurry." There, she'd said it. She'd thought it for days, now she'd said it.

It was the last thing Ross had expected to hear. For a moment he could only stare.

"You did say you'd take me places I'd never been," she reminded him. "And I've never been to a rodeo."

"What about the circuit?"

Cody stirred, and Paige shifted him, patting his back while searching for words to express what, until now, had only been inklings. "After my last competition, a good friend suggested I get away for a month, longer if possible. I resisted his advice. It sounded too drastic, that much time. Now I think he was right. I don't—" *Miss it, don't even think about it.* She met Ross's eyes over the top of Cody's head and knew she was looking at the biggest *don't* of them all. *I don't want to leave you. Not yet.* "I don't think I'm ready," she said instead. "So, if it's okay with you, I'd like to stay a while."

Ross rose up on his elbows. He didn't know what to say. He'd promised Faye this wouldn't happen. It was a promise he couldn't keep. No more than he could keep the hope from building that she might put off leaving indefinitely. That was dangerous. If not now, the day would still come when she'd go. A while, she'd said. How long was that? A month? A summer?

Head cocked, Paige watched him. His expression changed subtly with his thoughts, not so much that she could read them, but enough for her to sense their disarray. She laughed softly, smugly. "That's the second time I've managed to surprise you."

Hard raps at the back door startled Paige. She racked the skillet she'd been rinsing and grabbed a dish towel, running it through her hands as she peered through the screen. If memory served her, the skinny teenager staring back was Sam Kelly's boy.

"Ma'am." He swiped his hat from his head, using it to gesture at a large crate resting near his feet. "Pop sent me to town on errands, and this here was at the post office. Has your name on it.''

''Mine?'' She pushed open the screen at the same moment Ross reached the back steps.

''Will,'' he said, greeting the boy. ''What've you got there?''

''Don't know, boss. It's for Miz Meredith.''

''Let's have a look,'' Ross suggested.

With a handy hoof pick, Will unhinged the crate to reveal a brass-trimmed trunk. Ross hunkered down to release its latches, though Paige had a pretty good idea what they'd find inside. Resentment turned to anger, anger to fury, as she gazed at the trunk's contents. Knee-high riding boots were tucked around a trim English saddle, bridles and bits stuffed in the corners. Paige thought that if she lifted the saddle she'd find the bottom of the trunk lined with her workout clothes.

''She's still making decisions for me.''

Ross cut her a glance. ''You've talked to Faye, I gather.''

''Last week, after the picnic.'' The phone call had been brief, as tense and disagreeable as Paige had expected.

Ross waited, but the firm press of her lips indicated she had nothing more to say on the matter.

''Can I take it inside for you, ma'am?'' Will asked.

''No, you can send it back.'' A curse hissed through her teeth as she whirled on her heels. ''Pack it up and send it back.''

Will's saucer-wide eyes blinked when the door slammed shut, his Adam's apple bobbing on a swallow. ''Guess I'll haul it back to the post office.''

''That won't be necessary,'' Ross decided. ''Take it down to the stables and stow it in one of the tack rooms.'' Because the boy was worrying his hat through his hands even as he nodded obligingly, Ross leaned closer, his voice a conspiratorial whisper. ''We won't tell her. If she finds out, I'll take the blame.''

With a grin, Ross turned toward the door. It wouldn't take much to turn her fury into passion. A touch, perhaps only a look. Somewhere along the way, she'd learned never to scream or shout, never to let emotion ruffle her control. For Paige, the only permissible release for anger was activity. Ross knew just the sort of exercise to help her vent all that energy.

Chapter Eleven

The name of the next contender blared through twin loudspeakers, igniting a fresh burst of cheers. A haze of dust hung over the bleachers, where the air smelled of roasted peanuts and damp, crowded bodies. Despite record-breaking temperatures, every seat was taken. Wallets opened readily to vendors hawking cold drinks and programs sold in pairs—one to read, one to fan.

Away from the arena, in the area called "back of the chutes," Paige sat on a stack of hay bales, knees to chest in the loose cradle of her arms. If she closed her eyes, she mused, if she didn't look but only listened—to the jingle of tack, the hum of anticipation—she might think she was at a three-day in Maryland instead of a rodeo in Montana.

Propping her chin on one knee, she did look. At riders and ropers claiming space along the fence of the livestock corrals, rigging bags open at their feet, equipment laid out on the rails. At a dirt-streaked steer wrestler thirstily chugging a beer. At penned calves, colorful chaps, shirtsleeves dripping fringe, and clowns with painted faces. It was her fifth rodeo; she was no less fascinated than she'd been at her first.

Spotting Ross, she watched him give his spur a quick spin before clipping it to his boot. His left boot. Always the left boot first, then the right.

Nothing could have surprised her more than discovering he was superstitious. As rituals went, his was rather tame, not half as peculiar as some practiced by equestrians: unpacking tack in a specific order, refusing stalls in a northeast corner, wearing the same pair of socks throughout a three-day—without washing them! *Dumb*. There was no other word for such nonsense, though she'd learned not to say so to Ross.

She'd also learned not to distract him with conversation when he was preparing to compete. That, and the intensity of his eyes in an otherwise expressionless face, reminded Paige of herself before a dressage test. She felt again, as she had often the past few days, that she'd traveled to a foreign land, only to find herself in familiar territory.

A week ago she'd have laughed at anyone suggesting this world could resemble hers, beyond the obvious fact that riders inhabited both. Now she thought the two more alike than different.

Tension crackled behind the chutes, just as it did behind the gates at a jumping arena. Officials thumbed time clocks, judges flashed scores. Away from the stands, competitors used the time between rounds to check equipment, compare notes and doctor injuries. They reminded Paige of eventers at the vet box, regrouping between phases. Some, she knew, would be satisfied with a good ride or a clean catch. Others wanted it all—the points, the lead and, ultimately, the prize. On this circuit it was a win at the year-end nationals and the title of World Champion All-Around Cowboy.

The air stirred, the slight breeze smelling of rain. Paige lifted her face to it, adjusting her hat to shade her eyes. Bits of conversation reached her from the passing traffic, talk of past rides and future shows, of lucky draws and lousy calls. She smiled. *No, not so different.*

"Tanner, you'll go fourth."

Paige sat straighter, suddenly alert.

Ross nodded to the chute boss without breaking his concentration. Taking his time, he applied rosin to the gloved palm of his left hand, patiently working it into the coarse leather. When he was satisfied with the glove's stick, he repeated the process on the customized rope that, for eight harrowing seconds, would be his lifeline.

His gaze wandered as he worked. Preoccupied, he glanced at the sky without noticing the rain-heavy clouds gathering on the horizon. He skimmed blindly over sweating officials cuing riders into their gates, over the sparkling tiaras of the rodeo queen and her court, over a freckle-faced kid begging autographs. Then his indifferent gaze swept over Paige, backtracked and locked.

Beautiful, he thought, amazed that she could look so cool when the mercury was soaring through the nineties. Cool, elegant, and breathtakingly beautiful. She wore a thin white blouse, neatly tucked, but with the sleeves rolled back. Against it her skin was smooth and golden. She'd bundled her hair under her hat, though a few stray wisps had escaped to trail down one cheek. Her knees were caught in her arms, her bent legs hiking the hems of her jeans to reveal the fancy stitching on the shanks of her new buff-colored boots. Ross considered them, one eyebrow climbing to an arch.

At his quizzical expression, Paige slid to her feet, clamping her teeth to prevent a wince. He'd warned her not to spend the day in boots she hadn't broken in. He'd only razz her if he knew about the blisters.

"Who'd you draw?" she asked, joining him at the fence.

"Devil's Due."

Her stomach clenched, though names, she knew, meant nothing. "Is he hard to ride?"

With a laugh, Ross tucked the rosined glove into the waistband of his chaps, then wiped the sweat from his brow on a sleeve before slipping his hat on. Rope in hand, he tossed an arm around her shoulders and turned toward the chutes.

"Well, is he?" she persisted.

"Wouldn't be here otherwise."

"But is he harder than most?"

Leaves a pen spinning, Ross had been told. Kicks high, lands hard. Likes to stomp a man when he's down. "No, not particularly."

Paige cocked her head to look into his eyes. They were carefully blank. "Don't get hurt," she pleaded quietly.

A glib response occurred to him, then vanished as he recalled the morning she was to ride cross-country. He remembered fearing for her life and needing her promise, no matter how empty, that she'd be careful.

"Deal." Feeling tension in her shoulders, he gave them a brief squeeze. "You don't have to watch, you know. It won't hurt my feelings."

"It's worse not watching. My God, is that him?" Black eyes wild with fury glared at Paige from between the chute's slats. His hide, a dark solid gray, rippled with flexing muscles as, with one powerful foreleg, he pawed the ground. *And Ross thought riding an obstacle course was madness!*

"His blood's real hot, Tanner," a familiar voice warned.

Ross looked over at Chris Cooper, an old friend and a trusted hand at working the chute. "So I've heard. Half Brahman."

"And the other half's crazy," Coop added, breaking into a grin.

Here, the atmosphere was tense, electric, full of noise and nerves. Paige stepped back, instinctively clutching her throat where her heart had lodged as Ross climbed over the chute to stand on the rails on either side of a bad-tempered bull. He looked, she decided, staggeringly confident and totally at ease. Paige was neither. She knew the danger, had seen the damage inflicted by horns and hooves. She heard the explosion of sound from audience and announcer as the gate opened for the first bull and rider. Her eyes never left Ross.

Ignoring the action in the arena, he dropped the loop end of his rope down one side of the bull. Coop hooked the rope, threading it with a weighted bell before handing it back to Ross. Slipping the tail end through the loop, Ross fashioned a handhold, adjusting it high on the Brahman's neck. Straightening, he stood above the chute, straddling its width as the second bull and rider were let loose.

He turned his head to watch, automatically pulling his glove from his waistband and tugging it on. Paige stared at his profile against the hard blue of the sky and seemed to fall in love all over again.

When the third chute opened, Ross turned away and took up the rope. One hand on the rails for balance, he bent his knees, easing himself onto the bull's back. Sweat beaded on his brow, seeped through his shirt. Beneath him, Devil seethed. There was no saddle or pad between them. Only thin denim on the insides of Ross's thighs where the chaps didn't reach. Through it, he felt massive muscles twitch with a rage-driven impatience for the gate to open.

Anticipation came first, then a powerful rush of adrenaline. With his heart beating fast in his chest, Ross ran his gloved hand up and down the rope, creating friction to heat the rosin and intensify its stick. When he gripped the handhold, Coop pulled the rope tight, then tighter. "Pinch it off!" Coop barked. Nodding, Ross wrapped the rope around the back of his hand, laid it across his palm and made a fist. "Anytime," Coop said, and Ross knew the third rider was finished, his bull flushed from the arena.

Ross slid into his fist, so close he could feel the welted seam of his jeans through the glove's leather. Thought by thought, he cleared his mind. The ride, he knew, would be a blur, impossible to plan or strategize. There wouldn't be time to register and respond. Only to act. Every move, every countermove, would be guided by instinct.

Paige sensed when Ross was ready. A heartbeat before he said the word, she knew it was coming.

"Outside."

Devil left the pen rocking and rolling, bucking, turning. Hugging the arena fence, Paige saw Ross pitch forward with a snap that sent his hat flying, the arm he held up for balance already pulling him back to the center of momentum. Furious, the bull wheeled and romped. Because Brahman will charge a horse as easily as a man, there were no mounted pickup men in the arena, as there were for bronc riders. Just a pair of rodeo clowns waiting behind brightly painted barrels for the moment they were needed.

Eight seconds. To Paige, they felt like eighty. Ross tucked, twisted, anticipating the bull's moves with incredible accuracy. Devil lunged, horns raking the loose earth as his back legs kicked high enough to show a white patch on his belly. Ross, vertical to the ground, hung on. With surprising agility, the beast spun to the left before his hind legs touched ground again, then whipped back with a hard right.

Paige heard the whistle and was able, finally, to breathe. Ross released his rope and flew with the next buck, miraculously landing on his feet.

Without a thought for the danger, the clowns rushed out to run interference. Limping a bit, Ross strolled toward his hat, scooping it up in the same instant Devil charged. He didn't look back when the crowd roared, but sprinted for the fence and vaulted over.

Drained, Paige turned her back on the arena. And that had only been the first round.

The skies opened on a deafening rip of thunder. Ross slowed the car as he approached the motel, where a No Vacancy sign flickered in the office window. Glancing in the mirror, he saw a hard, driving rain flatten a wheat field and cross the highway. He turned into the crowded parking lot seconds ahead of the deluge and lucked into a space only three doors down from their room.

"Key!" Paige called, laughing over the sound of rain pounding the pavement, pelting the cars.

Digging the key from his pocket, Ross lengthened his strides. He couldn't have run if a rabid dog had been nipping at his heels. He unlocked and opened the door, kicking it shut as the storm hit full force.

"Feels like an oven," Paige gasped, the smell of pine-scented detergent overwhelming in the trapped heat. The room was small and thriftily furnished with a bed, dresser and nightstand. A coat of paint had been slapped on the walls sometime in the past year, perhaps to make up for the worn spots in the carpet. It looked like any of a hundred styleless rooms she'd stayed in over the years—except for a truly unique lamp shaped like a cowboy boot.

Ross didn't bother to try the air conditioner—it had wheezed its last sultry breath the night before. Crossing the room, he pushed faded curtains aside and, with three forceful tugs, managed to raise the sticky window halfway. It was enough, Paige decided, lifting her arms to let the cool air wash over her. Beyond the glass, the rain fell in sheets, so thick she could no longer see the blinking blue neon sign atop the drugstore across the parking lot.

Paige turned, dragging the hair off her neck as Ross walked to the bed. She noticed that he was favoring his left side. He sat and pulled his boots off, grimacing with the effort.

"You need a soak," she said, and headed for the bathroom. "A good hot soak."

Ross lay back and closed his eyes, cursing the pain in his ribs and left shoulder. To take his mind off it, he concentrated on the sounds coming from the bathroom—Paige spinning the taps, the creak and groan of ancient plumbing, water gushing from the spout. Tub filling, he heard her move to the sink and run the faucet, open the mirrored medicine cabinet, dig through her makeup case. Ordinary sounds, he thought. Ordinary, but intimate and oddly soothing.

"Here, take these."

Reluctantly Ross opened his eyes. She stood before him, a glass of water in one hand, two aspirins in the other. "Uh-uh. I'd have to move."

"You'll have to move anyway, to get in the tub."

Pushing up with his good arm, Ross took the aspirins and tossed them back dry. "When did I get too old for this?" he muttered.

"Are you kidding?" Returning to the bathroom, Paige shut off the water. "That last fall would have crippled a high school fullback."

"Dismount. It wasn't a fall, it was a dismount."

"Naah. It's a dismount when you land on your feet," she called back. "On your head, it's a fall."

"Yeah, but I won," he said from the doorway.

Glancing up, Paige saw his reflection in the steam-clouded mirror. She caught the glint of pleasure in his eyes, and felt a sudden, indefinable twinge. Envy? Regret? Then his image fogged over, and the strange feeling slipped away.

"Get in," she ordered, stepping out of the small bathroom so that he could step in. "Sink all the way down."

She left him, closing the door behind her. He'd taken care of her once. Now it was her turn to pamper. Dragging his slicker down from the top shelf in the closet, she threw it on and pocketed the key he'd left on the dresser. Outside, she had to fight the wind to pull the door shut, then hug the slicker to keep it from being torn away.

For a long time, Ross didn't move. It hurt to move. Hell, it hurt to breathe. Every muscle in his body ached. The steamy water helped, but it was going to take more than a soak to make him feel human again. Lance's Jacuzzi could do it, he mused, with the jets on full blast and the water heater set at scalding. Then he laughed, amused to find himself coveting one of Lance's self-indulgent toys. Dammit! It hurt to laugh.

He shut his eyes and slipped lower in the water. Time to go home, he mused. Muscles beginning to relax immediately tensed. And Paige? Will she think the same once they were back at the ranch? That it was time to go home? She'd already stretched her two weeks into five. He didn't know the exact dates of the Pan-American Games, only that they were scheduled for late summer. Six weeks, seven at the most. How much longer could she put off training and still hope to compete?

Until that moment, Ross hadn't realized how completely he'd forgotten that she would leave. Or how unprepared he was to accept it. Cursing himself, he leaned forward and pulled the plug on the cooling water. Before the tub had finished draining, he spun the shower taps.

How much time did they have? he wondered as the steam began to roll and the hot spray beat relief into his left shoulder. A day? A week? She hadn't mentioned the circuit since the picnic, or her plans after the rodeos. The sensible thing to do was ask her. Yeah, right. He was in love with her, for God's sake! Where was the sense in that? How could he ask her if—*when*, he corrected—*when* she planned to leave, when the thought of letting her go was impossible to contemplate? With a grunt of self-derision and a gesture of pure frustration, he shut off the water.

Hitching one towel at his waist, Ross rubbed a second one over his hair and wondered how Faye was holding up. Though Paige phoned her with dutiful, if reluctant, regularity, he doubted she'd given Faye any more indication of her plans than she'd given him. Limbo, he thought, with a grim smile. He was living in limbo. He liked it even less than living in Louisville.

Then he stepped into the bedroom and felt, suddenly, as if he'd stepped into a dream.

She'd lit candles. Six of them, stubby and white and smelling of camellias. The storm had waned to a patter on the roof, a whisper at the window. He saw Paige at the foot of the bed, folding the top sheet back on itself. One of his T-shirts hung loosely from her shoulders to skim the tops of her thighs. Wavering candlelight played over her long, slim legs.

"Feeling better?"

"You went out?" he asked needlessly. Her clothes were a soggy heap on the floor, her hair damp with rain. "For candles?"

"No, for liniment," she said as she circled the bed. "But they'd sold out. I'm not surprised. Every motel on the strip is filled with banged-up cowboys. It's a pretty small drugstore." Lifting the sheet at the fold, she turned it back again. She leaned over the bed to smooth a wrinkle, her movements hiking the T-shirt. Ross followed the hem with his eyes, his mouth suddenly dry. "The candles were an afterthought, to help you relax. Come on."

"And what?"

"Lie down." His expression was so dazed, she laughed. "I'm going to give you a massage."

Intrigued, he stepped closer, stopping short of the bed as she lifted a pink plastic squeeze bottle from the nightstand. "What's that?"

"Body lotion. Unscented," she added when he drew back. Filling her palm with some of the silky cream, she offered it to him for a sniff. "See? You won't smell pretty. I promise."

Unconcerned with how he might smell, Ross stretched out on the bed, reaching to trail his fingers down her thigh when she approached.

"Uh-uh, cowboy. Turn over," she ordered.

With a small laugh, he obeyed, rolling onto his stomach. Her knees sank into the mattress, her skin brushing his sides as she shifted to straddle him. Her weight settled just below his waist, loosening the towel. He should have removed it, he thought hazily. Already he could feel the bottom sheet soaking up the dampness. Then her hands slid up his back, spreading lotion, and he couldn't think at all.

He gave a quiet moan as her thumbs pressed rotating circles on his neck, untying knots at the base of his skull. Working out from the center, she kneaded his arms until they felt too weak, too heavy, to move. He couldn't have made a fist if his life had depended on it. When her hands glided back to his shoulders, he stiffened, anticipating renewed pain from the wrenched muscle. But her fingers were skillful, gentle, applying just enough pressure to relieve the tension without aggravating the injury. Ross closed his eyes, drifting in the sensations of soft rain and melting wax.

"Feel good?" she whispered near his ear.

"Mmm... Great hands," he murmured. "Somebody oughta give 'em a trophy. Call it the Best Damned Hands Award." Her smoky laugh stirred his body, even as his mind began to float.

Paige filled her palm again, holding the lotion so that it warmed in her hands. He had a beautiful body, lean and hard and strong. Smoothing cream onto his back, she explored the shape of him, freely, leisurely, lovingly. His muscles were taut, perfectly sculpted beneath skin tanned by the sun. She saw the slight discoloration of a bruise just below his left shoulder blade, and traced it with her fingers. Something they had in common. In their separate ways they were both athletes, driven to compete, determined to win. And with the battle scars to prove it. Surface stuff, she thought with regret. Hardly enough to build a life on.

Not tonight. She wouldn't let reality intrude on this night.

Scooting down, she slid her hands over his thighs and calves, the crinkle of leg hair tickling her sensitized fingertips. He tensed as she probed a knot just below the back of one knee. Over his groans of protest, she kneaded the tender area until the bunched muscle loosened and she felt him relax again.

One by one, the candles guttered out. Darkness amplified the sounds of distant highway traffic, plopping raindrops and their unsynchronized breathing. His deep and slow. Hers shallow, quicker. Leaning forward, she pressed a kiss to the center of his back. Slowly her lips moved over him. Mouth open, Paige feasted on the taste of him. She was sliding down, nibbling the firm skin at his waist, when he rolled over.

He reached for her, dragging her up to capture her mouth in a hard, demanding kiss. Passion for passion, she matched him, pouring herself into the kiss before pulling away. She could feel his hands at her waist, tugging on the T-shirt. Raising her arms as she sat back, she let him drag the soft cotton over her head.

Naked, she straddled his waist. So bold and proud and beautiful, Ross could only stare. The only light was the watery reflection of blinking blue neon from the drugstore across the parking lot. It flashed on her skin, on her incredible face, on the pale hair tumbling over her shoulders. So perfect, so regal. A vision of class, in a room that had none.

When he reached for her, she resisted. Placing her hands over his, Paige lifted them from her shoulders, pressing them into the pillow on either side of his head. Eyes open, she kissed him, softly, thoroughly, the ends of her hair brushing his chest. Though his mind was swimming, Ross sensed her desire to lead rather than be led, to take rather than be taken. And so he lay still, the blood pounding in his head, as her hands and mouth journeyed over him.

She hadn't known the act of seduction could be so exciting. So powerful. Paige was heady with it. The power to make his taut muscles pliant, his strong body weak. The power to make him want—her, only her, all of her. She touched him and he quivered. She nipped and he groaned. Passion thickened the air, dark and tinged with madness. Her own needs were building, straining her control. Yet she was patient, agonizingly patient, taking her time to arouse, tease, torture.

Minutes might have passed. Or hours. Ross had no awareness of time, only of losing his grip on sanity. Crazed and desperate, he tossed her onto her back. She gasped beneath him, fighting for air. Her eyes were as wide and wild with need as he thought his own must be. She arched when he plunged into her, releasing a sound of exquisite, nearly unbearable relief.

The madness seemed only to grow, engulfing them. Caught in a storm of passion, they were hurled through time and space. High and fast, deep and dark. Until, spent, they collapsed, lost but for each other.

Paige sat at Ross's desk, which was piled with ledgers, staring at the phone. Her fingernails made clicking sounds as she drummed them on the polished oak surface. Stalling, she held out her hand and studied the shell-pink tips, expertly, expensively, manicured. Cat had talked her into getting the works at the local beauty shop. Her toes were pink-tipped, as well.

It didn't look like her hand, she mused. All soft and painted. Turning it over, she saw that her palms were smooth, free of calluses. She'd have to start over, working through painful blisters to toughen them again. Which brought her back to the reason she'd sat down at the desk in the first place.

Heaving a sigh, she lifted the phone and dialed. She dropped it back in the cradle before the first ring.

What was the point? Conversation would be stilted, her words a repeat of the past. "Yes, Faye, I'm coming back. No, I don't know when. Soon." Every time she said those words, she felt a dreadful tug of guilt for lying to Faye. Not only did she not know *when* she'd return to Maryland, Paige still didn't know *if*. Growling her frustration, she stood away from the desk and shoved her too-soft, too-pink hands into her back pockets.

Somehow she'd thought her decision would be obvious the moment she'd returned to the ranch. But she'd been back a week now, and was no more certain of her future than she'd been two months ago.

Restless, she wandered through the house. Bored, she decided. Not restless, just bored.

Pillows were plumped, floors swept, tables waxed. In the sparkling kitchen, where a pot roast simmered on the stove and the washing machine chugged quietly behind closed doors, she gazed out a window at the vegetable garden. No weeds to pluck. No ripe tomatoes, either. Deciding she needed to be outside, she headed for the back door, grabbing her hat from its peg on the way.

She walked without destination, thinking only that she had to keep moving. In time, she arrived at the collection of weathered buildings that until now she'd viewed only from the second-floor windows. During the weeks of branding, they'd been a hive of activity. Now, with the cattle out to pasture and work focused on the harvest, the area was quiet.

With no one around to object, she indulged her curiosity, opening doors and peeking through windows. The first building she entered was the mess hall, where fifty could easily be fed in a single sitting. Unvarnished benches were tucked under tables covered with red-checkered oilcloth and stainless steel cauldrons hung over a ten-foot grill. The air, warm with trapped sunlight, smelled heavily of bacon and burned coffee.

Crossing a dirt-packed courtyard, she cracked the door to the bunkhouse. Inside, the walls were lined with serviceable metal lockers and military-style bunk beds, most stripped down to bare mattresses. Though unoccupied, the distinct smell of sweat-laced tobacco smoke made her feel like an intruder, and she pulled the door shut again.

Wherever she went, a sense of order prevailed—a place for everything, and everything in its place. There was a barn with hay bales stacked to the rafters. Another filled with sacks of grain. The largest structure housed tractors and plows; the smallest stored tools. While dust was inevitable, dirt was not tolerated.

At the last building, double doors twice her height were already open. The scents reached her before she crossed the threshold—hay and horses, leather and liniment. Smiling, she stepped inside. The light was dim and the air cool. The sounds—ruffling whickers, hooves clopping, the crackle of bedding—were as pleasing and peaceful as she remembered.

Responding to her footsteps, one of the horses dipped its head into the aisle. Scooping a handful of oats from a bucket she passed, Paige approached the inquisitive chestnut.

Anticipating a treat, the Thoroughbred pranced excitedly. Paige laughed at the familiar sensation of a warm velvet muzzle nipping grains from her palm, then curved her hand to the horse's satiny cheek. As she stroked the sleek neck, she saw that the mare was carrying, her sides bloated with the growing foal. Ross's broodmares. She'd nearly forgotten about his ambitious but misguided breeding program.

Only four of the eight stalls seemed to be occupied: Dutch doors open at the top, brass plaques engraved with names nailed to the latched bottom halves. It pleased her that he'd named them. He hadn't bothered with his cow ponies, calling for them by a descriptive pairing of sex, color or temperament—"the bay mare" or "that stubborn buckskin."

In a double-size stall two doors down from the chestnut, she found a dapple gray mare and her dusky foal, lazily feeding. Leaning in, Paige studied the spindly-legged colt and judged him to be about two months old.

"So you're the first of his new line," she crooned. Handsome, she decided, though looks hardly mattered to

Ross. "Can you think? It's what your owner is hoping for, you know?"

Ears perked, the colt tipped its head, then tossed it up and down, as if responding to her question. Ross just might have something, she thought whimsically.

At sounds from across the aisle, Paige turned and immediately recognized the Irish-blood filly she'd last seen trotting from the auction ring in Kentucky. Magnificent. Truly magnificent. She glanced at the plaque tacked to the filly's stall door and didn't know whether to laugh or cry. Etched in bronze was the name Small Fortune.

"And worth every penny," she murmured, approaching the skittish horse. Fortune maintained her distance, standing proud, almost haughty, in the middle of the stall. Though tangles had been combed from her black mane and tail, a film of dust dulled the rich red hue of her mahogany coat. "God, you don't belong here," Paige whispered.

"Something I can do for you, ma'am?"

Startled, Paige turned toward the voice. She recognized the squat, balding man as someone she'd met at the picnic, though his name escaped her. "Would it be all right if I turned her out?"

"Sure. Ride her, if you like. Boss said you could take your pick."

"He did?"

"Yep. About a month, six weeks ago. I'd given up on your coming down, though. Anyway, tack room's the last door on your left. Holler if you need anything. I'm usually close by."

Not until his footsteps had died away did Paige head down the aisle. Six weeks? Had it really been that long since she'd ridden a horse? Well, Mark Harrison had said she wouldn't forget how it was done. Perhaps it was time to find out if he was right. Then she opened the tack room door and nearly tripped over her trunk.

Her first instinct was fury. Was it contagious? Did everyone associated with her think they knew better than she what she wanted? First Faye, then Travis and Mark. Now Ross!

She'd told him to send it back. Why hadn't he? Outwardly fuming, she unlatched the trunk. Inwardly she was just a little bit grateful and wondering if Faye had thought to pack her grooming tools.

The air was warm, with a soft breeze blowing. Ross cantered a broad-shouldered mustang through scrub and brush, appreciating the uncommonly pleasant weather. As a rule, July scorched the last drop of moisture from earth. But the past four weeks had been exceptionally mild, with temperatures in the low-to-mid-eighties and brief but frequent cloudbursts. Tomorrow would mark the first day of August. Forecasters were already predicting an end to the respite with warnings of a hot, dry month.

Ross wasn't overly concerned. Graze was plentiful and in prime condition. Still, he'd given orders to move the herds closer to water. Now, heading back from a line camp, he enjoyed a rare, solitary ride.

Slowing the mustang to a walk, he looped the reins loosely around the saddle horn and tapped up a cigarette. Free to wander, the horse ambled toward the grassy shade of a lone cottonwood at the top of a rise.

As he cupped a match, Ross heard the rhythmic cadence of pounding hooves and looked for the source. Below, in a small, protected valley, Paige and Small Fortune were galloping full tilt. The wind whipped at her champagne hair and lifted the ebony mane of the Irish-blood filly. Splashed with sunlight, they were a vision of gold and flame.

Spectacular. Tearing across a Montana plain, she was every bit as spectacular as he'd once imagined. Cigarette forgotten, Ross watched her, ignoring the fact that her boots were knee-high leather, her saddle English instead of Western. Expertly she adjusted Fortune's gait, circling to set up for a jump.

It was then that Ross frowned.

She was maneuvering a course. A crude but painstakingly planned course. There were jumps made of tree limbs and hay bales, obstacles built of discarded fifty-gallon drums. She'd made this. Some time ago, he realized, zeroing in on the twisty path of trampled grass connecting the jumps like a dot-to-dot figure.

Paige sailed beautifully over a tricky two-part obstacle, landing without a hitch. He might have admired her skill if he hadn't been so baffled. She'd kept this a secret from him. For days—no, for weeks. She'd excluded him. *This part of my life has nothing to do with you.* The message couldn't have been clearer if she'd shouted the words at him.

Ross felt the anger flow through him. Flicking the cigarette aside, he took up the reins with a jerk that startled the grazing mustang. He wheeled the horse on his hind legs, spurring him down the slope, nursing his anger, knowing that if he didn't he'd have to deal with the hurt.

That night, he was quiet through dinner. Not just quiet, Paige decided, but cool and pointedly curt with her. He responded only to direct questions, with answers as short as he could possibly make them. Totally bewildered, she asked what was wrong, but he said only that he had ranch business on his mind. Silent, he pushed away from the table, his food barely touched, and left the kitchen. Surprised, confused, Paige listened as his footsteps carried him out the front door, feeling as left out and distant from him as if he'd physically shoved her aside.

Tipped back in one of the porch rockers, Ross told himself he was behaving like an ass. It wasn't like him to be spiteful, yet that was precisely what he'd been, giving her a taste of her own medicine. Acting like a pouty five-year-old, he chastised himself.

His anger was justified, he told himself. It was his ranch, his valley, his horse, dammit! So why hadn't he known what was going on right under his nose? There must have been clues—riding clothes in the closet, the smell of horse in her hair. Now he remembered her grabbing a pot on the stove a few weeks ago, and jerking back with a hiss of pain. There'd been blisters on her hand, new and raw. He recalled telling her not to do heavy-duty housework, that there were plenty of men around to call on. She hadn't explained the blisters. But then, he hadn't asked.

Stupid. Ross raked a hand through his hair, then left it curled at the back of his neck. He'd been so incredibly stupid. More than he'd wanted anything in his life, he'd wanted to believe that she'd forgotten about winning an Olympic gold medal, that she'd decided the prize was no longer worth the price. And so he had convinced himself it was true. He'd started planning a future, including the sons and daughters to whom he'd eventually pass on the Triple T. He'd imagined them in Paige's arms, with Paige looking as lovely and content as she had on that summer afternoon when she sat under a tree cradling Cody Anderson. Everything, all of it, had suddenly gone up in smoke.

The screen door banged shut as Paige stepped out. Moving only his head, Ross gazed through the darkness. She stood in the spill of light from the doorway, gazing back. He saw her open her mouth, hesitate, then shut it again. She strolled to a support post at the edge of the porch and glanced up at the sky.

"Beautiful night," she said.

Though her words were casual, Ross heard determination. She wasn't going to slink away just because he was behaving badly. "Enjoy it while you can. We're expecting a hell of a heat wave."

Distance. Paige sensed it, but didn't know how to bridge it. If she crossed the porch and stood toe-to-toe with him, she thought, they'd be no less far apart. She heard the scrape of a match, and turned to see his face in the brief glare of the flame.

He met her eyes as he shook out the match. "I was thinking we should have Mary and Cat to dinner soon. How's Saturday?"

"Saturday." He used to ask the same sort of searching questions when they'd first returned to the ranch. If he suggested they take in a movie on the weekend, it was his way of asking if she'd still be here then. "Sure, Saturday's fine." Her way of saying she planned to stick around.

Looking out over moonlit gardens, Paige hoped he wouldn't ask questions she couldn't answer. She was getting enough of that from Faye. She prayed that he wouldn't probe and push, or demand that she make her choice.

"You miss it."

Though it wasn't a question, it demanded a response. Paige shut her eyes briefly, then turned to face him, arms crossed protectively in front of her. "Some of it."

He nodded, then startled her with a lopsided smile. "The applause."

Because of the smile, she laughed. "Yeah. It's the best part."

Ross watched her, and waited. He'd given her an opening, cracked the door, let some light in. The rest was up to her.

What? What did he want? Paige clung tenaciously to her composure, even as she felt it disintegrating. She began pacing the length of the porch, the knock of her boot heels abrupt and emphatic in the evening quiet. For a time, she'd been sure, dead sure, that her life on the circuit was over. Then she'd gone on the road with him, rodeo-hopping. Packing up, moving on, driving through. It was a familiar way of life, one that in the past few years had begun to drain her. Not this time. She'd enjoyed it, even the string of tacky motel rooms, and realized there were parts of it she missed— the energy and nerves and pulsing excitement, the close-knit camaraderie and competitive spirits. Yes, she missed it.

For the first time it occurred to Ross that she was as much in the dark as he. In that moment, he wanted to shake her as much as he wanted to comfort her. With no other woman had he felt the need to rage and protect at one and the same time. She stopped pacing, shook her head and sighed, seeming to lose energy with the expelled breath.

He ached for her. And for himself, because he thought he knew what she would do, even if she didn't yet know it herself. "I've got a mountain of paperwork to wade through." Ross flicked the cigarette over the rail as he left the rocker. "I'll see you upstairs later?"

"Sure." Given the tension, Paige hadn't expected the depth of emotion in his eyes. He framed her face, gently, his palms on her cheeks. Tipping her head, he covered her mouth with his in a soft, sweet, heart-stirring kiss.

"You don't have to wait up," he said, his lips brushing her forehead. "Get some sleep. You look tired."

The moment the door shut behind him, Paige pressed her fingertips against her eyes, hoping in vain to stop the flood of tears. It was impossible to choose. Impossible. Either choice demanded an unthinkable sacrifice. Stay here, with Ross, but give up the dream of a lifetime. Follow the dream and lose Ross. And so she'd made no decision at all. Stuck in a frustrating paralysis of indecision, as time ran out and the deadline grew closer.

It was late when Ross finished up at his desk. It had been over an hour since he'd heard Paige lock the front door and climb the stairs. The grandfather clock began chiming. Midnight. He wasn't in the habit of waking people in the middle of the night. He toyed with the phone cord, then decided to place the call.

He listened to half-a-dozen rings before a groggy voice answered. "Faye, Ross. Sorry to wake you."

"Paige—"

"Is fine." He heard her expel a breath that was both relief and anger.

"I assume you know about time zones. It's two o'clock in the morning."

"I didn't think this call should wait." Satisfied that Faye had shaken off sleep and could hold a lucid conversation, he got straight to the point. "When does she have to be back if she's going to ride in the Pan-Am Games?"

"Two months ago," she snapped. "Though I guess tomorrow will have to do."

"What if she isn't there tomorrow? What's the latest she can show up without being disqualified?"

"She doesn't know you've called me, does she? Of course she doesn't." He heard the flick of a lighter, then Faye dragging on a cigarette. "Okay. She has to be at the games in time to ride her events. If she isn't there, she's disqualified. That's in two weeks—twelve days, actually. But just because she's there doesn't mean she'll be ready to compete. God knows what shape she's in. She hasn't trained in months."

"What about Absolute?"

"He's been getting three workouts a week, with some of the best riders on the coast. Now, I've answered your questions, you answer mine. When will she be here?"

"I don't know that she will," Ross said. "Honest, Faye. It's up to Paige. I just wanted a sense of the timing."

"Let her go, Ross," Faye pleaded.

"She isn't chained to the bedposts," he snapped. "She's free to go whenever she wants."

"Then make her go. She's your guest. Guests don't stay where they aren't welcome."

"That would be cruel, Faye." Though Ross couldn't swear he hadn't given the idea consideration.

Faye sighed, then muttered a bit to herself. "Let me tell you what cruel is, Ross. Cruel is giving your life to something, then having it snatched away. Cruel is letting someone get lost because you think they have the right to wander down the wrong road. She's going to wake up one morning and look for someone to blame. It just might be you."

Ross woke to the sound of his own heart beating. He knew before he opened his eyes that it was the middle of the night, and that he was alone in bed.

It didn't surprise him to find her gone. The smothering heat of the past week had made uninterrupted sleep impossible. Eyes adjusting to the darkness, he glanced toward the bathroom, assuming Paige had sought relief with a cool shower. But there was no sliver of light under the door, no hiss of water. Curious, he touched the sheets on her side of the bed. Too cool, too dry. He figured she'd been gone for an hour at least.

Then the pulsing rhythm altered, and he realized the muffled beat wasn't the echo of his heart, but was coming from outside.

Tossing warm covers aside, he walked to the open window. He saw them in the first paddock. Paige and Small

Fortune, dancing in the moonlight. Pressure, like the squeeze of a vise, built in his chest as he watched her take the elegant filly through the precise, unhurried steps of a dressage test.

Was this what their life would be like if she stayed? Would she always be two distinctly separate people—one athlete, one woman—with neither of them truly happy or satisfied?

He stood, watching her complete the seven-minute program, and knew it was time for her to go, that somehow he had to help her take that first deciding step, and that it would be harder than anything he'd ever had to do.

Damned heat. With a jerk on the lead line, Paige slowed Fortune down to a walk. The sun was too brutal for anything more than an easy workout in the paddock. A run through the obstacle course would have been a risk to both their lives. She cursed the heat again and wiped a sleeve across her brow to catch the sweat trickling from under her hatband.

In addition to the heat, there was the friction between herself and Ross to contend with. It was nameless, formless, yet it seemed to build daily. At first she'd ignored it, hoping it would smooth itself out. Now she accepted that there was going to be a confrontation, though about what she wasn't sure.

Ross stood inside the open stable doors, undetected in the dimness. He watched her as he stood leaning against the doorjamb. Her jeans and faded shirt were coated with dust, and her face was streaked with it. One had to look long and hard to find the elegant equestrian of two months ago. When she hissed a curse, he studied her expression. Her frustration was with more than the heat. She was an emotion-filled bomb waiting to explode. Perhaps it was time to light the fuse.

The arena dirt was soft and deep, yet she heard his approach from the moment he stepped from the stable. Despite the underlying tension, her first reaction was pleasure. "Hi." She brought Fortune to a stop and reeled in the excess lead line. "Playing hooky?"

"No." He tipped his chin, indicating the horse. "I've come for her."

Paige immediately stepped back, away from his outstretched hand. Instead of giving him the lead line, as his gesture demanded, she tucked it behind her back. "No. You can't."

"I can't what?"

"Breed her. Put her to one of your cow ponies."

Her obvious disdain made it that much easier for Ross to push on. "It's time she earned her keep."

It was hardly an unreasonable position for him to take, yet Paige was instantly offended. "You told Matt I could take my pick. I've picked her." With a firm grip on the lead line, she turned and began walking, pulling Fortune along behind her.

In three strides he stood before her, blocking the entrance to the stable. "She's off the circuit, Paige. It's over for her. Every person, building and animal on this ranch has a purpose. Hers is to breed and produce cow ponies. I have no use for a showpiece."

He couldn't have stunned her more if he'd slapped her. His eyes were cold, his voice was blunt, and his message was painfully clear. "You're not talking about Fortune. You're talking about me."

Her anguish was almost more than he could stand. "I'm talking about a horse. If you see yourself in anything I've said, I can't help that."

She might have taken comfort in his words if there had been the slightest hint of sincerity in his voice. "I have no purpose here. That's what you're saying. I don't contribute. Apparently you have no need for me." Just as her parents had had no need for her. A showpiece; just a showpiece. Mechanically she lifted her arm and handed over the rope. "It's time I left. I seem to remember a life I have to get back to."

The pain threatened to overwhelm him. Ross watched her walk away, looking as if she'd shatter into a thousand pieces at the barest touch. This was for the best, he told himself. He was a man with roots and responsibilities. She'd only been passing through on her way to a dream. If she'd stalled much longer, she might have missed her chance. And lived the rest of her life wondering what might have been, could have been, eventually growing as bitter and unforgiving as Faye was now. That, he knew, was something neither of them could have lived with.

Chapter Twelve

Ross hadn't known the hurt would run so deep, or that with time the pain would grow rather than diminish. Exhaustion was his only defense. He worked from dawn to dusk, seven days a week—with the cattle, with the horses, on fences, in fields. He thought of her constantly.

The heat held, so he wasn't the only one riding the range with a short fuse. For the first time since he'd taken over the ranch, his men rode the other way when they saw him coming. Life was tough enough without being drafted into joining Ross in whatever backbreaking, mind-numbing labor he'd chosen for himself that day. Two men had quit; Ned Foster had willingly registered for college.

Still he thought of her.

The worst part of the day was when it ended, and he had nowhere to go but home, to the huge, unbearable emptiness. Yet he refused Aunt Mary's offer to move back to the ranch. He didn't feel up to being gracious or polite. By the end of the third week, he'd established a routine that reduced to a minimum the hours he spent in the house. He rode onto the range at sunup, ate with the men at the mess hall and spent his evenings puttering in one or the other of the outbuildings.

And thought of her.

At half past ten, Ross climbed the back porch steps. He noticed, with utter indifference, that he'd forgotten to turn off the kitchen lights that morning. He pushed open the door, tossing his hat onto a peg on the mudroom wall. Then he heard the muffled clatter of someone stacking dishes, smelled the distinct aroma of home-cooked food. Heart pounding, he hurried into the kitchen, saw her, and stopped dead in his tracks.

"Go home, Cat."

The disappointment was crushing. For an instant, one terrible instant, he'd lost her all over again.

"Well, finally," Cat said, ignoring his inhospitable welcome. "I've made dinner. Just soup and rolls, but then, I never was much of a cook. Ross? What are you— Ross!" Using a pair of pot holders, he'd taken the soup from the stove and was heading for the back door. "Don't you dare!" Cat shouted.

With a tremendous clatter, soup, pot, lid and pot holders flew out the door to crash down the porch steps. When Ross returned to the kitchen, Cat was standing with her arms crossed and one foot tapping.

"That was a bit dramatic, don't you think?"

"Haven't you heard? My temper's in rare form these days. Now go home, Cat."

"No." She'd hoped the rumors of how drawn and haggard he looked had been exaggerated. She saw now that they were not. "People are quitting around here."

"Never hurts to cut out the deadwood."

"Even Pete? I don't think he's going to put up with too much more of you. If he quits, Aunt Mary says she'll have to get Lance back here to run the place."

There wasn't an ounce of belief in the look he gave her. "Nice try."

"Dammit, Ross, you're miserable, heartbroken. How will I decide who to blame if you won't tell me what happened?"

He paused to light a cigarette, then opened the refrigerator and helped himself to a beer. It seemed they were going to do this whether or not he wanted to. "There's no one to blame." He pulled a chair out from the table, popped the top on his beer and took a long pull. "She came for a visit and stayed longer than expected. Now she's gone back to her life, as we both knew she would. End of story."

"But you're in love with her," Cat argued. "You know you are."

"A mistake." Suddenly exhausted, Ross scrubbed a hand over his face. One little slip, he thought wryly, but one very big mistake. "Go home, sis."

"Wouldn't it help if I stayed for a while? So you won't be alone?"

"Leave by the front door, you don't want to slip in the soup."

After grumbling for a minute or two, Cat departed. Ross drained his beer, then grabbed another before heading upstairs. When he reached the landing, he turned left, heading for his childhood bedroom, where he'd been sleeping for the past three weeks.

He walked into and across the room, ignoring the lights but turning on the TV. The noise helped him fall asleep, kept him from thinking. According to the all-news-station anchorman, the president was enjoying a weekend at Camp David. Ross stepped into the adjoining bathroom to start the shower, then returned to hear an update on the latest third-world uprising. He opened the closet, eyes on the screen, then turned and snarled a curse. Empty. No shirts, no slacks, no shoes. Aunt Mary. Impatient with her stubbornness, he yanked on a dresser drawer. No socks.

Fine, so he'd sleep naked. Walk through the house naked. Dammit, he'd go down the lane for the morning paper bare-ass naked! Maybe then she'd realize she couldn't tell him where to sleep, and stop moving his clothes back to that room.

When he fell asleep, a weatherman was charting high-pressure systems; he woke to a recap of the day's baseball scores. Rolling over, he squinted at his wristwatch: 3:00 a.m. *Gonna be another one of those nights,* he decided. Propped on pillows, he lit a cigarette, took a swallow of flat beer and watched Cecil Fielder knock one out of the ballpark. After a shot of the stadium scoreboard, the scenery changed. Another grassy arena, more cheering fans. Then he saw Paige. Stunned, he sat up straighter. His eyes stung suddenly, and he had to blink her back into focus.

She was one of four standing on a raised platform, all of them dressed alike in white breeches, red jackets and black velvet helmets. They were waving to the audience with one hand, showing off gold medals with the other. The camera closed in on Paige, her face alone filling the screen as the sportscaster continued his commentary.

"... Paige Meredith, the last of her teammates to ride cross-country, covered the course in record time, saving the team gold for the United States..."

Ross looked his fill. He'd hoped to get a better look at her eyes, convinced he'd be able to tell if she was happy. But she was gone, replaced by a sweaty tennis player leaping into a serve.

Paige slid a gold stickpin through folds of white silk, securing the snowy stock beneath her chin. The mirror she gazed into was chipped around the edges and foggy with dust. Her hands were steady, her eyes were wide and unwavering. Beside her, Annie Jackson was swearing around a mouthful of bobby pins while struggling to roll her hair into a bun.

"Here, turn," Paige ordered. Starting over, she pulled a brush through the girl's shiny chestnut mane. "It's too clean." Paige twisted the hank of hair, then began rolling it up. "Pin. Don't wash it before a show. If it's a little bit dirty, it'll stay better. Pin."

"Gross," Annie mumbled.

Paige laughed, smoothing hair back with one hand. "The night before is okay. Just don't wash it the morning of a show. Pin. Hi, Faye,'' Paige called when the door swung open. ''What's up?''

''Ride times, judges.'' After a quick survey of the room, Faye settled on the least dirty chair. ''You know the routine.''

Paige scrutinized her handiwork, then reached for a can of hairspray. ''So what have you got?''

Gesturing with her eyes, Faye indicated Annie. Paige nodded her understanding, though she had to bite down on her lip to keep from chuckling. It seemed silly to be so hush-hush with coaching instructions, even if Annie *was* the competition.

''How do I look?'' Annie asked, twisting to view her backside in the mirror.

''Here.'' Paige straightened the girl's top hat, flicked a speck of lint from her shoulder and smiled. ''Perfect.''

''Thanks.''

''Good luck.'' Annie left, and Paige slid her smart cutaway from its hanger. Faye made short work of her notes, flipping through five pages before beginning her rundown of the judges.

''Smithy favors elegance.'' She shot a quick, critical look at Paige, then shrugged. ''Try.''

Paige simply laughed. It was the tan. Faye had been horrified when she showed up looking as though she'd spent the summer baking on a beach. Now she was just plain angry that Paige refused to wear sunblock twenty-four hours a day. She would, eventually, if only because it was better for her skin and health in the long run. But for now, she liked the look of it.

''We're athletes, Faye. We live, work, play, even sleep in the sun. Tanned skin is an occupational hazard. Just be thankful I didn't break out with freckles.''

Paige grinned at Faye's reflection. And, though she struggled not to, Faye eventually chuckled. ''Nice,'' she said as Paige withdrew pristine gloves from their protective envelope. ''You look nice.'' Faye opened the door, then hesitated at the threshold. ''Paige, that night in Kentucky, you said you didn't know what you wanted to be when you grew up. Did you find out?''

Paige felt a surge of emotion, though her smile never wavered. "Yeah." More important, she'd discovered there was a vast and significant difference between what she wanted to *be* and what she wanted to *do*. Competing at horse shows was something she wanted to do. Just as winning a gold medal at the Olympics was something she wanted to do. But what she wanted to *be* was happy. And loved, needed. A wife. Oh, yes, she wanted to be a wife, and a mother. Paige felt the tears that were all too ready to flow if she allowed them. She swallowed hard. To prevent Ross's image forming in her mind, she looked over at Faye. "Yeah," she repeated, the word sounding like a sigh. "I know what I want to be."

Faye waited, dejection replacing curiosity when Paige said nothing more. "Well . . . good. I'm glad."

Paige watched her leave, then shut her eyes. Their relationship had changed in ways that frustrated and saddened Faye. Paige understood, even sympathized. She loved Faye. Would always love her. She regretted the hurt and pain she was causing her. It was simply unavoidable. Their needs were different, as were their goals. Faye wanted to control; Paige wanted to find her own way.

To that end, Paige would no longer live at Gentry Farm. Recent events had demanded all her time and attention. No sooner had she returned from the Pan-American Games than she'd had to prepare Mr. Divine for this weekend and his CCI international qualification. That accomplished, her schedule was clear until the worlds in October. Four weeks. Plenty of time for her to find her own place. Home, she corrected. Her own home, and her first. Perhaps then she could put the past behind her and get on with the rest of her life.

Paige stepped out of the dressing room, into sunshine, tugging her gloves on as she took a long look at her surroundings. It was good to be back.

* * *

The dressing room was crowded, the babble of voices reflecting relief and elation at an event that was over. Paige pulled a T-shirt over her head, tucking it at her waist before zipping her jeans. Her formal clothes were already stuffed in a laundry bag, her ribbons clipped to its handle. Third place. Not so long ago, she'd have beaten herself up over anything less than first. Today she was satisfied with third. Satisfied? Thrilled! Third was all Divine had needed; third was what he'd gotten. Mission accomplished.

With the laundry bag over her shoulder, Paige reached for her hat and slipped it on. The mirror reflected more than one set of raised eyebrows. Cowboy boots were familiar enough on the circuit that hers went unnoticed. Not so a ten-gallon Stetson. Most of her fellow athletes had gotten used to it. Just as they'd gotten used to finding her in the stands between events, at parties after. She was rediscovering old friends, making new ones. It was a start.

Outside there was the usual clog of vehicles. Vans were being loaded with equipment, trailers with horses. Everyone, it seemed, wanted to be the first to clear out. Paige stopped at her own trailer long enough to drop off the laundry bag and tell Steve she'd be at the hotel, packing.

Because the day was beautiful, full of sun and birdsong, and the hotel close, Paige decided to walk.

"God, I love that hat. Wanna sell it to me?"

With a grin, Paige looked over her shoulder at Mark Harrison. "First my horse, now my hat." She slowed while he caught up and fell into step with her. "I doubt it'd fit, what with that swelled head. Speaking of which, where'd you decide to display your gold medal?"

"Hung it over the john. Honest," he said at her look of skepticism. "Now I can stand there and stare at it several times a day, and no one's the wiser." When she laughed, he tossed an arm around her shoulders and gave them a squeeze. "There's something I haven't heard in a while. Been rough, huh?"

"Yeah, but I'm healing. Nothing's broken. A few bruises. Big bruises," she conceded when she saw his doubtful expression. "They'll fade."

Though she hadn't confided in Mark, she hadn't needed to. Her absence from the circuit had had all sorts of rumors flying. Among them, that she'd run off with a cowboy. Not much point in denying it, particularly since she'd come back wearing a Stetson.

"You'll be fine. Just you wait," Mark said as he walked with her into the hotel lobby. "Hell, you got over me, didn't you?"

"Not completely," she told him, sliding quickly into an elevator car before the doors shut. She turned back in time to see him blush and shuffle, and was still smiling at the memory of it as she unlocked her door. The grin and the memory vanished the moment she stepped into her room.

Roses. Dozens and dozens of yellow-gold roses. She wanted to scream, to shout. Hands trembling with anger, Paige removed her hat and flung it and the room key on the bed. How did he do it? *Why* did he do it?

What did she care? It was his money wasted, not hers. She wouldn't look at them. How could she not? They were everywhere. She'd throw them out the window. But instead of grabbing the nearest vase, she withdrew one long-stemmed bud from the bunch and touched it lightly to her lips. When they arrived after the Pan-Am Games, she'd searched each bouquet for a card, a message. There'd been none. The concierge had called the florist for her, but learned only that the order had been phoned in from out of state. No message.

"Whoever told you where I was," she muttered, "should have mentioned I didn't win."

"Ah, but you were magnificent. Absolutely magnificent."

The rose slipped out of her fingers as she whirled. There, in a deep chair tucked in the corner, was Ross. Her first instinct was to throw herself into his arms. But then all that she'd learned since she'd left him rushed over her. And the emotions. Pain, confusion, rage, resentment. What he'd done was unforgivable.

"How did you get in here?"

If the look in her eyes was any indication of her feelings, Ross might have thought she wanted him dead. But for a brief moment when she'd touched the rose petals to her lips. In that moment, he'd seen into her heart, and the agony he'd been living in had begun to fade. "A little charm, and a big tip. Not to mention two hundred roses." He stood and walked toward her, stooping to pick up the rose she'd dropped. By the time he'd straightened she'd moved as far away from him as the room allowed.

"Why are you here?" She threw a hand out, stopping his forward progress. "No, don't come any closer. Say what you've come to say and then go."

"Not without you."

"Excuse me?" She lifted a brow so that her expression matched the coolness of her voice.

The ground was shakier than he'd expected. Ross knew she'd been hurt, that he'd been the one to hurt her. But the depth of the rage in her eyes baffled him. "I've come to take you back to the ranch."

"You've decided this, have you?"

Suddenly furious with her icy disdain, Ross grabbed her by her shoulders. "You belong there, dammit. I miss you."

"Perhaps you should have thought of that before you decided I *didn't* belong there."

Ross was stunned and, for a moment, speechless. Paige took advantage of his surprise to pull out of his grip. "What the hell are you talking about?"

"That little scene you played out in the paddock." She'd managed to get across the room, with the barrier of the bed between them. "Did you think I was so stupid that I wouldn't figure it out? It may have taken me a while, but I got it eventually. You wanted me to leave, and knew just what to say to make it happen." Tears glimmered in her eyes, trembled in her voice. "You used my past, my pain, things I'd told you about myself."

"Paige—"

"Did you breed her, Ross? Small Fortune? Or did you just take her back to her stall?" His silence was answer enough. "If you wanted me to go, you only had to ask."

"I didn't want you to go. I love you, Paige," he said quietly, desperately. "I love you."

His words didn't soothe, but sliced at her heart. "Then why? Why?"

"The Pan-American Games. The Olympics. I didn't want you to miss your chance." If he'd thought selfless motivations would soften her, he couldn't have been more mistaken.

"So *you* decided? You decided what I should do with my life, then manipulated me into doing it." There were so many conflicting emotions running through her, Paige found it impossible to stay in one place. She paced the room, keeping to her side of the bed. "Is that love, Ross? I know Faye thinks it is. My parents, too. But do you? You love me, but you don't talk to me. You love me, but you don't share with me. You love me, but you don't ask what I feel, think? What I want? I love you." There were tears in her eyes now, glittering on her lashes. "Yes, I do. I love you. And because I love you, I couldn't do what you've done. I couldn't decide your life for you, then go behind your back to pull it off."

"No?" He'd listened with a growing sense of panic to all she had to say. He might be guilty as charged, but he wasn't alone. "You didn't build a cross-country course? Don't shake your head at me. I saw it. I saw you on it, you and Small Fortune. Riding dressage at two o'clock in the morning. Where were your riding clothes? Not in our bedroom. How many nights, when I asked about your day, did you not tell me you were training?"

"That's...not the same," she argued, not entirely convinced herself. "That was my life, not yours."

"You *are* my life." To prove it, he dragged her into his arms and kissed her. God, he'd needed to touch her, taste her, for too long. She didn't resist, but responded with a helpless moan as she wrapped her arms around him. "Without you, I have no life," he murmured. Her head was

on his chest, his cheek resting on the top of her head. "
never meant to hurt you. I just didn't want to see you los
your dream."

Paige sighed, then eased out of his arms. "My decision
My dream to lose."

"That's it." He barely resisted the need to shake her. In
stead, he put his hands on her shoulders and shoved her into
the chair. "You want to make a decision about your life
Fine. Marry me."

"What? No." Shaking her head, Paige gazed up at him.

"No, you won't marry me?"

"No, you can't...I can't..."

"You can't marry me?"

Paige shot out of the chair. Her heart was beating too
fast. Her head was spinning. "Dammit, Ross, you don'
know what you're asking."

"I know exactly what I'm asking. I'm asking you to
marry me. And I'm not leaving until I have your answer."
It wasn't quite the proposal Ross had had in mind. Excep
that she looked as if she'd plopped herself down in a fiel
of roses. "Is there anything about this decision you'd like
to share with me, talk about?"

He's serious, Paige realized. But it was impossible. Wasn'
it? "Ross, the next year is going to be hell. You have no
idea."

"It's going to be hell whether or not you marry me
Would you rather be lonely while you're going throug
hell?"

"My horses—"

"I've got stables."

"My training—"

"I've got plenty of corrals. We'll convert one. And tur
one of the buildings into an indoor ring for winter."

She gazed up at him. Afraid, so afraid. "I'd always be
leaving to go on the road."

"And coming back home again."

Home. Paige closed her eyes on the word. *Home.* Was i
possible?

"Paige." She opened her eyes, those fathomless, fabulous eyes. "I want you in my life, for the rest of my life. I want to laugh with you and fight with you. I want to make love to you every night and wake up with you every morning. And the times I can't be with you on the road, I'll be at the door when you come home. What do you want?"

"To be happy." Suddenly, it was that simple. Paige left the chair, smiling as she went into his arms. "And loved. Needed."

"You are," he vowed.

"A wife."

"Is that a yes?"

"Yes," she told him with a laugh. He pulled her closer for one long, satisfying kiss. "Oh, and I want to be a mother," she added with a sigh.

"We'll work on it."

* * * * *

MONTANA
Mavericks

**Stories that capture living and loving
beneath the Big Sky, where legends live
on...and mystery lingers.**

This April, unlock the secrets of the past in

FATHER FOUND
by Laurie Paige

Moriah Gilmore had left Whitehorn years ago, without
a word. But when her father disappeared, Kane Hunter
called her home. Joined in the search, Moriah and
Kane soon rekindle their old passion, and though the
whereabouts of her father remain unknown, Kane comes
closer to discovering Moriah's deep secret—and the child
he'd never known.

Don't miss a minute of the loving as the passion
continues with:

BABY WANTED
by Cathie Linz (May)

MAN WITH A PAST
by Celeste Hamilton (June)

COWBOY COP
by Rachel Lee (July)

Only from **Silhouette®** where passion lives.

Silhouette

SPECIAL EDITION ™ ®

And now for the powerful conclusion to the trilogy

This Time, Forever

by Andrea Edwards

It began with A RING AND A PROMISE (SE #932), continued with
A ROSE AND A WEDDING VOW (SE #944) and finally,
in A SECRET AND A BRIDAL PLEDGE (SE #956),
a last pair of star-crossed lovers hope to be reunited.

U.S. Marshal Mark Miller was endangered witness Amy Warren's only
protection. The trouble was, Mark made her feel as unsafe as a woman could
be! But there was also something strangely familiar and compelling about
how he made her feel.... Could this be her chance at a forever?

A MAN FOR MOM
Gina Ferris Wilkins
(SE #955, May)

Struggling to keep a business afloat plus taking care of
the kids left little room for romance in single mother
Rachel Evans's life. Then she met Seth Fletcher. And
suddenly the handsome lawyer had her thinking about
things that were definitely unbusinesslike....

That
SPECIAL
Woman!

Meet Rachel—a *very* special woman—and the rest of
her family in the first book of THE FAMILY WAY
series...beginning in May.

"The perfect Mother's Day gift...for your
very special mom!